Further Off
the Mark

Further Off the Mark

Will Stebbings

Matador
9 Priory Business Park,
Wistow Road, Kibworth Beauchamp,
Leicestershire. LE8 0RX
Tel: (+44) 116 279 2299
Fax: (+44) 116 279 2277
Email: books@troubador.co.uk
Web: www.troubador.co.uk/matador

ISBN 978 1783062 102

British Library Cataloguing in Publication Data.
A catalogue record for this book is available from the British Library.

Typeset in 10pt Aldine401 BT Roman by Troubador Publishing Ltd, Leicester, UK

Matador is an imprint of Troubador Publishing Ltd

Printed and bound in the UK by TJ International, Padstow, Cornwall

GIFT

I would like to use this opportunity to thank Holly Ormrod-Stebbings for her excellent cover design for both this novel and for *'Off the Mark.'*

I am also indebted to Janet Veasey who expertly played the role of proof reader and prevented several gaffes from escaping my notice.

AUTHOR'S NOTE

'*Further Off the Mark*' is the sequel to '*Off the Mark*.' In the unlikely event that you've never read '*Off the Mark*' or perhaps it's been a while and you've forgotten the plot, it is probably worthwhile providing some background so that '*Further Off the Mark*' makes better sense.

The central character, Mark Barker, lives in the fictitious West Norfolk town of Sanford. '*Off the Mark*' begins in 1965 with Mark leaving an all-boys grammar school and obtaining a 'Junior' position at Gresham Installations, a London overspill company that manufactures and installs office partitioning. He has led a very sheltered life and at first struggles in his new adult world. Even more, he struggles with members of the opposite sex. I don't wish to give away too much information about '*Off the Mark*', in case you have yet to read it, but suffice to say, that Mark meets some interesting characters in his quest to get 'off the mark', particularly the female of the species.

Because both novels are set in the sixties, there are many pertinent observations of that decade and Mark's love of soul music should interest anyone with a penchant for that genre. Although the story is set in a fictitious town, Mark's exploits take him all over Norfolk and bring many real locations to life, albeit as things were in the sixties, so that lovers of anything Norfolk will feel at home.

So '*Further Off the Mark*' is a continuation of Mark's story, introducing new characters and situations, but also building on some of his previous relationships. In '*Off the Mark*', I tried in many cases to use quirky headings for each chapter – in some cases with a hint of humour. In '*Further Off the Mark*', I have taken this a step further by adding a twist that each heading is the title of a sixties soul record and representing the content of its chapter. To illustrate this further, on the following page, I have listed the Chapter titles with the names of the recording artists who brought these wonderful songs to my attention. This does not mean you have to be a lover of Soul music to enjoy the novel.

'*Off the Mark*' was my first full novel and writing it was a completely new experience for me. I found writing '*Further Off the Mark*' to be an even more enjoyable experience. I hope this comes across to you, the reader.

Chapter Titles	Artiste(s)
1. Giving Up on Love	Jerry Butler
2. Saturday Night at the Movies	The Drifters
3. What Now?	Gene Chandler
4. A Woman, a Lover, a Friend	Jackie Wilson
5. You're All I Need to Get By	Marvin Gaye & Tammi Terrell
6. At the Club	The Drifters
7. Don't Look Back	The Temptations
8. Dance to the Music	Sly & the Family Stone
9. Your Mother's Only Daughter	Smokey Robinson & the Miracles
10. What Does it Take (to Win Your Love)	Junior Walker & the Allstars
11. Getting Mighty Crowded	Betty Everett
12. Hello Stranger	Barbara Lewis
13. I Can't Help Myself	The Four Tops
14. You Really Got a Hold on me	The Miracles
15. Breaking Down the Walls of Heartache	Johnny Johnson & the Bandwagon
16. Things Get Better	Eddie Floyd
17. Only the Strong Survive	Jerry Butler
18. Out of Left Field	Percy Sledge
19. Take Me In Your Arms and Love Me	Gladys Knight & the Pips

CHAPTER 1

Giving Up On Love

'Paedo! Paedo! Paedo!' the group of noisy drinkers called out, whilst pointing their fingers at an embarrassed fellow sitting next to an equally embarrassed young lady.

'Do you know what that's all about, Mike?' Mark asked of the smiling landlord.

'It's about the age difference between that chap and his girlfriend,' Mike replied in a low voice. 'He's about forty and she's just turned twenty.'

'That doesn't make him a paedo,' said Mark, with a note of annoyance.

'No, I agree. And what's more, it's ruining their tenth anniversary.'

Mark had just taken a swig of his beer as he worked out the arithmetic, with the result that he very nearly returned the contents of his mouth over the bar, but he just managed to avoid doing that and caught the glint in Mike's eye.

After a couple of little coughs to make sure he wasn't going to choke, Mark said 'That's not actually true, is it?'

'No. His name is Peter Doe and he sometimes has to write it as P. Doe, so they all think that's funny. I bet he's ever so grateful to his parents. But it gives me the opportunity to tell my little joke. You've got to have a laugh, haven't you? Anyway, I haven't seen you in here, lately. Where have you been, mate?'

Mark took another sip of his beer before answering, rather hesitatingly. 'I've been going out with this girl from Heacham. So we've been frequenting the pubs in that area.'

'So how come you're not out knobbing her tonight?' asked Mike in his usual coarse manner.

Mark inwardly cringed at the term, especially as their 'knobbing' hadn't been too brilliant, anyway. 'We packed up a couple of weeks ago,' he said, reluctantly.

'Ah, that's pissbodical, mate. So you're back on the market, then?'

'I'm not in any hurry. Women always mess you around. You should know. You're always finding your wife in the Bricklayer's Arms.' It was Mike's own little joke, because his pub was called the Bricklayer's Arms.

'That's all right as long as I don't find her in the Carpenter's Arms. That's disloyal on two counts,' said Mike. 'Take my advice. You need to get right out there, again. It's a bit like falling of a bike. You need to remount as soon as possible to get your confidence back.' That was probably nearer the truth than Mike realised because Mark's confidence had been really hit by his failure with Jenny.

'What about that lovely little Debbie Pope? If you had the chance, you'd have to give her one, wouldn't you? It would be rude, not to.' Mike used to work at Greshams before taking over the Bricklayer's and like every other red-blooded male at Greshams, was attracted to Debbie with the cute little turned-up nose and green eyes.

Despite Mark's previous infatuation with Debbie, he'd never previously entertained lustful intentions. He just wanted her as a girlfriend, but that was before he'd met Jenny and had been introduced to the pleasures of the flesh. But he knew how someone like Mike thought, so he joined in the banter. 'Yes, she is lovely. If I had to give her marks out of ten, I'd give her one. But she won't go out with anyone she works with. I can't say I blame her. There's always someone ready to poke their noses into other peoples' affairs.'

'Yes,' said Mike, 'I miss poking out around into everyone else's business. 'Cause before her, you were after that Karen woman, weren't you? Now she really had a body on her. Not everyone's cup of tea, I admit, but fantastic legs. Not a lot up top, though. Always a shame in my book, but wonderful strong hips – full of kids.'

Mark couldn't help picturing Karen's wonderful strong hips and remembering her sitting on his lap, with her incredibly firm buttocks squirming around. 'The last I heard,' said Mark, 'was that she was about to get married.'

'What else is happening at the old place?' asked Mike. 'And how are you getting on as a surveyor?'

'I'm not a surveyor,' came the terse reply. 'I'm a bloody dogsbody. I fetch crappy coffee from the crappy coffee machine; I do crappy filing for anyone who's too lazy to get off their backside and I'm at everyone's beck and call to hold their crappy rods when they go out on site. I don't even have my own crappy rod. When I ask for my own sites, I'm told Dougie gets all the small sites as he's still classed as a trainee.'

'So it's going all right, then' said Mike.

'No, it's bloody not! At least when I worked in Payroll there was a purpose to my job. I thought this was going to lead to a career.'

'Well, I'm glad I asked. Excuse me; I'd better serve this gentleman. 'What will it be, Arnie? The usual? Because you usually have the usual, don't you?'

Mark had a look towards the pinball machine which was still occupied and he didn't fancy waiting any longer, so he finished his drink and decided to leave, giving Mike a little wave as he left.

'Keep your chin up, Mark. Remember every silver lining has a cloud,' Mike called out loud from the other end of the bar. Mark remembered that Penny always used to say that when he worked in the Payroll department. And *As one door closes another door shuts.'*

Mark felt as low as he had ever been. He thought his affair with Jenny was going so well and he was happier than he had ever felt before. Then it all came crashing down that one evening when she wanted to meet at a pub in Geldby, a small village approximately midway between Heacham and Mark's home town of Sanford, as though it were neutral ground. Normally, when they went out together, it would be arranged on the previous date, because Mark wasn't on the 'phone at home. Then Mark would drive to Jenny's house to collect her, but this time she had 'phoned him at work, sounding very subdued. 'Shall I pick you up?' he asked, not suspecting what was happening.

'No, I'm going to borrow mum's car. I'll see you at 7.30 tonight.' Then put the 'phone down before Mark could enquire further. He thought it all a bit strange, but still didn't suspect anything sinister. After all, Jenny always seemed to be the one driving the relationship. She was 18 months older and being a divorcee, was much more experienced in so many matters. Mark had not yet turned 20 and had led a very sheltered life.

When he arrived at the pub, she was waiting in the car park in her mother's little mini, which had been christened 'Ethel' because the number plate contained the letters 'EFL.' Mark still thought it was silly to give a car a name. On that basis, his car would have to be called 'BAH'.

It was just turning dark and there was a chill in the air. Mark went to give Jenny a hug and kiss as usual, but she just backed away and said 'Let's go inside.' Mark didn't like this.

As they entered, all the locals stared as they usually did in a Norfolk country pub. Jenny turned and said 'Let me buy the drinks. What will you have?' Now that really was strange. Jenny often bought him a drink, but only after Mark had already bought at least one round.

They found a quiet table by a draughty window and they both took an initial sip of their drinks. 'Mark,' she said. 'Do you remember me asking that if you ever decided to end our relationship, that you would promise to do it face to face? Well, I'm not going to be hypocrite. This is why I asked to meet you, tonight.'

Mark's head starting swimming around. He had guessed that something was amiss, but not this, surely not? All he could say in a trembling voice was 'Why?'

'There's someone else.' She paused for just a few seconds. 'I haven't always been a hundred per cent honest with you. When we first met, I told you I'd gotten divorced because my husband had been unfaithful. That wasn't true – although he did have a fling later; after he'd discovered that I'd been having an affair. There was this chap I worked with who was married with 2 children. He wouldn't leave his wife because of the children. I tried to break it off several times and when I first met you, I thought I had finally moved on, so there was no point in telling you. And I shall be forever grateful to you for helping me through that period, even though you knew nothing about it. Your friendship really helped.'

'Friendship?' thought Mark. 'Was that all it was?' But he couldn't speak. He was literally dumbfounded.

'Anyway,' she continued, 'his marriage has become so strained that he now feels it's best for the children if it ends. And I've been seeing him again. I have enjoyed our evenings together, Mark, but it's something else when I'm with Joe. He's able to wine and dine me because he earns decent money. It's not your fault you can't afford to treat me very often. He's also arranged a weekend away in Paris, which you could never do.'

Mark finally found his voice. 'I get a raise at the end of this month. I was going to take you for a meal somewhere.' It sounded pathetic, but he couldn't think of anything else to say at that point.

'I'm sorry, Mark. That would have been nice of you. But it's not just about things like that. I always enjoyed your company.'

'Was it about sex? I know that was never satisfactory.'

'No, Mark. Again, that wasn't your fault. But it was a waste of time in the back of your car.'

There had been one occasion when Jenny's parents have gone out for the evening and they had made use of Jenny's bed. This didn't seem spontaneous enough to be truly satisfying. A better opportunity presented itself when Mark's elder sister asked him to baby-sit and Jenny accompanied him. Barbara insisted they help themselves to the drinks cabinet and the mood was helped by a decent stereo system with a selection of Dionne Warwick and Nat King Cole LPs. Both instances could be classed as 'proper sex', but they only made them both more frustrated that it couldn't have been repeated. Mark still considered himself sexually inexperienced and his sex life with Jenny had consisted predominantly of heavy-petting in the car. They often talked about arranging a night away in Derbyshire, because it had long been an ambition of Mark's to take Jenny to see Monsal Head. But their relationship had started in the autumn, gone through the dark days of winter and just as spring had arrived, it was now all over.

Mark wanted to try to persuade Jenny to change her mind, but he knew it was a waste of time. Not only that, but he was starting to feel really angry about the way he had been used. He grabbed his drink quiet violently and she could tell there was a degree of anger.

'You must hate me, Mark,' she said. 'I was hoping we could still be friends.'

'I don't know what I'm thinking at the moment. I'm not sure I believe it all. How often have you seen him while we've been going out together?'

'Only in the last month. Are you still going to play badminton with us?'

'Are you?' he asked abruptly. Mark had just realised that over the last few weeks, he and Jenny had been kissing and cuddling in his car, while she had started seeing this Joe bloke again.

'I'd like to,' she replied, 'but not if you think it's going to be awkward.'

'No, you carry on. I'm sure there's somewhere nearer to home.' He didn't believe that, but apart from the 'awkwardness' as Jenny put it, he didn't want everyone else at the club to see him, knowing they'd split up.

'I think I'm going home, now,' he added and gulped down his last mouthful of beer and stood up to leave. Jenny left her half-finished glass of cider and also stood up. Mark walked out, but did just hold the door open for her, without looking back.

'Goodbye, Mark,' she said as he reached his car. 'I am sorry the way it turned out.'

'Goodbye, Jenny.' He waited until he knew her car had started successfully before moving off himself. He was still gentleman enough to ensure she wasn't going to be stranded in the middle of nowhere.

The irony was that Mark had never been certain that Jenny was the person with whom he wanted to settle down. Since those first few very enjoyable dates, the world had still turned. There had been no new stars in the sky; no angels singing in Heavenly choirs. But she did radiate happiness and it was always wonderful to be in her company. With all the other girls with whom he had developed an infatuation, it had been unrequited, and he would have moved Heaven and Earth for a date with each of them, but with Jenny, he had never had to work at it, so he'd never really appreciated what he had. He suspected he would now – once the anger had died down.

* * * * * *

After Mark's trip to the Bricklayer's, he went straight home. He wasn't sure what he would have achieved by drinking on his own, but he was fed up with moping about his parents' home. His old mate Dougie used to be a regular at the Bricklayer's, but since getting married, Dougie was spending more and more time at home with his wife and new-born little girl, and it had been a long shot to expect him to have been there.

The truth was that Mark had indeed developed very strong feelings for Jenny without ever realising the fact. Despite his anger directed towards her, his whole body ached to be with her again. At times, he wanted to drive to Heacham in the hope of seeing her, but he knew it wouldn't achieve anything, just as he knew that if he went to the badminton club, seeing her would do no more than make it even harder to get her out of his mind. He just had to live through this period of pain.

'You're back, soon,' said his mother as he walked in.

'I only popped out for a quick drink at the Bricklayer's,' he replied.

The rest of the family were watching television, so Mark went into the front room to play some music suitable for his mood. The first and most obvious record was 'Giving up on Love' by Jerry Butler. It perfectly summed up his mood, as did the Curtis Mayfield song on the flipside – 'I've been trying', where Jerry imploringly sings that he doesn't understand *'Why can't I be your only man?'* 'Mr. Pitiful' by Otis Redding was obviously just self-indulgent, but his 'I've Been Loving You Too Long (to Stop Now)' deserved a play. Ironically, the song was part written by Jerry Butler.

What would Mark do without his music to keep him sane?

He started to think hard about how he was to turn his life around. His social life had always suffered its ups and downs. His friendship with Gary had ceased quite suddenly when Gary started going out with Jean, in much the same way as his social life with Dougie had deteriorated once Dougie married. The football season had come to an end, with a similar outcome to the previous season, where Mark's Saturday club won nearly every match and his Sunday club (Greshams) ended rock bottom again. Tennis had re-commenced on Fridays. At the moment, that was the only occasion Mark went out anywhere – and that was very dependent upon the weather.

And then it struck him. Of all the girls he had tried to date over the last few years, there was only one that had always shown promise if the timing was right. He had twice asked Jane for a date, but each time she had been seeing someone else, but on the first occasion, she had said 'What a pity you didn't ask me a few weeks earlier.' To his mind, that left the door open. She wasn't the most beautiful woman he'd ever met, but she had a certain appeal to him. She was tall, well-built and with plenty of curves, albeit in a slightly overweight sort of way. Despite the fact that he'd always fancied Jane, he'd never developed an infatuation with her as he'd done with other girls he'd fancied. And that suited him while he was still nursing his feelings for Jenny. He wanted a social life again, preferably with female company with no strings attached.

Tomorrow, he would get hold of her number from the telephone directory and call her in the evening. 'I wonder what's on at the pictures,' he thought.

CHAPTER 2

Saturday Night at the Movies

'Hello Jane. It's Mark Barker.'

'Who?'

'Mark from Greshams.'

'Oh, yes, Mark. Sorry. I didn't know your surname. How are you?' She sounded quite pleased to hear from Mark.

'I'm fine, thank you,' he lied. 'I hope you don't mind me calling you like this out of the blue. It's been a while since I last saw you and I was wondering if you would like to come out with me sometime.'

'Umm. Well, yes; all right, then. When did you have in mind and where are we going?'

'Any time suits me, apart from Friday.' Mark didn't want to risk his Friday tennis as that was his only current social activity. 'I thought we might go to the pictures, if you don't mind a "Carry On" film. It's all I could find, but I could do with a laugh.'

'I don't mind a "Carry On" film, as long as I haven't already seen it. Which one is it?'

'It's the latest one – "Carry On Up the Khyber".'

'Well, I haven't seen that one. Why do you say you could do with a laugh?'

'Oh, I won't bore you with all that,' he said. Why did he have to go and say such a stupid thing? 'It's mainly problems with my job. Do you want to make it Saturday? The film is on at the Majestic in Lynn. It starts at 7.30.'

'Yes, Saturday is fine. Will you pick me up?'

'Well, I wasn't going to make you walk. How about 6.45 from your house? I'd rather allow plenty of time to get there and buy our tickets.'

And it was all arranged. Normally, when Mark tried to date someone, he would get extremely nervous, but whether he was just gaining more self-confidence as a result of dating Jenny, or whether he wasn't going to get too upset if Jane had said 'no', he really didn't know. There had been a time when he would have got very excited at the prospect of a date, but this date wasn't that important to him – and that was a very big mistake.

Mark had always placed his women on a pedestal, but his attitude towards Jane was all wrong and out of character. She had done nothing to deserve this.

He was thinking that if things went well on Saturday, he might try a little seduction, because he was missing that aspect of his relationship with Jenny and he would quite like to explore Jane's curvy body and compare it to Jenny's.

* * * * * *

Mark had first met Jane during the time before he owned a car, when he would regularly get a lift home from work with Margaret and her husband. Margaret was an elderly lady who worked in Accounts and she lived in the same road as Jane. Mark had enjoyed being squashed next to Jane in the back of the Mini Countryman and he'd noticed that she had made no attempt to avoid him as they were thrown around at the fast corners.

As Mark drew up outside Jane's house, she came out of her front door before he even had time to switch off his engine. He knew his 1959 Ford Anglia wasn't going to make an impression, but he couldn't afford anything better at this time. At least he had finished paying for it. When his mother had learned of his small pay rise, she demanded extra housekeeping from him, and by the time he'd paid some extra income tax, there hadn't really been much of an increase. So he would have to keep his Anglia a little longer yet.

He leaned over to open the door rather than get out like he used to do with Jenny; the first of many mistakes he was due to make that evening.

'You're nice and prompt, Mark,' Jane said as she sat down.

'I've always liked punctuality – it's almost an obsession with me, so thank you for being on time, yourself.' It was as near as Mark was going to get to paying Jane a compliment all evening. He had intended to start by saying how nice she looked and how pleased he was to see her again, but she had led the conversation in a different direction. However, as he drove off, he did say 'I've finally managed to get a date with you when neither of us is going out with someone else. I take it you're not seeing anyone else at the moment?'

'Well, there is a chap I've been seeing, but he's at University in London and it's not that serious. What's your situation?'

'I've just finished with someone. That was serious – or so I thought.

9

She had other ideas. I hope you don't mind going over to Lynn. I've seen the film at the Odeon and the place has too many bad memories for me. Anyway, the Majestic is nicer.'

Then Mark went quiet. He realised he'd said the wrong things. But before he could change the subject, Jane said 'You sound like you're on the rebound.' It was intended as a throw-away line that didn't require a response, but, unfortunately, Mark did respond. And before he knew it, he was telling all the details about the way he'd been treated by Jenny. He didn't stop until they pulled into the car park at the back of the Majestic. Jane had been looking for the right opportunity to change the subject, but Mark never gave her chance.

As they walked round to the front entrance and mounted the steps, Mark said, 'Anyway, I'm sure we'll enjoy this film. Do you want go upstairs or downstairs?' Jane was hoping she would enjoy the film, because so far the evening had been a complete let-down.

Once seated and while they were waiting for the film show to commence, Jane asked 'Did you ever ask Pauline to go out with you?' That struck Mark as a very strange question to ask. Mark met Pauline at more or less the same time as Jane, because like Jane, she used to wait in Reception for a lift home – in Pauline's case with her father who worked at Greshams. Mark would engage both ladies in conversation while he too was waiting for his lift, but at first regarding Pauline as being totally out of his league, especially as at the time, she was engaged to be married.

'I did, actually. But only after I had already asked you. If you remember, you were seeing someone else at the time.' Mark didn't want Jane to think she was second choice, even if she had been. The truth was that he thought he would have more chance of success with Jane.

'And did you go out with her?'

'Nearly. She said 'yes' at first, but then changed her mind at the last minute because she was about to emigrate with her parents and didn't want to get involved with anyone at that time. Why do you ask?'

'Because she told me once that she would like to go out with you, but was afraid that you were too shy to ask.'

This was a bombshell to Mark. It did take him ages to ask Pauline, mostly due to lack of opportunity but also because, at the time, he was too obsessed with Karen. However, Pauline was so gorgeous that he felt it would have done his credibility a power of good just to have been seen in her presence. Marks out of ten would have been ten just on looks alone. If only he'd asked her out earlier. Mark had never possessed any confidence in his appeal to the opposite sex.

'I'm curious,' said Jane. 'Why did you just say *only after you'd already asked me?*" Surely, you would rather have gone out with Pauline?'

Was Jane just fishing for a compliment? Mark didn't know how to respond without either telling a blatant lie or appearing to be rude. He was rescued by the sound of a cockerel crowing, which announced the start of Pathé News as the lights dimmed and the curtains were drawn back. Mark was hoping Jane wouldn't later push him for an answer. To say 'Because I thought I had more chance with you,' wouldn't have sounded very nice.

During the main feature, Mark realised that Jane was only the second person he had ever dated, so he thought he ought to start taking this seriously. The film would have lightened the atmosphere, so perhaps there was still time to have a bit of fun. He would invite Jane for a quiet drink afterwards. He had an interesting little anecdote lined up if he could just fit it into the conversation.

Meanwhile, Jane had already decided that this evening had been a mistake. However, by the time Mark asked her if she fancied a drink, it had been quite a while since either of them had drunk anything, so she agreed to a very quick drink. Mark suggested the Riverside Bar off the Tuesday Market Place. He always found this to be one of the more suitable places to entertain a lady when in King's Lynn.

While Mark was ordering the drinks, Jane took in the atmosphere of the Riverside Bar with its Lobster pots and fishermen's nets draped from the ceilings and walls.

'This is the first time I've been here,' said Jane. 'It's nice' and she started to relax.

Jane was drinking a half-pint of bitter, which Mark found quite endearing for some strange reason. While they both took a few sips of their beer, Mark had his first real chance to assess Jane's appeal. Even before this evening, he had never really had chance to study her that closely. She was wearing a plain knee-length brown dress. In fact, Mark had never seen Jane in bright colours. She did actually have quite an attractive face without being particularly glamorous. She had high cheekbones, deep brown eyes, a high forehead with her long reddish hair swept back. Mark thought she would have looked better with some of her hair left over her forehead. She had several freckles, which Mark guessed also covered most of her body. She also had a very faint moustache with no attempt to disguise it with make-up. Even this, Mark found to be endearing. She was very tall – about five feet ten, he thought, with broad shoulders and a pleasantly proportioned bosom which pointed in the right direction. She may have been a little overweight, but because she sat upright and always walked with a very upright stance, Mark felt she carried her weight well. On a scale of one to ten, Mark would award 8 or 9, but he certainly wouldn't mind giving her one. However, she wasn't Jenny. She was probably more attractive than Jenny and probably had a better figure. But she wasn't Jenny. She had shapelier legs than Jenny and as far as Mark knew, she didn't have affairs with married men, but he couldn't help wishing that he was with Jenny. Whenever he had been with Jenny, he wanted her because she had a certain 'sex appeal', which wasn't immediately apparent with Jane. Nevertheless, he knew he ought to capitalise on the fact that he was on a date with an attractive woman.

'I don't think that film is going to win any Oscars,' said Mark, 'but you know what you're going to get with a 'Carry On' film.'

'Yes, it was entertaining,' agreed Jane. 'Silly, but entertaining. I don't think they actually filmed in Asia, do you?'

'I think I read that some of it was filmed in Wales. They certainly didn't bother with historical accuracy. Anyway, I've got this funny little story,' he added. 'Jenny worked in a school and one evening, just before Christmas, we got invited to a party in Castle Rising. Practically everyone there worked at the school. I found myself stuck talking to this woman – I think she was Deputy Head or something. And she asked if I was a teacher. I said *"No, surely you can see I don't look intelligent enough to be a teacher."* She said, *"Do you think these teachers look intelligent, then?"*

I said *"Oh, yes. I'm sure I could pick out all the teachers here,"* So she challenged me to do it – and I did. I went round the room picking them out one by one. When Jenny re-joined us, the woman said *"Do you know your boyfriend is clever. He just picked out all the teachers in the room"*

When the woman left us alone, Jenny said *"You wicked person. I'd already told you who all the teachers were."* It was a bit of a boring party, and I thought I'd have a bit of fun. As you've probably noticed, I'm not that good at small talk.'

'I don't think I am,' replied Jane, wishing Mark would find a subject that didn't involve his precious Jenny. 'I think I'd rather stay at home with a good book. Which reminds me – do you think we should make our way home, now?' Mark got the message. He hadn't had chance to practice his seduction technique, and the truth was he didn't feel particularly seductive. And Jane hadn't given him any signs of encouragement all evening.

Both of them were fairly quiet on the way home. That last remark had stifled the conversation. Just before they reached Jane's road, Mark said 'I'm sorry if I haven't been very good company tonight. As you said yourself, I'm on the rebound.'

'You just need a bit more time, Mark. Thanks for asking me out.'

★ ★ ★ ★ ★ ★

Over the next few days, Mark realised how he'd messed things up with Jane. He re-lived the evening and every little conversation and he found it added to his woe. He knew he had made a fool of himself and he also knew that Jane must hold him in very low regard. If he had only conducted himself like a sensible human being, he might have been able to look forward to some further evenings with an attractive woman and the chance to enlarge upon his experience with the opposite sex. Now he was back on the shelf and he only had himself to blame.

He decided he had to call Jane and apologise. He wouldn't attempt another date with her, but it might improve her opinion of him, because Mark didn't like anyone to have a low opinion of him.

So he tried to call her one evening. The first time, her father answered and after a short delay, her father announced that she wasn't at home that evening. Mark wondered if she was deliberately avoiding talking to him. But he tried again a few days later. This time, Jane answered the 'phone, so she couldn't pretend to be out.

'Don't worry, Jane. I'm not going to ask you out again; much as I'd like to, though. But I'm not going to put you through all that again. I just wanted to apologise for my behaviour the other night.'

'In what respect?' Jane asked, although she knew what he should be apologising for.

'Well, in short, not paying you enough attention and being too absorbed in my own problems. I've wanted to go out with you for such a long while and then, when I finally got the chance, I blew it. I can assure you that I am normally better company than that. I know I'm not one to sweep a girl off her feet, but I can do a lot better than that.'

'I was a bit surprised,' said Jane, 'Because whenever I've seen you in the past, I always thought you could be quite amusing, so I don't think you were really yourself on Saturday.'

'No, I wasn't. Anyway, as I said, I'm not going to ask you out again. Not now anyway. I'm going to stay away from girls for a little while, until I think I can treat them properly. So please don't judge me on Saturday's events.'

'No, I think I'm more likely to judge you on tonight's conversation. It is nice of you to call.' That sounded nicely put he thought.

'I just didn't want you to think badly of me. I would like to give it another go, but just not yet. Perhaps I'll just bump into you sometime and take it from there.'

'Yes. I hope you can sort your life out,' she said.

'Right then. I'm glad I called to get it off my chest. It's been bothering me. I'll just say goodbye for now.'

'Bye Mark. And thanks for the call.'

Mark did feel better for that, but he also still wanted to go out with Jane. Ironically, he had just improved his chances of another date by saying he wasn't going to ask for one. He wondered how long he could leave it before he tried again. At least two months, he thought – probably a bit longer. By then, Jane would probably being going out with someone else. In the meantime, he certainly didn't want to mope about the house feeling sorry for himself. Perhaps he could get into the departmental Darts team. That would get him out of the house for at least one extra night a week.

CHAPTER 3

What Now?

'Mark! Go get some coffee,' said Ian Beddington.

'Sorry! Is that the same as 'Go get some coffee, *please*?'

'No! It's the same as 'Go get some coffee, *now!*'

'Sorry. My powers can only be used for good,' Mark replied obstinately.

'Your powers will cease to exist if you don't do as you're told.'

'Then who's going to do all your filing?'

'We'll employ some other little insignificant toe-rag.'

'And here's me thinking I've made myself indispensable.'

This banter was typical of the conversations in the Surveyors' office. Mark was immune to the insults and the bullying, but it always brought home to him that his job would continue to bring frustrations for the foreseeable future. He knew from his experience in the Payroll office that he was capable of performing work of a high standard if he was given the opportunity and the responsibility, but the Surveyors' office was currently overmanned, so he could expect no immediate change in his fortunes. He had been looking out for new positions at the local Labour Exchange and in the 'Situations Vacant' column of his local paper. So far, nothing suitable had presented itself. There had been a surveyor's job in Fakenham, but he couldn't honestly expect to get that as he hadn't done any actual surveying. And he certainly wasn't going to apply for a position as an office junior.

It was time he did something about his situation. He decided to confront his manager, Reg Stanmore.

He knocked on Reg's door, which was almost always kept open to the adjoining Surveyors' office. 'Reg, can I have a word about a couple of things? You've always said your office is open if I have any concerns.'

'Of course you can Mark. Would you like Pat to leave us alone?' Pat was Reg's secretary.

'No, it's not that personal. I could do with another rise, but that's not what I want to talk to you about.' Mark knew that with the company restricting pay rises, Reg had done well to get Mark any sort of rise back in April.

'When I joined your department, I thought I was going to train to be a surveyor. But so far, all I seem to do is filing and fetching coffee. When am I going to get my own contracts?'

Reg didn't have to think very long before replying. 'As you probably know, the company is struggling to pick up new contracts at the moment, so there just isn't that much work around. I'm afraid I have to ask you to just stick at it for a while longer. It seems the company are going to start making and installing aluminium windows. The design team have already come up with the designs, and Stan and Ali are working on the prototypes.'

'That will be another fine mess, then,' Mark said.

Stan Wilkinson and Yousef Khan worked in the New Products workshop. Some wag in the factory had christened them Stan and Ali. Yousef didn't understand the joke. In fact, Stan wasn't too pleased either.

'There are several other companies starting to get in on aluminium windows, but we've got a good established sales force,' Reg added. 'So that should generate some new contracts, but it will be some time before we as surveyors see the benefit of it.

'What happened to that curtain walling that was going to be the next big thing?' Mark asked.

'No one was interested in buying it. You said there were a couple of things you wanted to talk about. What's the other one?'

'I'd like to get into the darts team. It's the Surveyors' team and I'm a surveyor – sort of.'

'We've already got 4 people. I can't drop someone just so that you can play.'

'But George is in the team and he's not a surveyor.'

'I'm still not going to drop him just so that you can play.'

'Well, if you're short, keep me in mind.'

'I will, but Dougie is first reserve.'

'I'm glad I came to talk to you. You did say your door is always open.'

'That's so you don't have to open it when you leave.' Reg thought he would match Mark's sarcasm with a little of his own, but then added 'If I can help you with either matter, I will, but I can't promise anything. I think Sam is going up to Doncaster on Thursday. You can go with him to help measure up. That will be something a little different.'

Sam Baggaley usually preferred to do his own measuring and in any case, Mark didn't always enjoy Sam's company, because he was half deaf and conversations were often difficult. But at least it was a day away from filing and fetching coffee. Mark went to tell him the good news.

'I would be glad of your company young Mark, but I've got some personal business to see to that day, so I want to go alone.'

Ian Beddington decided to stick in his oar. 'You're not supposed to carry out personal business when you're out on company business. So you can take Mark with you on Thursday!' He deliberately spoke loud enough for Reg to hear from the next office. Ian was a very conscientious individual who did not suffer fools gladly.

'I didn't realise you were now in charge of the department,' replied Sam.

From the adjoining office, Reg called out 'Sam. Would you mind taking Mark with you on Thursday?'

'My pleasure,' came the reply and then Sam turned to Mark and added 'I'll pick you up at 7.30. I'll need directions to your house.' Sam wasn't being deliberately unfriendly, but he was a bit of a loner and didn't always join in with the office banter. This was partly down to his need to wear a hearing aid. Mark thought Sam may have had plans to take his girlfriend out for the day, but if they were going to Doncaster, Mark thought he was probably doing her a favour.

* * * * * *

Later that same day, Mark bumped into Paul Sturridge. Paul worked in the costing department and had been largely responsible for introducing Mark and Jenny at the badminton club in Hunstanton.

'I haven't seen you at badminton, lately,' he said to Mark.

'I play tennis in the summer,' Mark replied. 'Are you still getting a good turnout?' Mark had immediately thought about Jenny and would welcome any news about her.

'Yes. All the usual people. A couple of them have asked me about you'

'Anyone in particular?'

'Tonya and Jenny.'

'You know Jenny and I have split up, don't you?'

'Yes, she did tell me.'

'And how is she?'

'She seems very happy – as usual, in fact. But she wanted to know if you're all right.'

'Tell her I'm all right.'

'And are you?'

'No, not really. But I'll survive.'

'Are you going to join us when the tennis is finished for the year?'

'I don't think so. It's a bit of a trek in the winter. I'll see if I can find a local club.'

'I'll tell Jenny you asked after her.'

'I'd rather you didn't. I feel pretty bitter about the way things turned out.'

'How can anyone feel bitter about Jenny? I thought you two always seemed happy together.'

'I didn't realise what was going on, so I find it quite easy to be bitter, but I don't really want to talk about it.' Actually, he did, but he knew it wouldn't achieve anything and this conversation was only going to disturb Mark's equilibrium all over again. It was still too early to contact Jane again. Even the lovely Debbie couldn't stir Mark to 'remount the bike' as Mike would have put it. It seemed strange to think that only a few months earlier, Mark had a crush on Debbie, but now he didn't think he would go out with her even if he had the chance (which he didn't!). She was lovely, but she no longer stirred Mark's ardour.

Mark's trip to Doncaster was mostly uneventful. His conversations with Sam were hard work as Sam's hearing aid seemed to be playing up. In any case, Mark knew that his conversations with Sam nearly always included discussions about women and Mark really didn't need that in his frame of mind. They'd finished their site visit by lunchtime and found a pub which sold unappetising bread rolls to accompany their beer. Mark challenged Sam to a game of darts, which Mark won surprisingly comfortably. His game had improved dramatically in the last year or so. The dartboard in the pub didn't have any trebles, so this took a bit of getting used to.

'You should be in the darts team,' Sam told Mark.

'Would you like to say that to Reg? I'd like to get in the team.'

Whether or not Sam did say anything to Reg, Mark never knew, but two weeks later Reg asked him to play in the team as he and Dougie had to go to London for the day and they couldn't be sure of getting back in time. The match was against the Despatch Bay who were currently top of the league and were unbeaten. The Surveyors team were mid-table, but unbeaten at home. Their home venue was the Bricklayer's Arms where Mark had done most of his playing in the last few months. The dartboard was tucked up a dark corner and the board itself was a bit spongy, requiring a certain technique to ensure the darts stayed stuck in. The home team that evening consisted of Ian Beddington, Noel (Billy) Bunter, George Harris (Mark's cousin and Company Accountant) and Mark himself. Ian was acting captain and would anchor the team. It was usual for the best player to anchor, whilst the second best opened, but when Ian realised that Mark did not have his own 'arrows', he feared the worst and decided to sacrifice him against the opposition's lead. Not having his own 'arrows' was not that much of handicap because Mark was used to the pub's chunky darts.

The match kicked off with Mark losing the first game after being stuck on double one for an eternity. His opponent, Danny Scott, worked as a labourer in the Despatch Bay. Despite winning the first game Danny was obviously not finding the conditions to his liking. Each player had to win the best of three games against his corresponding opponent. Each game was 301, starting and ending with a double.

In the second game, Mark got his lead double first time, whilst Danny struggled to get started and before long Mark had built up a big lead, leaving him just 32 to throw. His first dart scored 16, grazing the intended bed, but serving as a marker for his next dart which entered the double eight to a loud cheer from the home team.

Both players started the third game well, but having got used to the conditions, Danny soon built a lead and narrowly missed his double top to win. Mark needed 161 to win and the odds did not look good. But he stood at the oche for a few seconds while he calculated his 'out'. The first dart went straight into the treble 19; the second quickly followed into the treble 18 and almost immediately his final dart entered the bull. Mark always found that if he could get his throwing arm into some kind of rhythm he could be more accurate – a bit like a gunfighter who might struggle to hit anything if he aims, but succeeds if he can draw quickly (or so they say in the films).

George, who was scoring, said 'Hold on, Mark. What on Earth have you done? Take your time.'

But Mark knew he had just won and was waiting for everyone else to catch up with his arithmetic. George was adding it all up and was poised to chalk the score when it dawned on him that Mark had scored the requisite number of points. 'That's it,' he called in a high pitched voice.

'It can't be,' said Danny. 'He's bust'

Mark held his hand out to Danny ready to be congratulated as soon as Danny had caught up. He wasn't a happy person when he eventually shook

Mark's hand and said 'Well done. What will you have?' But it wasn't with any degree of grace.

Billy Bunter was next and he lost quite badly, but George won his game against their weakest player, so the team were guaranteed at least a draw.

The last pairing was Ian Beddington against Red Miller – a lorry driver and feared union activist, who sported a thick red beard and constantly smoked a smelly pipe. As soon as Red started warming up, he was criticising the dartboard and the cramped conditions, even though everything was perfectly legal. Ian quickly took the lead, due in part to the fact that Red's darts kept falling out of the board. And indeed, Ian won both games convincingly.

'You wait 'till you come to our place, with a proper board,' Red said as he begrudgingly shook Ian's hand.

Mike, the Landlord had laid on a spread of sandwiches and the away team were invited to help themselves, but Danny said they were expected at their own pub. After the opposition had left, it was generally agreed that it was bad form not to stay and be sociable, but their company was not missed. So the home team tucked in to the food and carried on playing darts among themselves with a game of Shanghai followed by a game of 'killer', which became quite intense but made all the more enjoyable due to the team victory against the league leaders. While this was all going on, Reg and Dougie turned up and were greeted with the great news. Everyone wanted to have their say about how the match was won. Then Mark chipped in and said out loud 'You should have heard old Red going on about the state of the board and the lighting and that was just in the warm-up. He kept going on about it all night, silly old git.'

'He's sat up the corner if you want to ask him,' said George, desperately trying to stop Mark saying anything else.

Mark looked towards the corner table and there sat Red with someone who looked like she might be his wife, both with a plate of sandwiches in front of them. They had stopped eating and were glowering at Mark.

Mark just said 'That was right, wasn't it Red?' He had to say something, but that was all he could think to say. Mark had never felt so embarrassed in his life before.

Red didn't reply, but carried on glowering. Mark decided not to say another word all evening, except that as he walked past Dougie, he said under his breath 'Shit!' Dougie gave him a big grin and patted him on his back.

A few minutes later, Red and his wife both rose, but as they left, they gave Mark another hard stare. Neither of them spoke. George called out 'Goodnight, Red. Thanks for the game.'

It was intended as a friendly gesture, but Red did not respond. Mark had made an enemy for life – a fact that would come back to haunt him later.

The next day, the office was buzzing with the news of the victory. The Buying Office in particular was pleased with the result because their team was second in the league and they were the Despatch Bay's chief rivals for the title. Barney Briggs, who was the Chief Buyer, made a point of visiting the surveyors. Mark always thought Barney looked like a cockney spiv from an Ealing comedy, but he was an extremely likeable chap, with his pencil moustache and sharp three-piece suit. 'Mark, my ol' son. I 'eard you beat Danny. He 'asn't lost all season. 161 finish! You're a star.'

'Call it home advantage,' Mark replied modestly. 'I'm sure they'd beat us 9 times out of 10.'

'Yeah, but you did it when it mattered, my son. And Ian beat Red. Well done, Ian'

'But it wasn't me who put his nose out of joint,' replied Ian. 'That was our diplomatic young friend here.'

'Yes, I heard. I hope you don't ever get involved in any union negotiations, Mark.'

'I doubt whether I'll ever get involved in any negotiations,' Mark replied.

Despite Mark's success, he was still only second reserve and it was another seven weeks before he was asked to play again. This time it was against the Buying Office at the New Inn in Flitcham. And they lost 4-0. Mark had to borrow some darts and he lost his game badly, but it was still an enjoyable evening. Barney was on particularly good form, both with his darts and his wit. He said 'I had to get my team fired up for this one. I told them if they didn't win, I was going to shoot myself. And then I was going to shoot all of them. That did the trick.'

Mark always attended the home games even if he wasn't in the team, because he could always join in the friendly games after the match was over. So he now had at least one more fortnightly social event to help him forget his romantic problems.

CHAPTER 4

A Woman, A Lover, A friend

Mark was walking through town one Saturday morning, just on his way to the local record shop to buy a new LP, when he walked past a young lady who looked familiar. 'It can't be,' he thought. It had been 4 years since they had last met and then he had only known her for a few days, but she had left some lasting memories. If she had been wearing a mini-skirt as she used to do, he would have been in absolutely no doubt, because she possessed the most fantastic legs that Mark had ever set eyes upon, but this young lady was wearing a maxi-skirt. He turned to follow her with a view to getting another look. Certainly from the rear, she looked the part. She was the right height and build. There was only one way to find out if she was the same person.

'Blodwyn?' he called. The lady turned and Mark's heart started thumping. It had to be. Why else was she acknowledging his call? She looked at him with the same lovely pair of green eyes, but without any sign of obvious recognition.

'It is you. I thought you'd gone back to Wales.'

'I'm sorry,' she said. 'I don't remember you, see.' Oh, that lovely Welsh voice.

'It's Mark … from Greshams. You must remember.'

'What's Greshams?' she asked.

'Where you worked for one week in 1965 – before you had to go back to Wales.'

'Oh, yes – Greshams. And you worked there, as well did you?' Was she just teasing him? Surely she remembered those personal conversations they had?

'Yes, and the last time we spoke, I asked you out and you were going to let me know your answer next time you saw me. So what's it to be?'

'I don't remember any of this,' she said. 'Are you sure it was me?'

'Oh yes. You used to try and embarrass me by talking about your legs.' There was still no sign of recognition. 'You used to tell me your boyfriend said you had fat legs and you asked me what I thought.'

'Did I really? And what did you say to that?'

Mark wasn't sure he wanted a repeat of those conversations, so he just said 'I disagreed with him.'

'Yes, you did, didn't you? It's starting to come back now.' She was teasing him.

'I thought you'd gone back to your Gareth?'

'Oh, yes. That was a big mistake. He started getting very possessive and on one occasion, he hit me. So I came back to my parents in Sanford. I have a cousin whose husband hits her and I'm not going to stand for that. He wasn't getting a second chance.'

'What about the baby?' Mark asked.

'What baby?'

'Weren't you expecting?'

'Certainly not. Where on Earth did you get that from? I've never been pregnant.' She sounded cross.

'Sorry, I'm getting you mixed up with someone else who worked at Greshams and then left to have a baby.' The truth is that it was only Margaret who had started a rumour about Blodwyn being pregnant and, at the time, Mark didn't believe it anyway.

'So I've been waiting for four years for you to tell me if you will go out with me. I've been saving myself for you.'

'I doubt that. The thing is I don't really know you. I don't go out with strangers.'

'Well, when I asked you before, you did say you would go out with me if you weren't already going out with Gareth. I'm still the same person I was then. The invitation still stands if you want to.' Mark was aware that his heart was still thumping. Here was one person who would certainly take his mind off Jenny.

'If I remember rightly, you were very shy back then,' she said.

'I still am. My heart is thumping, you know.'

'Do you have a car?'

'Yes.'

'I like to go to the Maid's Head in King's Lynn on a Saturday night. If you come and pick me up, tonight, you can take me there.'

'That's great. I'd rather take you somewhere quieter. It's not very easy to talk to each other in there.' Mark had only ever been in the Maid's Head once and it had been very busy and very noisy.

'We can always go somewhere quieter later on. It's got to be the Maid's Head. I usually meet some friends in there.'

'All right. Where do you live?'

'23 Compton Drive, on the Northfleet Estate.'

'I know Compton Drive. It's just round the corner from our football pitch. How does 7.30 sound?'

'Make it eight o'clock. No one gets there that early, see.'

'Right then. Number 23.'

Mark had a strange feeling about this date. Blodwyn was definitely still a tease, but she had those legs! Legs that he thought had been lost to lucky old Wales. So it had to be worth her little games. He didn't like this new fashion for maxi-skirts. What happened to the 60's sexual revolution? If things carried on like this, blokes like him would be getting their thrills from a glimpse of ankle. He wasn't happy about going to the Maid's Head either. How was he meant to seduce her with all that noise? But he was determined to seduce her; even if it took a few dates to achieve. He couldn't think of anyone with whom he would rather spend an evening. And at that moment, that included Jenny. It may have been just a physical attraction, but what was wrong with that?

★ ★ ★ ★ ★ ★

At two minutes to eight, Mark pulled up at number 23 and knocked on the door. Blodwyn answered. She was wearing a white knee length dress which revealed a few inches of her lovely firm bosom. Mark remembered how white clothes showed up at the Maid's Head. There was some weird lighting that made anything white look luminous and Blodwyn would know that. Still at least, it wasn't another horrible maxi-skirt. And he wouldn't have been very happy if she had been wearing one of her very short mini-skirts for all the world to ogle at her all night.

He opened the passenger door for her and she said 'Oh, I remember you were always a gentleman. Thank you.' So much for her bad memory.

Mark had a sly look at her wonderful calves as she entered the car and made herself comfortable. Oh yes. Just as he remembered them.

As he sat down himself, he said 'You look lovely.' He felt a little embarrassed about this, but he recalled how he wished he had paid a compliment to Jane and still regretted not doing so.

'Why, thank you. I'm sorry I'm not wearing a mini-skirt. I know you like looking at my legs, but I've thrown all my short skirts away. I've never liked my legs and I only ever wore minis because that was the fashion.'

'She's already turned the conversation around to her legs,' he thought to himself. He had to steer the conversation away from her legs or he'd get one of those pyramids in his trousers like he did last time she talked about her legs. And that would be very embarrassing – although he hoped for a pyramid at some point during the evening, but not now.

'I didn't just ask you out for your legs, you know. You've lots of other things going for you,' he said as he started the car and moved off.

'Like what?'

'Well, there are your lovely green eyes, for a start. I'd want to go out with you just for your eyes. Then there's your lovely Welsh accent. There's something about a Welsh accent. Just with a woman, of course. I can't say Harry Secombe's ever done anything for me.'

'So if I speak to you softly and ask you to spend lots of money on me, would you?' She had deliberately softened her voice. She was in teasing mood again.

'Probably, except that I haven't got much money.'

'What if I really wanted something you couldn't afford?'

'I'd go and ask for a raise,' he said, thinking that this was a silly game.

'Do you still work in the Wages department?' she asked.

'No, I'm a surveyor now.' He wasn't going to admit to being a *Trainee* surveyor.

'That sounds like a lucrative career.'

'Well, I'm still building up to a lucrative career. What are you doing, now?'

'I work at Jacksons the wholesalers in town – in the accounts section.'

'And what do you like doing in your spare time?'

'Socialising; going out with friends.'

'Do you play any sports?'

'I quite like a game of tennis. I'm not very good, though.'

'Right answer', thought Mark, then said 'There's a group of us from work who play down the rec. every Friday. You would be most welcome to join us.'

'I might do, but, as I said, I'm not very good, see.'

'I wasn't when we started, but I soon improved. What about badminton.'

'I've never played badminton.' Mark decided not to push that option.

'Do you watch any sport – like football?'

'Don't like football. I like rugby. Big rugged men with big rugged thighs.'

Mark decided not to push that option either.

And the conversation continued in a 'getting to know each other' vein for the rest of the journey, with no further mention of legs. And they were soon parked in the Tuesday Market Place. While Blodwyn was doing something in her handbag, Mark walked round to open the passenger door for her. 'Oh, thank you, kind sir. I could get used to this treatment.' Mark was hoping there would be plenty of opportunity to do so. He wasn't going to leave anything to chance this time.

The Maid's Head was already busy and noisy. Mark fought his way to the bar to order a Babycham for Blodwyn and a small beer for himself. When he returned to Blodwyn, she was already busy talking to some girlfriends and made no effort to introduce Mark. He felt like a spare part at a wedding. He tried to stand next to her, but she was leaning towards her friends to talk in their ears and there wasn't space for Mark. This carried on for at least ten minutes until a tall good looking chap in his mid-twenties approached the group and Blodwyn broke away from her friends to talk to him. At first, Mark thought her body language indicated a certain frostiness, but then she seemed to visibly relent and they stood very close together talking in each other's ears.

Mark didn't like the look of this. With her bright white luminescent dress, Blodwyn stood out from all the other women in the room and was receiving lots of admiring looks, but no one was watching as intently as Mark. After a few more minutes, she turned towards Mark and pointed towards him for the benefit of her new companion, who looked at Mark with interest.

After a few more minutes of this, Blodwyn returned to Mark. He felt a wave of relief, but it was short-lived, because Blodwyn said 'I'll make my own way home, and started to walk away.

Mark grabbed her hand and stopped her. 'What do you mean? Where are you going?'

'I'm with my boyfriend over there.'

'Wait a minute!' But she was already walking away.

Mark just stood there watching her wonderful body walk back to this boyfriend and probably out of his life. He had been used. How could anyone behave like this? Maybe she didn't know for certain that this boyfriend would be there, but Mark now understood why she didn't want to go somewhere of his choosing. Now he stood there like a lemon with half a glass of beer and looking forward to a journey home on his own.

He finished the beer and pushed his way back to the bar to return the glass. 'You're not the first,' he heard a female voice say beside him. Mark looked to his right to see a woman was talking to him. 'I saw her do the same thing three weeks ago. When I saw her come in with you, I suspected the worst. She's the original prick-teaser.'

'She's done this before?' Mark asked, wanting to ask so much more, but knowing it would be hard work with so much noise around him. Before the lady could reply, he also asked 'Do you know him?'

'Oh, yes. He's Terry ...' Mark didn't catch the last name and he wasn't really interested, but he leaned closer towards the lady to hear what else she had to say. 'He lives in Terrington and I live in Clenchwarton. Everyone knows him. They've been going out together for months, but they keep splitting up and getting back together again.'

The lady seemed to be totally alone. She had a very friendly face and was holding an empty glass. 'Are you on your own?' he asked.

'Yes. Are you going to buy me a drink?'

'Can we go across the road to somewhere quieter? I think I want to get away from here.'

'All right,' she said returning the empty glass to the bar and following Mark outside.

'Is the Duke's Head all right?' Mark asked seeing the hotel next door.

'It's a bit dull. Let's go over to the Stable Bar.'

The Stable Bar was next to the Riverside Bar and part of the same hotel complex. Like the Riverside, the Stable Bar had a 'theme'. Mark had never been in a stable, so he didn't know how authentic it was, but it was quiet and relaxing.

'I'm Maggie,' the lady said, taking a sip of her vodka and orange.

'Mark,' replied Mark, pointing to himself.

'Was that the first time you'd been out with Blodwyn?'

'Yes. I worked with her about 4 years ago. She was a right tease then, so I half expected a struggle with her, but I didn't expect that sort of behaviour. You say you've seen her do this before?'

'Yes. Three weeks ago and I ended up talking to that poor unfortunate chap as well. Second-choice Maggie they ought to call me.' Mark was too honest to contradict her. Maggie wasn't in the same class as Blodwyn – at least not as far as looks and figure went, but class came in many forms. She was about twenty-five years old, he thought. She didn't use a lot of make-up. Mark couldn't put a name to her hair style, but it reminded him of Marilyn Monroe in 'Some Like It Hot' except that Maggie wasn't anything like Monroe, neither in looks nor figure, but she seemed to have a permanent smile. In any case, Blodwyn had highlighted that looks aren't everything.

'So do you live in Sanford, Mark?'

'Yes. Did the other chap from three weeks ago live there as well?'

'Oh yes. You've got to hand it to Blodwyn for attracting blokes with cars. I wish I had her looks. But we're all the same with the lights out. I've got better legs than Blodwyn. Old Thunderthighs we call her.' Maggie probably thought a chap like Mark preferred slim legs.

'I always think personality and character are the most important things,' Mark said. 'Not that you're not attractive,' he added quickly, thinking she might have taken his remarks as an insult. He quickly changed the subject. 'So you know this Terry chap then, do you?' Mark felt in need of confirmation of the some of the things he thought he had heard above the noise of the Maid's Head.

'Oh yes. He lives in Terrington and I live in Clenchwarton. Both villages know each other's business. He fancies himself as a bit of a ladies man and he's been out with other girls even while he was going out with Blodwyn. She finds out, splits up and still goes back to him. I went out with him about 2 years ago, but not for long. He always wants the latest model. So when, a few months ago, Blodwyn turned up at the Maid's Head, all legs and a skimpy mini-skirt, he was straight in there.'

'She told me she's stopped wearing mini-skirts.'

'That's probably Terry. He can be a bit possessive.'

'She was telling me about another old boyfriend who was a bit possessive and she packed it in with him.'

'Does that mean you are you hoping you're still in with a chance?' Maggie asked.

'Oh no. She's not going to mess me about again. I do have some pride, you know.'

'Good for you, Mark. Anyway, let's talk about something else. I heard a good joke at work yesterday. A man was walking along the road when he saw two council workers with spades in their hands. The first one dug a small hole, then the other one filled it in again. The first one dug another one a few yards further along and the second one filled it in again. After a few more holes like this, the man had to ask what they were doing.

"We're planting trees. There are usually three of us, but our mate's off sick."

'Oh good one, ' said Mark with a chuckle. How refreshing to find a woman who can tell jokes. He had to follow up with one of his own, so he told a variation on Mike's 'paedo' joke, but without the reference to 'P. Doe'.

The two of them spent the next twenty minutes swapping jokes before getting to know each other a little better. Mark found out that Maggie worked at Cooper Roller Bearings near the Southgates, so it was the right side of town for getting a bus from Clenchwarton. Unfortunately, she wasn't interested in any sports – watching or playing. Nor did she share Mark's taste in music. But she was good company and it was with disappointment for both of them when she said 'I'll have to make a move if I don't want to miss the last bus. I had to thumb it a couple of weeks ago. I didn't enjoy that.'

'I should think your parents would worry about that, wouldn't they?'

'My father doesn't care as long as I take my pill each day,' came the surprising remark.

'She's on the pill,' thought Mark. At least if he was to further this relationship, he wouldn't have to mess about with those horrible condoms. He hated them. But he wasn't too sure if he would want to further the relationship – except that Maggie was very good company and he wouldn't mind enjoying her company another time. He'd come out that evening with lustful thoughts for Blodwyn and her wonderful body and he still felt a little sexually frustrated. He wasn't sure if his opinion of Maggie measured up with thoughts like that. Nevertheless, the least he could do was to offer a lift to Maggie. Clenchwarton was the wrong direction for him, but she had saved his evening. And he felt compelled to tell her that fact.

She had no hesitation in accepting his invitation and thanked him for his kind comments. They were soon on their way out of town and into the Fens.

When they stopped outside Maggie's house on the edge of the village and close to the flat open countryside, he turned to her and said 'Once again, I'd like to thank you for saving my evening. I've really enjoyed meeting you.'

29

He was about to ask if they could meet again, when she said 'Do you want to come in for a coffee?' Mark actually wanted to go home and have a fantasy about Blodwyn's legs to get rid of his sexual frustrations, but it seemed rude to refuse the invitation, especially if he wanted to see Maggie again.

'Thank you. It will be all right with your parents, will it?'

'Oh, they'll be in bed. They always go to bed early.'

Inside the house, Mark was told to take a seat while Maggie made the coffee. She left a single table lamp switched on offering subdued lighting. Her parent's lounge was cosy and looked very Victorian, with lots of ornaments and with pictures hanging from the picture rail. Mark sat on the settee and when Maggie returned with the coffee, she sat beside him, kicked off her shoes and folded her legs up under her, whilst she cradled her mug of coffee. 'This is cosy,' said Mark, meaning the room, but Maggie thought he meant the two of them sitting together and she moved a little closer, nestling her head against his shoulder, still holding her coffee. Neither of them spoke,

When Mark had finished his coffee, he looked for somewhere to deposit his mug. The best place was a table so he had to stand up to do this, taking Maggie's mug with him. She stood up as well; then draped herself round his shoulders, taking Mark by surprise. His arms gravitated to the small of her back, which felt deeply indented and completely different to Jenny's. He found himself pulling Maggie even closer and their lips met. After about a minute's passionate kissing, Maggie said 'You're a randy bugger, aren't you?' Being this close, he had been unable to disguise his pyramid. It had been a long time without sex and he felt like a wild animal in season. Maggie returned her lips to his and after a few more minutes, said 'Are you going to take your clothes off?' and proceeded to remove hers.

'Are you going to let me have sex on the first date?' asked Mark incredulously, realising it made him sound like some naïve schoolboy.

'I can't let you drive home in that condition?' Maggie made it sound like she was stopping him from going out and raping someone.

'What about you parents? What if they come in?'

'They won't. They wouldn't dream of disturbing us.' Mark realised that this was not an unusual situation for Maggie, and that bothered him a little, but he was feeling incredibly randy. Moreover, he didn't have to worry about finding a condom, so he did as she said and removed his clothing, whilst she removed hers. She then threw down the cushions from the chairs and settee and lay down in front of him, totally naked, all breasts and milky-white thighs.

This was, without doubt, the best sex that Mark had ever enjoyed. It was a little rushed because he was concerned that Maggie's parents might disturb them, but the sensation of sex without a condom added to his enjoyment. He even stopped half-way to try another position, but Maggie insisted on finishing off underneath.

They dressed and sat down on the settee together.

'Do you feel better, now?' Maggie asked.

'No, I feel sore,' Mark replied with a grin. 'No, that was wonderful, thank you. I hope it was all right for you.'

'Oh yes. That makes you number 137.'

'Pardon?'

Number 137. I keep a diary of all my conquests.' Mark couldn't believe that she had had that many men, or that she would keep a record. Even stranger was the fact that she told people about it. He suddenly had second thoughts about wanting to see her again. He worked out the arithmetic in his head. If she lost her virginity at say 17, and she was now 25; that's 8 or 9 years activity. That's an average of over 15 a year. And he'd had only 2 partners.

Maggie nestled up to him again and they both sat there for several minutes before either of them spoke. Mark felt he ought to think about going home, but he didn't want it to appear that he'd had his pleasure and was ready to abandon her. No, he had enjoyed his evening, so why was he being such a prude? He would ask her out again. In any case, she might say 'no'. She might be ready to look for number 138. So he went for it.

'Can I see you again?' he asked.

'Of course you can, love,' she replied.

'Are you doing anything tomorrow evening?' Mark was thinking that if he had to travel to Clenchwarton, he would rather do it at the weekend, and he didn't want to wait until the next weekend.

'I can't do tomorrow. It's not fair on my parents.'

'Why is it not fair on your parents?'

'I can't expect them to babysit every night. They're very good as it is.'

'Babysit for whom?'

'My son.'

'You have a son?'

31

'Yes, I have a son. He's six years old.'

'Are you married – or divorced?'

'No. The father was married – still is, in fact. I didn't know he was married at the time. He's been good about it moneywise. Does that mean you don't want to go out with me, now?'

Mark didn't answer straight away. His motives for going out with Maggie had nothing to do with a long term relationship, so her being a mother shouldn't make any difference.

Before he could answer, Maggie said 'Your hesitation tells me everything. You'd better go, Mark. Thanks for the lift home.'

'Hang on. I haven't answered, yet.'

'You don't have to. I've seen it all before.'

'No, I was just thinking about tomorrow. The football season is starting and this is the last weekend when I know I will have Saturdays and Sundays free. I've been meaning to take a trip to the seaside while I still can, but I've never got round to it. If we go out together for the day, you can bring your son with you.' Mark realised that he wasn't going to be able to enjoy any carnal pleasures, but a day at the seaside with Maggie and her son would surely be better than sitting around at home. 'Had you got any plans for tomorrow?'

'No, Mark. That's very nice of you. Richard loves the seaside. It will be a lovely surprise for him.' And she threw her arms around Mark. 'Where shall we go?'

'Hunstanton, I suppose. We can go to Old Hunstanton to spend some time on the beach. Then later, we can have fish and chips on the green for lunch and take him on the funfair. Shall I pick you both up at 10.30?'

'What a lovely person you are, Mark.'

'If that's all sorted, I'd better get home and get some sleep. I'll see you tomorrow.'

On the way home, Mark mulled over the days' events. When he'd woken up, he had been feeling full of gloom and despondency. His trip into town was solely to buy a new LP which sometimes helped cheer him up. After a chance meeting with the lovely Blodwyn, life suddenly looked rosier. He knew if he was to get over Jenny, he had to get out more. Yes, he wished that things with Blodwyn had gone better, but that relationship never stood a chance of working. He didn't want to pursue a long term relationship with Maggie, but she would fill a valuable part of his life until Jenny was totally out of his system. He thought of the Jackie Wilson song 'A Woman, A Lover, A Friend' because that was how he viewed Maggie.

And the trip to the seaside was something he had spent most of the day hoping for with Blodwyn, so it all fitted in nicely. Except that he wouldn't now see Blodwyn in her swimming costume. With that thought, he decided that when he got home, he would have one final fantasy about Blodwyn in that fictitious costume.

CHAPTER 5

You're All I Need To Get By

It was a fine sunny day. Mark lay on a towel next to Maggie as they both watched Richard making sand castles and digging holes in the sand.

'Happy as a sand boy,' said Mark. 'I've never understood that expression. What is a sand boy? Whatever it is, it's quite appropriate for Richard.'

'You should have seen his little face light up when I told him to pack a bucket and spade because we were going out for the day,' Maggie said. 'This is his first trip to the beach this year. It's probably going to be his last now. We've done well with the weather. I'm going to change into my costume. Are you?'

'I never thought to bring one. The forecast wasn't too good. I hope this weather lasts.'

Maggie had brought a huge beach towel and disappeared under it. After a lot of squirming, she emerged in a one piece blue costume; her dignity intact. Mark couldn't resist having a good look and Maggie didn't seem to mind. The one thing he noticed with pleasure was the shape of her bottom as she lay face down for a spot of sunbathing. Jenny had always bemoaned the fact that she didn't really have a bottom at all. It had been quite flat, which was always a major disappointment to Mark. He had to stop comparing his girlfriends to Jenny, but at least here was one reason to be pleased.

After a while, Mark started to feel a little bored. He wanted a kiss and cuddle, but he knew they couldn't do that in front of Richard, and the sight of Maggie's bottom made him feel frustrated, so he announced that he was going to stroll down the beach for a little while. Maggie was happy to lie there, keeping an eye on her son, who was making good progress with his hole in the sand. Mark wandered among the rock pools beneath the impressive cliffs, looking for any interesting wildlife, but not finding anything of great significance. He looked towards the pier and fancied walking towards it, but decided he ought to return to Maggie and Richard.

After a few more minutes of sitting next to Maggie, he asked if anyone was hungry. Richard wanted to carry on with his digging, so Mark said, 'If we go and have some food now, we can go to the funfair afterwards.'

'Funfair! Oh, great!' said Richard.

Maggie asked if she could just have a quick dip in the sea. She said she didn't know when she would get another chance for a little swim. Of course Mark agreed, saying he would stay with Richard who was told he could play in the sand for a few minutes more.

The tide was starting to come in, but Maggie still had a short walk to the sea. After a while, she returned dripping wet and Mark couldn't resist admiring the effect of the swimsuit adhering to her shapely form. He thought she looked better in a swimsuit than in the nude.

Maggie dried herself and told Richard to gather up his bucket and spade while she performed her contortion act under the towel.

There was a big queue at the chip shop, but once they were all sat down in the middle of the green looking out over the pier, Mark felt a lot happier. Somehow, fish and chips tasted so much better at the seaside and as far as Mark was concerned, this was sure to be the highlight of the day – except that the sun went in and it started to cloud over.

'Are we going to the fair, now?' Richard shouted with excitement.

'Yes, we'll walk along the prom,' Mark replied.

Mark and Maggie strolled along the promenade, holding hands. With Richard dancing happily beside them, they must have looked to all the world like a contented married couple. Halfway along the promenade, Richard spotted an ice-cream kiosk and asked his mother if he could have one. 'Why don't we have one on the way back?' Mark said, thinking that might be an incentive to get him to leave the fair if they had problems persuading Richard to leave.

'Can I have some candy-floss, then?' the youngster enquired.

'You're not having both,' his mother replied before Mark could say anything. Mark remembered the time, when he was younger, how he had made himself sick by eating too much before going on the Mart at King's Lynn. He didn't want any sick children getting in his car, so he was glad of Maggie's support.

Just as Mark had guessed, Richard wanted to go on every ride and it was only the promise of an ice-cream that convinced him to leave. 'The ice-cream man will be packing up soon,' he said to Richard, which had the desired effect.'

'You're good with children, Mark,' Maggie said, as she squeezed his hand.

'I've got two young nephews, so I've had a little practice.'

Mark didn't want to make a habit of going out with Maggie and Richard as 'a family'. The truth was that he wasn't enjoying the day as much as he had hoped and Maggie had been much more fun when there were just the two of them. But he saw this day as an investment in their relationship, with the promise of more intimate moments to come in the ensuing months.

When Richard showed reluctance to go home, Maggie told him that if he made a fuss, Mark wouldn't take him out again. Mark actually had no plans to take him out again anyway, but he didn't say anything.

In the car, Richard started sulking. Mark asked him 'Do you know any jokes?'

'No,' came the abrupt reply.

'Here's one,' Mark said. 'What has a bottom at the top?'

'I don't know,' Richard replied.

'A leg.'

Maggie laughed, but Richard wasn't amused. 'Why is that funny?' he asked.

'Because you get a bottom at the top of your leg, don't you?' his mother explained and repeated the joke. 'What has a bottom at the top? A leg!'

A few minutes later, Richard asked 'What has a foot at the bottom?

'We don't know,' came the impatient reply from both adults.

'A leg,' Richard said and then started giggling.

'Very good,' Maggie said, and then whispered to Mark 'Just humour him.'

A few minutes later, Richard asked 'What has a hand at the bottom?'

'Is it an arm?' Mark answered with a note of boredom in his voice.

'Yes!' Richard replied and then started giggling all over again.

Mark was very relieved when they got back to Clenchwarton where he was invited in for a cup of tea, which he was pleased to accept. As he finished his cup, he asked Maggie if she wanted a little walk around the village. He saw this as their first chance to be alone all day and he wanted to ask her out again. While they were walking along, Maggie pointed the conversation towards the fact that very few of her previous boyfriends had shown any interest in her son. 'I need to find someone who is prepared to take both of us on,' she said, wistfully. Then when Mark didn't respond, she asked 'Do you want a family, Mark?'

'I think I'm still a bit too young for that responsibility. And I'm a long way off being able to support a wife, let alone a family.'

'In that case, Mark, I don't think I should see you again.'

Mark wasn't expecting that. He had taken Maggie for a good-time girl and was quite happy to take advantage of that, but thinking about it, he could see her point of view. He had misjudged her. She wanted to take her responsibility seriously.

'Can't we just be friends? I would happily stand aside if someone else came along.'

'No, I think that would just confuse Richard. He needs a father and I need him to have a father. All his friends have fathers and that must have an effect on him. I'm sorry to end like this. I've enjoyed being with you and I think you're a lovely kind chap, but let's not waste each other's time.'

'I'm very sorry about this,' replied Mark. 'I could easily tell you lies and convince you that I want a family, but you would soon realise that's not true. And it's nothing against Richard. You have a lovely little boy and he does you credit. I will want a family at some point, but the timing has got to be right.'

''I know,' said Maggie. 'And I appreciate your honesty, but I'm quite a bit older than you. Time isn't on my side. You can go out and get another girlfriend tomorrow.'

'I don't think so,' Mark replied.' I haven't had much luck getting girlfriends and even less luck keeping them.'

'But you've dated two girls in two days. How many do you want, you greedy bugger?' Maggie said, trying to lighten the mood.

'Yeah, but if you think about it, I didn't actually date Blodwyn. I was just her bloody chauffeur. And meeting you in a bar doesn't count as dating someone.'

'You shagged me. Doesn't that count, then?'

'Yes, of course it does, but I think you shagged me, actually,' Mark replied with a grin, also trying to keep the mood light. 'And I may have gone out with two girls in two days, but both of them have dumped me. Anyway, you've made your decision and I can quite understand it. I'm just disappointed.'

★ ★ ★ ★ ★ ★

The next few months in Mark's life were quite uneventful. The football season had started again. He had retained his place in goal for Northfleet in the upper tier of the Sanford Saturday League and for Greshams in the lower tier of the Sanford Sunday League. He hadn't been selected for the darts team again, so his social life was very restricted. His weekend with Blodwyn and Maggie had been a mild distraction in his efforts to get over Jenny, which had seen a slight improvement, mainly in the fact that he was sleeping a little easier and had more of an appetite for his food. What struck Mark about his situation was that life had been painful during the period of his infatuation for Karen, but once she had left his life, he got over her quite quickly. But the situation with Jenny was almost the opposite. He decided that his attraction to Karen must have been mostly physical. After all, she did have a fantastic figure; whereas Jenny's figure, although perfectly acceptable, was nothing special. And yet he still ached to be with her.

He did feel he was now better equipped to deal with another date with Jane, but he wasn't going to 'phone her for fear of rejection. If, however, he were to meet her in town, he probably would try again; except, that he didn't meet her. And he did crave female company.

There was a film at the local Odeon that he wanted to see. It was 'You Only Live Twice,' with Sean Connery. He had missed it the first time around and thought it would be a while before he'd get another chance. But he didn't want to go alone. He asked Dougie if he wanted to go, but Dougie had already seen it. It was probably a long shot, but the only other person he could think of was Maggie. What did he have to lose? He didn't have her telephone number, but he knew she worked at Cooper Roller Bearings.

Reg's secretary, Pat, had a local phone directory at her desk, so as soon as Mark knew that Reg wasn't in his office, he went to borrow the directory. He didn't want Reg to know he was making a personal call in office time. Mark always enjoyed some friendly flirting with Pat. She was in her middle thirties, married with two children. She was quite wide-beamed and bustled about the office, tolerating the jibes and sexual innuendos from the all-male surveyor's office. Ian Beddington always described her as built for comfort, not for speed. Mark agreed with him in secret, but Ian actually voiced his thoughts to her face.

Mark gave Pat a quick squeeze of her surprisingly firm hips as he asked permission to use her book. 'Hello,' she said. 'Are you up to something furtive?'

'Yes,' he said. 'I've got to phone my girlfriend. She keeps accusing me of stalking her. I say "girlfriend"…' and he left the sentence hanging for comical effect.

'Well, if she's not your girlfriend, it sounds like you are stalking her.'

'Yes, I know. It was just a little joke.'

'Well, I'm sure she doesn't think it's funny. I thought you'd have gotten over her by now. You need to know when to move on.'

'Thanks, Pat. Do you know the STD code for King's Lynn?'

'It's 0553', she replied. He wrote down the code and the number on a piece of paper and returned to his desk before Pat could accuse him of other crimes against the female population.

Mark couldn't make outside calls from his 'phone without asking someone on reception to connect him, so he decided to use the payphone which was situated in the factory, next to the canteen. In any case, he wanted some privacy for this call. He thought he ought to warn Ian Beddington that he'd be away from his desk for a short while and told him what he was going to do.

'I want you to file these papers as soon as possible,' he said. 'So don't be too long with your personal affairs.'

Mark picked up his waste bin from under his desk and placed it on his desk. 'Just leave them in my in-tray,' he said.

And then the usual banter ensued whereby all the surveyors criticised the attitude of the younger generation. After putting up with this for a few minutes, Mark took umbrage when 'Billy' Bunter joined in. As far as Mark was concerned, Billy was a waste of space. Whenever the two of them had been out on site together, Billy always seemed determined to do the least amount of work possible. So as Mark got up, he turned to Billy and said 'I don't know what your problem is, but I bet it's hard to pronounce.'

Near the payphone, Mark bumped into little Jenny from the Metal Shop. Jenny always liked to flirt with Mark. He still remembered how she had totally embarrassed him on his very first day at work. But Mark had a lot more self-confidence these days and now he enjoyed it. 'Hello Mark! How's your love life?'

'Up and down, you know. But it's all right on "hole". How about you?'

'I get by. My little Jack has got a job here now you know. He's in the Panel shop.' Jack was her husband.

'I'd better watch my step, then.'

'Yeah, he'll soon give you what for.'

'Oh, really. I wouldn't know which way to turn.' Mark had met Jenny's husband and he was a little fellow, so Mark and Jenny often had a little joke about his stature. Her favourite little joke was talking about Jack popping out to stretch his legs, but coming back the same size.

'How's the surveyor's job going?' Jenny asked.

'Not very well. I'm just a tea-boy, really.'

'That's a shame. Everyone said you did a good job in Wages. My money was always spot on when you did it. It's been wrong several times since you left. Why don't you put in for that job on the notice board?'

'What job?'

'They want a couple of Time and Motion men. They say they'll train people up if they haven't got any experience. Go and have a look at the board.'

'I will. Thanks, Jenny.'

But first, Mark wanted to call Maggie. He didn't know her surname, so he just asked for Maggie in Purchasing. 'Hello Maggie. It's Mark.'

'Hello Mark. It's nice to hear from you. How are you, love?'

'I'm all right, thank you. How about you?'

'You know me; always got a smile on my face. I often hoped you might call.'

'Really? I wondered if you would like to go to the pictures one night. Just as a friend, as it were.'

'Do you know, I would, my darling. I really would.'

'Any particular night?'

''Any night suits me.'

'Shall we make it Friday? I hope you haven't seen 'You only Live Twice.' It's on at the Odeon in Sanford.'

'I've never seen any of the James Bond films. I'm sure I'll enjoy it.'

So they made the necessary arrangements and Mark went to find the notice board.

The job in question was titled 'Work Study Engineer.' There was no reference to a status of 'trainee' or 'junior'. The ideal candidates (two were required) would have experience of working in one or more areas of the Factory, but anyone with the right attitude would be considered. There were a few details about the company's plans to introduce an incentive scheme into the Factory and the successful candidates would also be responsible for studying all production activities with a view to recommending efficiencies. Full training would be provided under the guidance of 'MANCON', an outside organisation who were in the process of providing management consultancy. Anyone interested should contact the Works Manager, Paul O'Connor.

As Mark was already in the Factory, he thought he'd just pop in to see the Works Manager's secretary to see if she could provide Mark with more information. Mark sometimes used to cycle home with Anne before she got married and they'd always got on well together, although he'd never fancied her.

'Paul's not around at the moment, but if you like, I'll tell him you're interested.'

'Yes, if you would, please. Do you know if there's much interest from anyone else?'

'Not that I know of. The job's been advertised for about ten days. I think some of the factory workers are suspicious that they'd been required to spy on their colleagues, but Paul doesn't see the job like that. The incentive scheme should be an opportunity for the workers to earn some extra money.'

'Or highlight people who aren't pulling their weight,' Mark added. 'That wouldn't make you popular.'

'No. Perhaps you being from outside the Factory might help your case. It's worth having a chat with Paul. I'll get him to contact you.'

That evening, Mark went down the Bricklayers for a pint and a game of darts with Dougie. It had been quite a few weeks since they had last been out together. While they were waiting for the dartboard to become free, they had a chat. Mark mentioned the Work Study job. Dougie thought Mark should go for it. He understood Mark's frustration with the surveyor's position and couldn't see it improving in the near future.

Inevitably, the subject veered towards members of the opposite sex, and Dougie, who knew of Mark's split with Jenny, enquired as to Mark's love life. Mark didn't want to say anything about his 'friendship' with Maggie, but he did say 'You'd have been proud of me a few weeks ago. I went out with 2 women on the same night and had a one-night stand with a woman.'

'Whooah! Markie boy! We'll make a lover of you yet. You're making me envious. I'm a happ... – I'm a married man now. I haven't dipped the ol' wick in for ages – apart from the missus, that is. I sometimes wonder if I've still got the magic touch.

I've had my share of one-night stands. There was this one girl called Virginia. I called her virgin for short... but not for long! You know I have a bit of a size problem with John Thomas.'

'Really?'

'Yeah, I'd love to have an eight-inch penis... instead of this great thing. Hey, the dartboard's free. Let's get in there, quick.'

After a few games, Dougie announced he had to leave and get home to see his little one to bed. He really had turned into a model husband and father.

Maggie had insisted that Mark should pick her up from the top of her road so that there was no chance of little Richard seeing Mark and getting the wrong idea. She greeted Mark with a great show of affection and told him how much she had missed him. During the journey to Sanford, she asked if Mark had been seeing anyone else, and, of course, he hadn't. 'What about you?' he asked.

'Nothing serious,' she replied.

'Does that mean you have seen someone, though?'

'I am up to 139,' she replied.

'And neither of them was serious?'

'No, it was just my dentist and his wife.'

'And his wife? A threesome?'

'Yes, it was fun. You should try it sometime.'

'No thanks. Isn't he in danger of getting struck off for doing it with a patient?

'He might do, if I complained. But I didn't. We went round his house and made a complete evening of it.'

'How many times have you done something like that?'

'Just the once. They do it all the time and they like to keep trying it with different people.'

'Do you just have a knack of meeting these weirdoes or do you go looking for them?'

'I think it's 'cause I'm always smiling. People find me approachable. After all, you picked me up in a bar.'

'Er...No, I think you chatted me up, if I remember rightly.'

Yet again, Mark felt uncomfortable about Maggie's sex life. And it made him feel unsure of this relationship. But 'wait a minute.' Wasn't he going out with her just for friendship? What concern was it of his that her morals didn't match his? After all, he'd hardly be taking her to the company's dinner dance, this year. In fact, he had no plans to go at all this time. At least he had taken Jenny to last year's to fulfil a long-held ambition not to go unaccompanied. So he just decided to enjoy the film and a night out.

In a quiet hotel bar after the film, Mark decided a heart to heart discussion was required. He started by asking 'What would you normally do on a Friday if I hadn't asked you out?'

'I would probably have gone to the Maid's Head', Maggie replied.

'Do you always go on your own?'

'Yes. I don't always leave on my own. The trouble is everyone there knows me, so if I do leave with someone else, it's probably an old boyfriend.'

Mark could imagine how that would end up. Maggie continued, 'I used to go with a few friends to the dances on the American airbase at Sculthorpe. The Americans used to lay on transport, but I haven't been for a couple of years. You know what they say – "One good Yank and they're down". Mark gave a little laugh, but he felt uncomfortable about this news.

'Look,' Mark said, adopting a very serious look on his face. 'I've enjoyed being with you again, but my situation hasn't changed. I don't see myself being in a position to become Richard's father, but I would like to do this again. Do you think we could just go out together from time to time? No ties. We're both free to see someone else if we wanted to?'

'Yes, my darling,' she replied with that smile on her face again. 'No one ever asks me to the pictures. So whenever there's anything we both want to see, one of us will ring the other at work.' Neither of them was on the telephone at home.

Back at Clenchwarton, Maggie invited Mark in for coffee and he felt happy to accept. While the kettle was boiling, Maggie disappeared for a few minutes and returned wearing a dressing gown. 'Is that a hint that you don't want me to stay for long?' Mark asked.

'Of course not, silly. I just needed to get out of that bra. I don't know why, but it was hurting my back.' It looked to Mark as though she was completely naked under the dressing gown.

Mark had decided he would not attempt to have sex that evening. He had told Maggie he just wanted to go out with her for friendship and he had every intention of sticking to that. Except that, as she sat next to him on the settee, he was aware of her lovely milky white thighs half exposed and she made no attempt to cover them. Mark finished his coffee and said he had better be on his way.

'Aren't you going to make love to me?' she asked, standing up with him and putting her arms around his neck.

'I thought we were just going to be friends?' he replied by way of a question.

'Don't you find me attractive?' and she pulled back her gown to push her ample breasts towards him. Mark's arms went round her back to feel that lovely little indent in the small of her back. And then they ventured further down to his favourite area.

She could now tell for herself that he did fancy her and they were soon engaged in some vigorous activity on the carpet. This time, Mark didn't feel the need to rush anything and it was even better than the first time.

When they returned to the settee for a cuddle, Maggie asked 'Do you ever feel like doing something a bit more adventurous?'

'You probably realise I'm not that experienced. To be perfectly honest, any sex is a bit of a novelty to me.'

'Tell me about your first time,' she demanded.

Mark didn't want to talk about his previous sex life, especially as his first time had been a confusing fumble in the back seat of his car. He hadn't actually considered this as proper sex, but Jenny had insisted that she had taken away his virginity – and he certainly didn't want it back.

'I was at school,' he lied. 'We did it against a tree. She was making all sorts of funny noises which I assumed must have been normal. But when we finished, she said "*You idiot!*"

I said "*I thought you were enjoying it. You were nodding and making all sorts of moaning noises.*"

She replied "*That's because you had my scarf caught up in it*"

Maggie laughed and said 'I don't believe a word of it. Have you never had a blow job?'

'I don't think I even know what it is,' he replied. He'd heard the expression, but couldn't think what on earth you would want to blow to get any form of pleasure.

'Perhaps another time,' she said. 'A lot of my boyfriends expect that, but it's not the sort of thing you want thrust down your throat.' Mark didn't understand the joke.

'Is there anything you've ever wanted to try?' Maggie asked.

Mark thought for a few minutes. It was one thing to admit that he wasn't very experienced, but he didn't want to appear to be totally ignorant, so he felt he ought to say something. 'Well, I've always thought it would be nice to do it in the open air.'

'If you think we're going outside this time of year, you can forget it,' she said with a laugh and a playful thump on his shoulder.

'I think we can leave that one for now,' he said with a chuckle.

This was the first of many similar dates. They would be spaced roughly 3 to 4 weeks apart, leaving them both free to pursue other partners, except that Mark had no success at all in this area.

CHAPTER 6

At the Club

Soon after Mark arrived at work on the following Monday, he received a telephone call from Paul O'Connor's secretary, Anne. She told Mark that Paul wanted to have a chat with him. It wasn't an interview; it was just a preliminary chat and could he present himself in Paul's office at ten o'clock?

Mark thought he ought to quietly tell Ian Beddington what was happening, but Ian was busy sharpening a couple of pencils in the office sharpener on the other side of the room.

'Percy Shaw,' Ian said, addressing the whole team. 'Now there's a genius. He invented the cat's eye, you know. He had this wonderful idea after watching a cat approaching him at night time and seeing the light reflected from his eyes.'

'Good job the cat was walking towards him,' chipped in Mark, who had heard the joke before.

'Or he'd have invented the pencil sharpener,' said Ian, before Mark could steal his punch-line.

As soon as Ian sat down at his desk and started rolling a supply of skinny little cigarettes to see him through the day, Mark approached him and spoke to him in a quiet voice as he didn't want the rest of the team to know what was happening.

Ian wasn't surprised that Mark was looking for another position and he wanted to give him some words of advice. 'You will find Paul O'Connor a very demanding boss and if you want to succeed, you will have to be prepared to make an effort. And you will be working under pressure. When he was a Contracts Manager, he was forever criticising the factory, saying materials were always delivered late and that the quality left a lot to be desired. So when the last Works Manager decided to leave, he challenged Paul to take on the job, which he did. I think he's turned things round, but he's ruffled a few feathers on the way. The general feeling is that it was him who forced Ron Hall to hand in his notice. Anyway, I doubt whether you'll get the job. They will want someone from the factory.'

'Well, as for pressure, you don't get much more pressure than making sure your payroll is always on time – and correct. I can't see I've got anything to lose by trying.'

'Well, good luck.' That was the first time Ian had ever strung a few sentences together without seeking to belittle Mark, and Mark should have felt a little encouraged by Ian's good wishes, but his comments about Paul O'Connor now made him feel anxious. Mark had never spoken to Paul, but he knew him by sight and his impression was of a very unapproachable individual. But to Mark's way of thinking, getting Ron Hall to leave was not a bad thing at all. Ron had a string of affairs behind him, including Karen. If it hadn't have been for Ron, Mark may have had more success with Karen.

It was with trepidation that Mark entered Anne's office. She told him that Paul was busy on the 'phone and asked him to wait. After ten minutes, Paul called him in and greeted him with a fierce handshake. Mark understood that Paul used to do a bit of amateur boxing at flyweight, but Paul was no longer a flyweight. He was very thickset with a dark shock of hair and a very strong chin. His broad nose showed signs of having been hit a few times.

'So why do you want this job, Mark?' Paul asked abruptly. He had a hint of a London accent, despite being of Irish descent.

Mark decided he wouldn't get anywhere by taking a half-hearted approach and he had spent a few days preparing for such a question. 'I want a job that is going to offer a future; is going to present me with a challenge whilst also being of great benefit to the company.'

'And you don't see that as a surveyor?'

'Maybe if I stick at it for 5 years, but I don't want to wait that long. At the moment, no one is giving me the chance to go forward. I'm the second of two trainees, so I'm little more than a junior and I've already had a stint as a junior in the Wages department.'

'You did a good job looking after my Works payroll,' Paul said. Mark was surprised that Paul even knew that Mark had existed whilst in the Payroll department and noted that Paul had said '*my* Works payroll' as though he owned the company; or at least, the factory. He continued 'My factory is operating at far less than one hundred per cent efficiency. So we need to make better use of the resources we have. That comes in two parts. One is to study the production techniques, cut out waste and, if necessary, modernise. The other is to give the workers an incentive to increase productivity. That comes with the introduction of a bonus based incentive scheme. The employee earns extra money – we get more output. Everyone wins.'

'What if someone doesn't make his targets?' Mark asked.

'You tell me.'

Mark hesitated for half a minute before replying. 'We have to find out why. No two people work at the same speed, so the scheme is going to benefit some people more than others. I would have thought if someone is swinging the lead, his foreman or chargehand should already be aware of that. Using an incentive scheme to get rid of people will only get everyone's backs up and make it unpopular.'

'You're absolutely right. And, of course, we have to work with the unions, not against them. So far, their reaction is low key, but not totally negative. So, no, there's no question of dismissing someone for not hitting his targets.'

'Although he… or she may be better employed somewhere else,' Mark added.

'That's a good point. In fact, I'm just on the point of doing that with one chap. Can I ask what you're earning?'

'Five hundred,' Mark replied.

'Five hundred pounds a year?' Paul asked incredulously.

'That's right.'

'You mean someone earning five hundred was in charge of running my works payroll?'

'No, I was only on three-two-five at that time. I started as a junior and got caught out by the pay freeze. I didn't get a rise until I joined the Surveyors team. If I got the Work Study job, would I be able to negotiate an increase?'

'You don't negotiate anything. I pay you what I think you're worth, but I won't be paying five hundred.'

Mark just nodded his head. He really wanted to know what sort of money he could expect, but now was not the time to pursue that question.

'So what do you think are your strengths and weaknesses?' Paul asked

Mark again took his time before answering. 'I think I have a clear methodical approach to problems. I'm very good with figures and I think I work well under pressure. I like to work efficiently. That's part of my nature. Just as an example – if I'm about to go upstairs at home, I don't like to go empty-handed.

'Weaknesses?' Again, he paused. 'At school, I was never very good at things like woodwork, so I don't know if that would work against me working in a factory.'

'Not necessarily,' Paul said, then after staring at Mark for a few more seconds, he continued. 'Let me put a situation to you. You've done a study that shows that a certain operation can be performed far more efficiently, but no one, including me, is prepared to do anything about it. What would be your next action?'

Mark had to think about this one. Then he said 'I would double check all my figures. And if I was completely sure of my facts, I would pester you.'

'And if I still failed to act?'

'I would go over your head – but only if I was absolutely sure.'

'You would have to be sure, but that's the right answer. I've been told I can be a bit of a bully, so I sometimes need someone to stand up to me.' Mark was hoping the situation never arose. He could believe Paul would be a bad tempered bully, but he probably wouldn't appreciate a wimpy 'yes-man' either.

'Do you have any questions?' Paul asked.

'Can you tell me how many people have applied?'

'No, that's none of your business.' But then Paul softened. 'Not many, if I'm honest. The next stage is a formal interview with a couple of chaps from MANCON. I will make the final decision, but they will do the interviewing and give me their feedback. You've heard of MANCON, have you?'

'I've heard of them. I know MANCON is short for Management Consultancy. It's a good job they're not called Consultancy Management.' Mark couldn't resist a little joke even though he doubted whether Paul would appreciate it.

'CONMAN, you mean? You're not too far from the truth. I don't understand how we've managed to create a company virtually from scratch, employing nearly three hundred people and continually making a profit and then some clever person thinks we need some glorified consultants. As you can guess, it wasn't my idea to employ them. But we'll see. We'll let you know when your interview is. I can't tell you when that will be.' He stood up and held out his hand to give Mark's another good crushing. At least Paul had indicated that there would be a formal interview, so Mark felt reasonably optimistic.

When Mark returned to his own office, Ian Beddington asked him how the interview went. Mark replied in a quiet voice, 'It wasn't an interview. But Paul did ask me a few questions. I think I gave a good account of myself, but MANCON will be doing the actual interview. And I don't know when that will be. Can you keep it all to yourself, please?'

Mark actually wanted to tell everyone, but he thought he ought to wait until something more definite happened. This was just the time when he wished he had a proper girlfriend with whom he could share such information. He considered calling Maggie, but he'd only just seen her and that would go against their agreement to only meet occasionally.

His social situation still needed a lift, so he decided to take advantage of the company's Sports and Social Club, which up until recently hadn't been particularly active. A few people had organised golfing days, which was beyond Mark's budget. And there had been a couple of fund-raising dance evenings, but without a partner, Mark had given these a miss. But now, there was a clubhouse. This had been financed by a contribution from the company, together with the funds from the dance evenings. In addition to this, there had always been a voluntary monthly subscription from each employee. Much of the construction labour had been provided by the employees themselves, but Mark had never felt he had anything to offer the project. He decided to pay the clubhouse a visit that evening. It was about three hundred yards along the road from the Factory on a piece of land that was deemed unsuitable for commercial use.

When he arrived, the only other persons present were Don Morley, a wood machinist, who Mark barely knew and his attractive wife Linda, who didn't work at Greshams and was therefore a complete stranger. Bar duties were carried out by different people on a rota basis. Don and Linda were manning the bar that evening, so Mark ordered a beer and exchanged pleasantries, before playing a game of darts by himself on one of the two dartboards. There had been a suggestion that the inter-departmental darts competition would be held here, but everyone preferred their own local venues. After winning three games in a row, Mark returned to the bar.

'I thought I'd better not hog the dartboard,' Mark said.

'No,' said Linda. 'It's a good job we've got a spare board.'

'Mondays are always quiet,' said Don, then after a pause, 'and Tuesdays, Wednesdays and Thursdays.'

'The record so far,' chipped in Linda, 'is six on a Friday – not all at once, fortunately. Or we'd never have coped!'

'You need to get the message across,' said Mark. 'Perhaps a couple of notices on the notice boards?'

Don replied, 'We need to offer something different to people's local pub. We've got the Table Tennis tables, but that's not enough to drag people out here. I had this idea for a discotheque type of evening – probably on a Saturday. I've got a good deck I can connect to a P.A. system; and a good selection of records. I think I'll try it out this week. I won't advertise it yet. I'll see how it sounds first.'

'I'll come and have a look,' said Mark. He knew he wouldn't be doing anything on a Saturday. 'And I'll pass the word around the offices, if you can do the Factory. Shall I have a go at doing a couple of posters?'

'That would be great,' replied Don and Linda, almost together.

'I'll let you have a look at them before I pin them up,' Mark added. 'I'll be off now, before my car gets trapped in by the next wave of visitors. See you, Saturday.'

'Bye,' said Linda, who didn't know Mark's name.

'Bye, Mark,' said Don, who did.

On Saturday, Mark waited until after eight o'clock, but he was still the first visitor to arrive. Don had already set up his equipment and had started playing some records, few of which Mark recognised, but at least they weren't the usual "Top of the Pops" type fodder. After Mark had ordered his first drink and bought one for Don and his wife, he rifled through Don's stack of records. They included records by Canned Heat, Steppenwolf, Creedence Clearwater Revival and Gary Puckett. So it seemed that Don's taste leaned towards American rock, but none of it sounded 'danceable' to Mark.

Don came over to talk to him. 'Sounds all right, don't it?' he asked at the top of his voice.

'Hang on,' replied Mark. 'I'll try the other side of the hall' and walked to the far end. He nodded and put his thumbs up and returned to Don, who was now joined by Linda. When that record finished, Don asked Mark what he thought of the record selection. 'It's not to my taste, but I'm not the one you have to appeal to. I do think you might need a broader selection, once the crowds roll in.'

'What do you like, Mark?' asked Linda.

'Soul music. Some of that would be ideal if people want to dance, but your stuff will probably appeal to a wider audience if they just want to listen.'

'I quite like some soul music, but I don't think we've got any, have we Don?'

Don shook his head. 'I could dig some out, if you like?' said Mark.

'Yeah, why not?' said Don. 'As you say, we need a broader selection. What have you got?'

Mark mentioned a few singers, some of whom were recognised by the other two people.

Just then, a young couple walked in, after first peering through the door to make sure they were in the right place. Mark recognised the chap as an apprentice Joiner. His companion was presumably his girlfriend. Linda dashed to the bar to make them welcome and serve them with drinks, whilst Don selected another record. Mark took a seat to one side of the hall.

A little while later, Daniel Peterson and his wife walked in to swell the crowds. Daniel worked in the Metal Shop and had once accompanied Mark to a football dance with his niece Rachel as a sort of blind date for Mark, which hadn't been very successful. Mark joined them at the bar to make them welcome. He had unwittingly become interested in making these evenings a success and felt the need to play a role as a host. When Don played a record that the young couple particularly liked, they started dancing; not on the dance floor, but to one side of their table.

Daniel and his wife did the same, just as another couple walked in. Mark didn't recognise this couple at all. They stood at the bar with their drinks in their hands watching the dancers. When the music finished, Daniel, recognising the new couple, approached them at the bar and suggested they joined him at his table. Mark now felt superfluous, so he ordered another drink and returned to his own table.

A few minutes later, the young couple got up to leave. Don told them to bring some friends next time, because the evenings would get better once the word got around.

Mark stayed a little longer, but when it became clear that no one else was going to arrive, he decided to call it a day. As he left, he told Don that he would get the posters finished as soon as possible and he would turn up again next week with some of his own records.

By Tuesday, Mark had completed two posters. He wanted them to really stand out and capture people's attention. He wasn't very good at art, so he found a picture of some people dancing and traced their outline onto a poster; then repeated the process on a separate poster. At the top of each poster in bright colours, he wrote *'Come and Dance the Night Away.'* On the next line – *'Saturday Night is Discotheque Night.'* At the bottom, he added details about the time and place, and that entrance was free. He took them round to the Wood Machine Shop to show Don, who was happy to use them, so Mark pinned one to the Factory notice board and the other next to the office coffee machine.

He also made a point of telling everyone he encountered during that week. So it was with some renewed optimism that he ventured out on the following Saturday evening. This time he arrived at 7.30 with a box of dance orientated soul singles. Don was busy setting up his equipment and Linda was manning the bar. In conversation with Linda, Mark learned that the Social Club committee had met to discuss the viability of keeping the clubhouse open during the week. It had been agreed to monitor the situation for another month.

Don started playing his own records and just before eight o'clock, the first couple arrived. By half past, there were about twenty people, but no one was dancing. Don asked Mark if he would like to try his soul records. So Mark picked out 'Dance to the music' by Sly and the Family Stone, which, because it was in direct contrast to the previous records, grabbed everyone's attention, and first one couple got up to dance, and then another followed. A minute later, two more couples joined them.

Mark knew he had to keep the momentum going, so he had 'In the Midnight Hour' ready to place on the single deck and switched the disks as soon as he could to keep everyone on the dance floor. A few more people took to the floor. The next record was by Sam and Dave.

By now Mark was feeling very pleased with himself and there were more people dancing than sitting down, so he played a second Sam and Dave number. Suddenly everyone left the dance floor. Why? This record was just as danceable. Perhaps, everyone needed a little rest, so for his next record, he flipped Otis' 'Respect' to play a ballad, figuring a smoocher wouldn't be so taxing; but still no takers.

Back to the dancers, then. 'Rescue Me' should be a guaranteed floor filler, but it wasn't, although two couples did eventually get up. By now, Don joined him and said 'You had them. What went wrong?'

'I've no idea. I thought I'd got the measure of them.'

'Let's see what happens if I play one or two of mine.' After the first three bars of 'Born to be Wild', the floor was occupied again. So Don took over the reins for half an hour, while Mark got a top-up from the bar. Daniel Patterson was at the bar, so they had a chat and Daniel invited Mark to sit next to him and his wife. There, they discussed why Mark's DJ-ing had faltered after a good start. It was felt that Mark's first few records were vaguely familiar to most people, but the two Sam and Dave records were not. As they were already on the dance floor, people continued to dance to the first one, but the second unfamiliar tune was too much, whilst all of Don's records were familiar.

For Mark's second stint, he had a Motown session which produced a more consistent result. A young lady approached Mark during this session and asked if he had any Beatles records, which produced an apologetic but negative response; as did a request for the Hollies, Kinks and Rolling Stones.

After everyone had left, Mark helped Don and Linda with the tidying up, while the three of them discussed whether the evening had been a success.

'We still need more people,' said Don, 'but perhaps the word will get round.' Then they discussed the music and Mark told them of his discussion with Daniel and his wife and how he had learnt something from that. He also mentioned the young lady's requests.

Don said 'We're never going to please everyone. So let's not try to play all types of music.' They agreed to repeat the event the following week, with much the same format.

★ ★ ★ ★ ★ ★

And the following week, the turnout was slightly better and some of the same people turned up, but the club still needed a bigger clientele to make it all worthwhile. In fact, the next few weeks produced much the same result. Sometimes the numbers were up, sometimes they were down. And the actual personnel varied as well. The people that Mark recognised were mostly from the Factory and none of his own colleagues could be persuaded to attend.

CHAPTER 7

Don't Look Back

It was nearly three weeks before Mark got his formal interview with the two people from MANCON. The interview was conducted in Paul O'Connor's office. The more senior of the two was Alan Barnes and he did most of the talking. Mark was informed that the other person, Tommy Bryant, would be responsible for the training of the two successful candidates and during that time, would effectively act as the Work Study Manager, whereas Alan would be an occasional visitor, as his responsibilities included several other clients.

Although classed as a 'formal' interview, Mark actually found it more laid-back than his discussion with Paul O'Connor. In fact, Mark had to answer very few questions as most of the meeting was taken up by Alan, and occasionally Tommy, telling Mark what his new job would entail. Moreover, Mark gained the distinct impression that a decision had already been made, since they both made more use of the expression 'what you *will* be doing' rather than 'what you *would* be doing.' And he was told that he would hear from them within a day or so, after seeing one more interviewee. So it occurred to Mark that Paul O'Connor had already made the decision for them.

And sure enough, he received a telephone call from Tommy the very next day, to say that they would like to offer him the position on a starting salary of £800, with a review after six months. Mark gave his response immediately. Tommy said the other successful applicant had already accepted, so they would like them both to start on the first of February 1969. Mark's new colleague would be a former joiner and his name was David Ross. Mark guessed that David must have joined the company fairly recently, since he didn't recognise the name from his time looking after the Works payroll.

Mark put the telephone down and looked across to Ian Beddington, who was already staring at him. Mark didn't say anything, but just sat there grinning. 'Well?' asked Ian.

'Well, what?'

'Have you got the job?'

'What job?'

'Do you want your tiny little knackers trapped in a drawer?'

'Yeah, I quite enjoyed it last time. Of course I've got the job. They know talent when they see it.'

'Now we can get some peace and quiet around here. Go and get some coffee. You're still our dogsbody until we say you can go.'

'It will be a pleasure, but I must go and tell Reg, first.'

But Reg already knew. So much for trying to keep him in the dark until the time was right. Reg had known all about it for three weeks and was very happy for Mark.

That weekend, Mark took Maggie to the cinema and told her the good news about his new job. When she asked if it meant a raise in pay, he just told her that there would be a review after six months. This wasn't a lie; it just wasn't the whole truth and nothing but the truth. He was afraid that if she knew he was to receive a substantial rise, she might consider his circumstances sufficiently altered to affect their long term relationship and he had no wish to mislead her.

He also neglected to tell her about the discotheque evenings, just in case she showed an interest in attending. Mark was not proud of his actions, but Maggie was not his girlfriend and their liaison was their little secret. He fooled himself that this was for her benefit as well as his.

The evening ended on her carpet as usual. Mark always felt like she was rewarding him for taking her out and he kidded himself that he deserved this reward. The truth was that he was just using her until something else came along.

Eventually, February arrived. The first working day of the month was Monday the third and Mark turned up for his new position as a Work Study Engineer. He was determined that this would be the start of a big change in his life and he would do all he could to make this move successful. He was also determined that whatever qualities the other new chap brought to the function, Mark would not be second best.

Paul O'Connor's office was the only room in the Factory that was big enough to accommodate the Work Study function which was due to grow in the coming months, so Paul and his secretary vacated the room in favour of a new temporary structure that sat above the Factory floor giving him a panoramic view over his domain. David Ross was already waiting when

Mark arrived, but there was no sign of Tommy Bryant, so they both introduced themselves and exchanged details of their respective backgrounds.

Before David had mentioned the fact, it was soon apparent that he had a military background. As Mark had entered their new office, David was standing 'at ease' with his legs apart and his hands behind his back. He continued standing in this position while they talked, with Mark perched on the edge of one of the desks and having no intention of standing 'at ease' or otherwise. David had recently completed twenty years in the army, where he had learnt his trade as a joiner and had only been at Greshams for ten months. He hadn't applied for the Work Study position. His foreman had recommended him. Mark wondered why, but didn't ask.

Throughout their conversation, it was apparent to Mark that David's sense of humour had been surgically removed by the army. Every time Mark tried to introduce a little whimsy into their discussion, David just stared back at him. He wasn't being deliberately unfriendly, but this aspect of his personality certainly began to annoy Mark. Working with David Ross was going to be very hard work.

Just after ten o'clock, Tommy did eventually arrive. He made no apologies for being late, but just explained that he had to travel up from Berkshire and would always be late on a Monday. But he soon got to work on the task of training Mark and David. Their priority was to introduce the incentive scheme into the main production areas of the Factory. So each of them was presented with a stop watch and clipboard. Tommy also introduced them to the pleasure of using a slide rule for calculations. Mark didn't understand what was wrong with good old-fashioned brain power.

Having only ever worked in the Factory, David had not come equipped with any stationery, so Mark offered to visit Sally who looked after the stationery supplies in the office block and he would get a supply for all their needs, to which David asked 'Can we make you I.C. requisitions?'

'Pardon?'

David repeated his question. Mark guessed what David meant, but he felt some strange compulsion to score some points. This was the real world; not the Army. And David needed to speak English; not Military.

Tommy intervened. 'That's a good idea, Mark. You can be responsible for all our stationery needs.'

'Wow!' thought Mark to himself. 'I've only just arrived and already I've been given a special responsibility.' He was so used to being sarcastic that now he was doing it to himself! But then he saw another opportunity to score points. He turned to David and said 'If I go and sort that out, would you like to fetch some coffees?' He resisted the urge to say 'You can be I.C. refreshments.'

David just stared back at Mark, but as he always looked like that, Mark didn't know if he had been offended or not. Tommy probably realised what Mark was up to and said 'We'll all go and sit in the canteen and have a coffee.' In any case, Mark remembered that there wasn't a coffee machine in the factory, so they had to go to the canteen for refreshments.

So that was the start of Mark's new career. In the next few months, he consolidated his training by establishing targets for all the various tasks in both the Metal Shop and the Paint Shop. David was responsible for both the Joiners Shop and the Wood Machinists. During this time, Mark built up relationships with all the foremen, the charge-hands and the operatives in the areas of his responsibilities. Mark was relieved that the Despatch Bay was outside of the scope of this exercise, because that meant he avoided Red Miller. The Metal Shop was represented by Red's union, but they had their own representative in the shape of a burly Irishman named Sean Rafferty.

Mark found it gratifying that his set of targets was ready before David's. There were mitigating circumstances for this fact, but Mark would have been mortified if he had been the one to lag behind.

Mark worked extra hard and seldom left work on time. He sought to ingratiate himself with Tommy, knowing that David was lacking in social skills, but Mark was no expert himself, especially as he didn't warm to Tommy, who seemed to be one of those 'ladies men' that Mark despised. It was no surprise when Mark discovered that Tommy, who had a wife and three children back in Berkshire, was conducting a secret liaison with someone at Greshams. He knew because of the whispered soppy telephone calls and the coded conversations Tommy had with Alan Barnes who visited once a fortnight. The name 'Mary' came up in conversations between the two of them but Mark didn't know of any 'Mary' at Greshams, so he suspected it to be an alias. At first, he guessed it might be Gail from the Typing Pool who had a string of conquests behind her, but one day he saw Tommy going out to lunch with Wanda, the director's secretary. After a while, Tommy stopped all covert operations and his relationship with Wanda became public knowledge. Mark always disapproved of extramarital relationships and was disappointed with Wanda's behaviour. She must have known Tommy would only be around for a few months.

Throughout this period, Mark continued helping with the discotheque evenings and regularly visited Maggie. On one occasion, just as the evenings were getting lighter, she persuaded him to give the pictures a miss, because she wanted to take him somewhere special. It turned out to be a clearing in the woods where they made love. She remembered Mark saying he'd always wanted to try it outdoors. Afterwards, she complained that it had been a bit rushed, but Mark explained that he was concerned at being discovered by passers-by and he was able to make up for it later on her carpet. The outdoor experience was also a disappointment for Mark and he didn't enjoy the sensation of a cool breeze blowing on his testicles.

One day he received a telephone call from her.

'Mark, my darling, I've just had a call from one of my old boyfriends who's tested positively for V.D. I'm going to pay a visit to the clap clinic for a check-up. In the meantime, I advise you to refrain from any sexual activity.'

Mark was shocked; although he shouldn't have been. He just said 'There's not much chance of me indulging, but thanks for the warning. I hope everything's all right with you.'

'I'm sure it will be, but best to be on the safe side. I'll call you again in the next day or so.'

Mark knew that Maggie had continued to see other men; some of them old boyfriends and some of them new people. She had told him her 'log' was now up to 145. He had been number 137. That's eight more chances of catching something. And that didn't include revisiting old boyfriends. Being on the pill was great but it didn't offer that sort of protection. He realised he had been a complete and utter fool. Now he had the worry of whether he, too, had succumbed to an infection.

Whatever the outcome of Maggie's tests, he had to end this relationship. It would be a wrench – not because of any deep attachment, but because it had been a convenient bit of fun. It was time to grow up. There was no point in trying to continue a relationship without sex, because they both enjoyed it too much to resist.

When Maggie called again a few days later, it was with the good news that her tests were negative. Mark thanked her for keeping him informed and told her he would see her again soon. He didn't want to end it over the telephone and there were no films worth seeing that week.

But the following week, he did meet her. After the film, they went to the Stable Bar and before Mark could broach the subject, Maggie said 'You're going to ditch me tonight, aren't you?'

'You're a very perceptive lady, aren't you? How did you know?'

'You haven't been yourself, tonight. I've been here before. Are you seeing someone else?'

'No, there's no one else.' Maggie smiled throughout. Mark still hadn't decided the best way to tackle the subject, but Maggie had saved him the bother. However, he felt that she was now in control of the situation

She continued smiling as she asked 'What's brought this about? Was it the V.D. scare?'

'In a way. It just made me re-think our whole relationship. It's not fair on you and it's not really what I want. The truth is I've been using you because I was on the rebound.'

'I think we've been using each other, so don't feel bad about it.

'I do, because I'm not like that. I don't think I am the type of person that just uses women. I usually abhor people like that. And you deserve better.' As Mark spoke the last sentence, he realised that, actually, Maggie deserved exactly what she got. But he couldn't despise her for that. That would make him a hypocrite.

'Tell me about this rebound thing. You've never mentioned it before.'

Mark started by telling Maggie about his disastrous date with Jane and explained that it was that experience that had prevented him from mentioning Jenny before. Then he moved on to talk about Jenny. It was the first time in ages that he had talked to anyone about Jenny and it felt as though he was cleansing his soul.

'And how do you feel about this Jenny, now?' Maggie asked when Mark had finished his tale of woe.

'I just feel bitterness. I don't think I'd cross the street to talk to her. She made me happy for a few months, but I spent a lot longer being unhappy.'

'And how will you remember me?' Maggie asked.

'With quite a bit of affection. You've always been great company and you're good fun. Moreover, you've helped me get through some dark days. In many ways, I would love to go on seeing you like this, but it's not right. I hope you can see that and don't hate me.'

'I could never hate you, Mark. And I think you're absolutely right. There's been a few times when I thought about whether we should pack it in, but I kept putting it off. And far from using me, it's been a relationship built on honesty. That's quite unusual for me. So many men have led me up the garden path and left me there. You're different.'

Then she asked 'Will you be looking for someone else?'

'I suppose so. To be honest, I've been so busy at work that I've been content with a limited social life. I've had my football at weekends and the occasional game of darts with people at work. We'll be starting tennis again soon. I'll just see how things go. I want to get a new car, so that will keep me occupied. I don't think I can trust the old Anglia much longer.

But as for girls – I've never had much luck in that department. I think, in the past, I've tried too hard. So perhaps I'll have more luck if I don't bother about it.'

When Mark dropped Maggie at her door, she invited him in for one last 'cup of coffee', but he declined. He wasn't feeling particularly randy that evening, so it wasn't too difficult to do the decent thing.

CHAPTER 8

Dance to the Music

The Discothèque evenings were still struggling along. There were evenings when no one wanted to dance and others that fared much better. The clubhouse was proving to be a white elephant, despite a lot of effort from a lot of people. The consensus of opinion was that its position on the industrial estate was the problem. Nobody lived within a mile of the property and it wasn't on the way home from anywhere, so few people could be bothered to make the effort. It was not cost effective to open on weekdays, so these had been abandoned, except for the odd occasion, such as a table tennis tournament.

But Don and Mark said they would persevere with the Saturdays for a little longer. Mark produced two fresh posters in the hope that these might attract fresh punters. After posting these on the notice-boards, there were a few new faces, but they were effectively replacing some previous attendees. There were a handful of semi-regulars such as Daniel and his wife, but they came mainly for the cheap beer and would have attended if there hadn't been any music.

One evening, there was a group of five younger people who did seem to enjoy the music and danced for much of the time. Among this group was a pretty young lady who approached Mark to say she liked the music he was playing and could he play *'The "In" Crowd'*.

'I don't think I've brought it tonight, but I'll just check.' Mark knew he hadn't, but still looked through his collection while he thought about what to say next. For some reason, he suddenly felt all nervous just like he did when he first left school. He should have been beyond all that by now. She was just a young girl talking about records. She wasn't trying to chat him up or anything – was she?

'No. It doesn't look like I brought it tonight. I can bring it next week, if you're coming.'

'I don't know if we're coming back next week. I can't drive, so if the others don't want to come, I can't get here.'

'Well, I'll make sure I do bring it, just in case. You'll have to try and persuade your friends to come. We're trying to build up the numbers and get a good atmosphere. It's free to get in. If this place was in London, playing music like this, you'd have to pay a lot of money to get in. And the drinks would be twice the price.'

She just smiled and was about to walk away when Mark said 'Feel free to see if there's anything else you want me to play.'

She gave him a nervous little smile and said 'Thank you.' Mark guessed she could only have been about seventeen years old and was very quietly spoken. As she looked through Mark's discs, she turned over each one to look at the flipsides as well as the top sides. That struck Mark as unusual, unless she was a real soul fan.

'Oh, I love this one. Can you play it?'

'*How sweet it is*?' asked Mark as she had presented it flipside up.

'No the other side; "*Forever*". I love that'.

So did Mark, but it wasn't a dance number. Still, it was time to turn down the tempo for a change. So he said 'O.K. My pleasure. Good choice.' And the young lady skipped away like an excited school girl. Perhaps the young girl wanted to have a smooch with her boyfriend.

As the requested Marvin Gaye record started playing, the floor emptied and Mark gazed over to the young lady to see if she was going to smooch with anyone, but she just sat there, clearly enjoying the record. At her table, there were three girls and two lads, one of whom Mark recognised as a trainee draughtsman. Mark seemed to remember his name as Micky something. The others were new to him and he hadn't seen any of them at the club before. Moreover, Mark was pleased to see the young lady didn't appear to be sitting close to either of the two fellows.

It was soon time for Don to take a turn at being the disc jockey, so Mark tidied up his records and went to the bar for a free drink. He was no longer expected to pay for drinks while performing. As Don's second disc started, the group of five prepared to leave. They had to walk past Mark to reach the exit, so he made a point of saying to the group as a whole 'Please come again. It's going to keep getting better every week as the word gets around.' He didn't believe it, but he did want to see the young girl again. How wonderful it would be to have a girlfriend who had the same taste in music! Her figure was a bit slimmer and flatter than Mark would have wished, but she was still young and would probably fill out. And she was attractive in a youngish sort of way.

But if she didn't turn up again next week, he probably wouldn't see her again. What could he do about it? He knew nothing about her. He didn't know her name. He didn't know where she lived and he didn't know if she had a boyfriend. All he could do was hope.

During the next week, Mark considered visiting the Drawing Office to talk to Micky, but he felt uncomfortable about doing this without knowing Micky's relationship with the girl. He had no business in the Drawing Office and now seldom even visited the Office Block, so he was unlikely to just bump into him.

The following Saturday, Mark made a point of taking 'The "In" Crowd' but didn't play it until 'she' had turned up, but Micky's group never showed, which meant Mark didn't play it. The week after that, the clubhouse was used for an end-of-season Football fundraising dance with a 'live' band. Mark's services as a DJ were not required. He did attend, without a partner as usual, to find the place heaving with noisy people and three volunteers manning the bar. Mark found this ironic, because the music wasn't so good to dance to and everyone had to pay an entrance fee, but he did admit there was a lively atmosphere, which just proved what the place could be like if well attended. Mark didn't stay very long – just long enough to show his support for the football team and to see if Micky had brought his gang.

On the following Tuesday, Tommy announced that Mark and David had been invited to view the new computer. This was another initiative that had been suggested by MANCON. Two existing employees had been trained to operate and program the machine, which was an NCR500. Mark had seen the vacancies being advertised, but that was one week after accepting the Work Study position, otherwise he may have applied. Several systems applications were to be written to run on the machine and the first of these was now complete. It was the Purchase Ledger system, written by James McDougall who used to work in the 'Take-off' department and he was going to give a quick presentation to several little groups of six people at a time.

Tim Peart, who used to be a buyer, was still busy writing the Payroll application, which was far more complex and, therefore, taking longer to write and test.

MANCON had recommended the NCR500 as suiting Greshams' needs, which didn't justify one of the more widely known and bigger IBM machines. The NCR was still a sizeable machine and needed a purpose built air-conditioned room to house it, together with an adjoining room where a young girl was busy punching data on a punch-tape machine, and where the two programmers were based.

As the group of six people assembled for the demonstration, Mark noticed that one of them was Micky from the Drawing Office, so Mark surreptitiously positioned himself next to him, with a view to talking to him at the first convenient opportunity. The machine was very noisy, so James gave a quick talk in the adjoining office before entering the glass-partitioned computer room on his own to operate the machine. He carried on talking inside the computer room, but unless you could lip-read, that was a complete waste of time.

As all the various lights flashed and the print carriage shuddered back and forth, Mark said to Micky 'It's impressive, isn't it?'

'Yeah, I hate to think what it cost.'

Mark was pleased to have broken the ice, because he'd never spoken to Micky before.

The presentation only lasted fifteen minutes, which was just as well because James McDougall's voice was monotonic and did no favours to the Scottish race.

As they were dismissed, Mark walked away beside Micky and asked if he was going to the Discothèque evening that week.

'I don't know. Sandy said she really wants to go again, but she lives in Peterborough, so if she is to go, someone has to put her up for the night.'

'Is that your girlfriend?' Mark asked.

'No, that's my mate's cousin. She was staying with him that night.'

'Is Sandy the young girl who came to talk to me?'

'Yes, that's Sandy. She's only seventeen.'

'So that wasn't her boyfriend with you that night?'

'No, she hasn't got a boyfriend at the moment. I think she's just broken off with someone, but I don't know her that well.'

Mark didn't think he ought to pursue the subject any longer. He just said 'Well I hope we do see you at the club again. It was packed last Saturday. It was the Football 'do'. You get a good atmosphere when there are more people.' Mark didn't mention the 'live' band. He thought it more likely that Micky would attend if he thought the numbers were improving.

'I'll see what we're all doing next week,' said Micky as they both went in different directions.

So Sandy lived in Peterborough. That wasn't very convenient. It was a good hour's drive from Sanford. Mark thought he ought to forget about dating Sandy. However, during the week, he reconsidered. After the experience with Maggie, and indeed, Jenny, it would be good to go out with someone less experienced – and safer!

But that Saturday, there was no sign of Micky or Sandy. At the start of the evening, Don had announced to Mark that this would be the last Dance evening. He was feeling very frustrated at the lack of interest and couldn't be bothered to keep setting up his equipment. So Mark would have to forget about Sandy. However, after a better than usual turnout, Don said he would give it just one more try the following week.

Mark obtained a lot of satisfaction from getting the punters up and dancing, but he always felt disappointed when the floor then emptied for no apparent reason. Since the same thing happened when Don did a stint, Mark guessed that some people probably only wanted to dance for a few numbers at a time, so he had grown to accept it.

As Mark had nothing else to do on a Saturday night, he would miss these evenings, so he wanted the last one to be as successful as he could make it. Whenever the opportunity arose during the week, he tried to drum up support for the last dance night.

When Saturday came around, he took all his best dance records and a varied selection of the more recognisable Motown singles.

The evening began quietly and Mark started with a selection of mid-tempo Motown records. There was no point in wasting his best dance records on an empty floor. A few people entered, but not enough to generate any sort of atmosphere. After half an hour, Don took over the deck and Mark went over to the bar to exchange small talk with Linda, but then a few more people walked through the door and required drinks. But there was still no sign of Micky or Sandy and Mark was resigning himself to another flat evening. It was warm in the bar, so he wandered outside for some cooler air. It was still just about light enough to see where a start had been made on turning over a stretch of land that was going to be Greshams' football pitch. It was on a slight incline so that would give the team a degree of 'home advantage', which might help them pick up a few extra points next season. It would also guarantee a good turnout in the bar for Sunday lunchtimes.

As he re-entered the hall, he could see another small group of people had entered while he was outside. It was Micky's little gang and there was Sandy wearing the same green dress she wore a few weeks earlier. Mark considered going over to speak to them, but he suddenly felt all nervous again. Not only that, but he didn't know three of them and he hardly knew the other two. But if he didn't speak to her that night, he would probably never see her again. Perhaps if he played some music, she might approach him again. Even then, he couldn't just ask her out, there and then. Why should she go out with a complete stranger?

Mark was sure that Sandy would want to hear Mark's records, so he went over to Don to see if he wanted a break. Don could easily have played Mark's records or Mark could have played Don's, but they both preferred their own sounds. Nobody was dancing to Don's records, so he let Mark have a try.

Mark started with *'The "In" Crowd'* and once the vocals had started, he looked over to Sandy to see if she was appreciating the fact that he was playing this just for her. She was just gazing into space at first, but then she caught Mark's eye, so he gave her a friendly 'thumbs up.' She responded with a little nervous smile.

Mark wasn't sure if this was a success or not. He could follow it up with *'Forever'* but that was just a little too obvious, and, in any case, out of step with the need to get people dancing. So he continued with a series of out and out dancers – *'Sweet Soul Music'* was followed by *'Soul Man'* and then *'Dance to the Music.'*

By now, there were a few people dancing, including the five people from Sandy's group, who were all dancing together with no clear pairing up of partners. It did give Mark a better chance to assess Sandy's appeal. She was about five foot eight or nine inches tall. She was quite slim, but she had the semblance of some minor curves in all the right places. She was definitely enjoying the music, but she seemed a little self-conscious in her movements. In all respects, she was different to each of the girls Mark had dated so far. And for that reason alone, he felt the need to pursue a relationship with her – but how? He was starting to feel desperate about finding a way to talk to her before it was too late. He didn't feel he knew Mick well enough to go and talk to him. He would just have to ask her for a dance, which meant getting Don to play Mark's choice of records while he approached her. And that meant he would have to tell Don what he was planning. But he kept putting it off.

When Don asked Mark if he needed a break, Mark asked Don if he thought it was time to play some slow numbers. Don said 'Why not? Some of the older people might like a bit of a waltz.'

Mark wasn't thinking about the older people. He said 'Would you mind doing me a little favour? I want to dance with someone. Would you mind just playing these couple of slow ones while I ask her?'

'Of course not. I bet I know who you want to dance with.'

Mark cued *'Forever'* by Marvin Gaye, which was the record Sandy had selected on her last visit. Almost immediately, nearly all the people who were dancing left the floor. That included Sandy's group, so Mark walked over to her.

'Would you like to dance to this?' he asked. He was breathing heavily. This was always the part of dating that he hated.

She looked to her companions for some reason and when they did not respond in any way, she turned to Mark and said 'All right.' But it was with some reluctance or so it seemed to Mark. She followed him onto the nearly empty floor, but a few other people joined them. He put his right arm around her back and clasped her right hand with his left, as though they were going to waltz. He wanted to hold her closer, but, after all, he was much of a stranger to her, so he didn't think it was appropriate.

'I thought as you like this record, you might enjoy dancing to it,' he said if only because he couldn't think of anything else to say. She didn't say anything. 'You like soul music then, do you?'

'Some of it,' she replied, but that was all she said. This was going to be hard work. Was she being unfriendly or was she just naturally quiet?

'Have you got many records?' Mark asked.

'I haven't got any. I listen to my mother's records.'

'So she likes soul music, then?'

'She likes the Tamla Motown stuff. I've been brought up on it. I like most of the records you've been playing.'

'Oh good. I'm doing something right, then. I think this is going to be the last of these dance evenings. It has never attracted enough interest, I'm afraid.'

'That's a pity. I don't like the rock music the other chap plays.'

'No, but a lot of people prefer that, so we mix it up a bit. And it's his equipment.'

Just then, the record finished and she wanted to separate, but Mark said, 'Can we just do this next one? It's one of my favourites. I'd like to know what you think of it.'

The record started with a femme chorus singing *'I can't stand to see you cry.'* Then Jerry Butler's mellow tones started.

At the end of the first verse, Sandy said 'He's got a nice voice. Who is it?'

'It's Jerry Butler. He's my favourite singer.'

'I've never heard of him. It's very nice. I bet my mother would like this.'

Mark thought he'd like to meet her mother, but one step at a time. His priority at that moment was to arrange to see her daughter again. He didn't want to rush things and scare her off, but on the other hand, he might not get another chance. They just carried on dancing without any further conversation. Mark wanted to hold her closer, but he maintained his position. It occurred to him that he had never danced with any of his girlfriends.

When the music finished, Mark released her and she started walking back to her table. 'Just a minute,' he said. 'Would you like to go out with me?'

'I live in Peterborough,' Sandy replied.

'I've got a car.'

'Would you drive over to Peterborough to see me?'

'Yes, I'd like to see you again.'

'Aren't there any local girls you can go out with?'

'I've been out with local girls, but I want to go out with you. I'd like to get to know you better. I know you don't really know me, but if I didn't ask you now, I'll probably never see you again.' Was she playing 'hard-to-get' or was she determined to find a reason to say 'no.'

'All right, then. I tell you what. Are you doing anything tomorrow?'

'I've got nothing special on.'

'If you could pick me up from Downham Road in the afternoon, you could take me bowling in Peterborough and that would save my mother a trip over to pick me up.'

'I'd like that. I've never been bowling, so you'll have to show me what to do. Do we need to book a lane?' Mark remembered his attempt to go bowling in Norwich with Gary and Karen, when they found all the lanes busy with league bowling and had to return home without touching a bowling ball.

'Not at that time on a Sunday. Make it four o'clock. My relatives always have a late lunch on Sundays. They live at number 33, on the corner of Wellbeck Close.'

'I know where Wellbeck Close is. I'll see you at four o'clock. Thank you for the dance.'

'How did you get on?' asked Don.

'Well, I've got a date for tomorrow. Thank you for your help with the music.'

By now, Don was playing his rock music again and Mark could see Sandy's friends getting up to leave. As she walked towards the door, Sandy turned towards Mark and gave him a little goodbye wave and he waved back. He just hoped she wasn't using him to get a lift as Blodwyn had done.

CHAPTER 9

Your Mother's Only Daughter

The journey from Sanford to Peterborough seemed to take an age. Apart from the Guyhirn straight, the roads were twisty and the conversation was laboured. Mark's attempt to get to know more about Sandy resulted in mostly monosyllabic replies. So he used the time to tell her more about himself. He thought she might be impressed when he described himself as a Work Study Engineer, but if she was impressed, she didn't show it. Mark decided that Sandy was just lacking in communication skills and he recalled how shy and awkward he was when he first left school.

Sandy gave Mark directions to the Bowling Alley, which was situated next to the Football Stadium. Mark remembered once seeing Peterborough United play King's Lynn at the Walks Stadium, when both teams were in the old Midland League. The Linnets were badly beaten that day. Peterborough were now in the Football League.

Sandy was right about the alley not being too busy at that time of day and they were soon ready to start bowling. As this was Mark's very first attempt, Sandy suggested they just book two games and she showed him how to pick a ball and how to score, although he had a rough idea, because he had seen the game on television.

In the first game, Sandy scored 95 to Mark's 53, with several of his attempts going down the gutter and he achieved no 'spares', but in the second, he managed to score 102 to her 98. By then, Mark's thumb was feeling sore, so he was ready to stop and Sandy was agreeable to stop as well. They both had a soft drink and Mark had a hot dog, which Sandy declined as she'd had a late lunch. Mark was pleased that during the game, they'd both had a laugh or two, mostly at Mark's expense, but he expected that and didn't mind.

'What would you like to do, now?' Mark asked.

'I think I ought to go home, if you don't mind. I've been away for two days and I have to go to work in the morning.' Mark did mind. He'd driven a long way and still had a long journey home and it wasn't yet eight o'clock. 'But I have enjoyed it,' she added.

'Are we going to meet again?' Mark asked.

'Yes, if you don't mind driving over again.'

'No, I don't mind. I hope my old car can cope with all this, though. It's time I changed it. There's been a couple of times when it didn't start first time. Are you on the 'phone at home, in case it lets me down?'

'Yes. I'll give you the number when you drop me off.'

As they drove over to Sandy's house which was in Werrington, on the outskirts of the city, Mark asked her what she wanted to do for the next meeting. He was going to suggest just going for a drink to get to know each other better, but she was such a quiet person that he decided that wouldn't be a lot of fun. 'We could go bowling again,' she replied. 'Or swimming; the pictures. I don't mind…anything.'

'The last time I went to Peterborough, it was to go train spotting. I don't suppose you want to do that.'

'No, I don't!' she replied, not realising it was intended as a joke.

'I didn't think you would.'

Mark, his brother and Mark's old friend Podge often visited Peterborough or March in the late fifties and early sixties, before all the steam engines were withdrawn from service. Peterborough was a haven for train spotting due to its position on the East Coast Mainline. March was also popular because of the nearby Whitemoor Marshalling Yard, which attracted freight trains and engines from all over the country. Whitemoor was less glamorous than the express trains in Peterborough, but there was still a great variety of engines, including the really big freight locomotives that could never travel on any of the railways in Norfolk.

'I don't really know Peterborough,' Mark continued, 'so I'm quite happy for you to tell me where to go. As it's a bit of a trek over here, it makes sense to get as much as possible out of a visit. So if we make it next Saturday, we could go for a swim in the afternoon, have a bite to eat somewhere and then go to the pictures in the evening. How does that sound?'

'Yes, all right.'

Mark said he'd try to get there for three o'clock. They were now pulling into Sandy's road in Werrington. It was a modern estate and Sandy's home was a semi-detached house with a small front garden.

Mark said 'Do you think I could use your toilet? I should have gone in the Bowling alley. I forgot I've got a long drive home.' Mark thought it was unlikely that Sandy would have invited him in for coffee. But once inside, her mother, who thanked him for saving her a journey to Sanford, did offer him a drink.

The first thing that struck Mark about Sandy's mother was the similarity of the two ladies. If anything, the mother was slightly more attractive, despite being obviously older. Mark estimated her to be in her late thirties. She was an inch or two shorter, but was slightly fuller in the figure and in all the right places. Where she differed greatly from Sandy was in her powers of communication, because she was soon in conversation with Mark.

'So you're the D.J. at this club Sandra goes to, are you?'

'Well, it's hardly a club and I'm hardly a D.J. I've been helping play records at our Company's Social Club's clubhouse; otherwise, 'yes'. I understand you're a bit of a soul fan yourself?'

'Oh yes. Sandra told you that, did she?'

'Yes. You could say it was music that brought us together.'

Sandy chipped in 'Mark, what was that nice record you played last night? I'm sure mum would like that one.'

'You mean the Jerry Butler record?' Mark asked rhetorically. 'Do you know Jerry Butler?' he asked of Sandy's mother. At that moment, he was paying more attention to her than to Sandy, but she was easier to talk to.

'I've heard of him, but I haven't got any of his records. Most of mine are on Tamla Motown – Marvin Gaye; The Temptations; people like that. Do you live in Sanford?'

'Yes, I do.'

'That's a bit of drive. I hope you've had a good time this afternoon.' Sandy's mother was fishing to see if Mark was going to carry on seeing Sandy, but didn't want to come straight out with the question.

'Yes, very enjoyable, thank you. It was my first attempt at bowling.'

'Are you staying for a bit of tea?'

'I've just had some food at the Bowling Alley, thank you.'

Again Sandy chipped in 'Will you be able to find your way back onto the main road?'

'I think so,' said Mark, sensing that Sandy wanted him to go for some reason. 'I'd better make a move. Thank you for the coffee, Mrs… Sorry I don't know your name.'

'Call me Angela. It's Angela Graham. Will we see you again?'

'Yes. I'm coming over next Saturday. We're going swimming; then off to the pictures if Sandy can find something to see.' He was still talking to

Angela rather than Sandy, but then turned towards Sandy while still talking to her mother. 'I don't know Peterborough, so I'm relying on her. Are you going to see me to the door, Sandy? Good-bye, er…Angela.'

'Good-bye, Mark. We'll see you next week.'

'We?' thought Mark to himself. He was obviously expected to be invited in again.

It was clear to Mark that he wasn't going to get any carpet activity on his trips to Werrington, but at the door, he did just turn to Sandy and give her a little kiss on the lips. It wasn't the best kiss he'd ever had. It was a bit like kissing an old aunt – totally lacking in passion. Perhaps Mark had just taken her by surprise.

As he drove home, Mark's first thought was that he was relieved that Sandy wanted to meet again and this wasn't a repeat of the episode when Blodwyn just used him to get a lift. He was also considering whether this relationship could actually work. The biggest stumbling block was going to be the travelling distance. He could only hope to meet once or twice a week. So what did Sandy offer that would make all this travelling worthwhile?

She was attractive and she had a similar taste in music. She was, in many ways, just the girl he would have wanted when he first left school and had no experience of girls at all. She wasn't divorced like Jenny. She didn't have children like Maggie. He doubted whether she fooled around with married men. She didn't work for Greshams like Karen and Debbie. And she was probably inexperienced, so little chance of catching a social disease. But was she the girl of his dreams? In any case, was that what he wanted at this stage in his life? Did he just want someone whom he could date for a little while or did he want a long term relationship?

Mark had so far found it difficult to talk to her, so having the same taste in music wasn't so brilliant if they couldn't discuss the subject. Her sense of humour was also a bit suspect. The only time Mark had seen her laugh was when he made a fool of himself bowling. Still, her mother was nice. Yes, very nice.

If they were going swimming next week, he would have to check that he could still fit into his trunks. He hadn't been swimming since the last term of school and he had put on about a stone in weight since then. At least he could look forward to seeing Sandy in her swimming costume.

With all this extra driving, he really would have to look for another vehicle. He was now earning a little more money, so he could afford to buy something half decent, but it would have to be on H.P. He quite fancied either a Wolseley 1500 or a Riley 1.5, both of which shared the same body shape, but so far, he hadn't seen one in good condition. Both vehicles were four door saloons with a nice walnut veneer dash, so they had a bit more class about them, without being too expensive to run.

It seemed like a very long week for Mark, but his new career was keeping him busy. His team was very nearly in a position to launch the incentive scheme. Mark had been helping David complete his set of targets for the Joiners' Shop and this involved the two of them working closely together. David never appreciated Mark's constant need to find humour in every situation and he didn't understand Mark's sarcasm, so one day David broached the subject.

'I find it hard to come to terms with this business of not taking work seriously,' he said to Mark. 'I seem to be out on a limb with this. It must be my army background.'

Mark replied 'I don't think it's a question of not taking work seriously. It's more a question of alleviating the pressure of work. You should try it. I don't think I've ever seen you laugh.'

'No, I never seem to get any of your little jokes,' said David.

'What does make you laugh?' Mark asked.

'That's the problem. I don't laugh.'

'Don't you laugh at anything on television?'

'I only watch television for news and documentaries.'

'Does your wife laugh at anything?'

'No, not really,' David replied. Mark wondered what life was like in the Ross household. David was just the sort of chap that would have been picked on at school. It was as well that they'd never had children.

'Okay,' said Mark. 'Try this. This is something that happened a couple of weeks ago when one of my uncles came round. He's about seventy years old, I would think. He's actually my great uncle… a bit of a character. He said something that had us all in stitches. He said that, these days, making love with his wife is a bit like playing snooker with a rope.'

David just stared at Mark, as he usually did when Mark tried to be humorous. 'So that is a joke, is it?' David asked. He wasn't being deliberately unfriendly. He really didn't have a sense of humour. 'Can you explain it to me?'

'No. As soon as you try to explain a joke, it's not funny. But just imagine playing snooker with a rope instead of a cue – and then see the analogy with making love when you're in your seventies.'

Just then, Tommy entered the room and saw the two of them talking seriously. 'Is there a problem?' he asked, suspecting a work-related problem.

'No,' replied Mark. 'We've just worked out that David and I share the same sense of humour. Well, we have to. He hasn't got one.' Tommy didn't laugh at this. He thought Mark was just trying to score points as usual. Mark could sense this, so he explained what had just happened, including his uncle's joke. This time Tommy did laugh, but David was still stony-faced. Well Mark had tried.

Then Tommy changed the subject. 'As we're almost ready to launch the incentive scheme, you two are going to need some help with calculating and recording the bonus, so Paul has agreed to start advertising for a bonus clerk. One thing we will need before she starts is a list of all the employees that are going to be eligible for bonus. That's probably something you can sort out, Mark, with your contacts in Payroll – a list of employees in each department.'

'So you'd like a list of employees broken down by age and sex. I think my uncle would be on that list.'

Tommy chuckled. 'No – just in alphabetical order within each area, thank you.'

David still hadn't laughed.

Then Tommy mentioned that he was expecting to start a new assignment in about two months' time and would be leaving soon. Mark wondered if Wanda knew that and how she would take the news. But he had no sympathy for her. He'd had too many bad experiences of women messing with married men.

During the week, Mark used his lunch-break to nip into town with the intention of buying a copy of the Jerry Butler record for Sandy, but the shop didn't have it in stock. So he asked the shop assistant to order it for him. When Mark went into town on Saturday morning to collect it, the assistant said it was now deleted and couldn't be ordered. Mark asked if they had any other Jerry Butler singles in stock, but they didn't, so he went home empty handed and disappointed.

It was a nice sunny afternoon when Mark set out for Peterborough. Apart from his quick trip to the record shop, he'd spent the rest of the morning looking around some garages to find a new car, but still without success. When he arrived at Sandy's house, he was greeted by her young brother Jerry, who invited Mark in and Mark was duly welcomed by Sandy's mother as well. 'Hello Mark,' she said. I have a little favour to ask. I hope you won't mind. I wondered if you and Sandy would take Jerry with you to the lido. He loves swimming and I never seem to have time to take him. If you do that for me, there'll be a nice meal waiting for you when you get back.'

Mark did mind. He wanted to spend some time alone with Sandy to further their relationship, but he found it very hard to refuse Angela. And at least he was going to get a free meal out of it. Mark assessed Jerry's age at around twelve. Jerry seemed friendly enough and thanked Mark politely.

Sandy appeared with her swimming gear and gave Mark a nice smile. 'You don't mind seeing '"*Ring of Bright Water*" tonight, do you?' she asked.

'That's the film about an otter, isn't it?' Mark asked.

'That's right. It starts at 7.15, so we need to be out of here by 6.45.'

'I love watching otters,' said Mark. 'I saw some a year ago at Great Witchingham Wildlife Park. They do things like swim on their backs while chewing a carrot. Then they'll play on the slides. I felt that they were deliberately trying to entertain the visitors. I could have watched them for hours.'

Angela said 'I hear it's a very good film. I'd like to see it sometime.'

'Can't you get your husband to take you?' Mark asked innocently.

'I haven't got a husband, Mark. Didn't Sandy tell you? He walked out on us five years ago.'

Mark felt dreadful. Sandy should have warned him. He was tempted to invite Angela to join them, but thought better of it.

'Anyway,' added Angela, 'you all get off and enjoy yourselves while I prepare your meal.'

At the pool, Mark tried to get undressed as quickly as possible in order to observe Sandy before she entered the water, but Jerry held him up and she was already swimming around. She was wearing a green swimming cap, which would enable Mark to pick her out if he decided to remove his spectacles, which he was reluctant to do, because he was in a strange place and everything would be a blur without them.

Sandy was a good swimmer and kept swimming up and down the length of the pool, until, that is, a young lad got in her way and she berated him for it. Mark thought that was a bit unnecessary and was surprised at her loss of temper, especially as the lido was primarily a leisure pool and was not really suitable for serious swimmers. Mark wasn't such a good swimmer and was tired out after swimming two lengths, so he resorted to swimming the occasional width, stopping frequently for a rest and a furtive look round at all the other ladies in their swimming costumes. Mark soon got bored of all this. Sandy was doing her own thing and ignoring him. Jerry had met a friend and so he, too, was ignoring Mark. Mark felt as if he may just as well have gone for a swim on his own at his local baths.

After what Mark considered was a long enough period of time, he approached Sandy as she entered the shallow area, forcing her to stop and talk to him. 'What sort of time will your mother expect us back?' he asked.

Sandy stood up, so that at last Mark could see her top half, glistening in the late afternoon sun as water drained from her slender figure. He never heard her answer. He had suddenly seen her in a whole new light. She looked like a green water goddess. His impression of her, up to that point, was that she was a bit too slim for his taste, but in that figure-hugging green swimsuit, she was perfection and he wanted to grasp her passionately in his arms – except that it wouldn't be right and proper.

'You look stunning,' he heard himself say. 'Green really suits you.' He added the last sentence so that it didn't sound like he was lusting after her body, even though he was, but she didn't appear to take offence.

'Why, thank you. Yes, a woman in a dress shop once told me that green is my natural colour – something to do with my skin tone and my green eyes.'

Mark could see that her eyes were actually brown, but with the merest faint fleck of green, so he didn't argue. He was still in awe of his water goddess. If only she would remove her cap so that her hair could tumble about her shoulders, the effect would be complete. He concentrated on looking at her lovely face, while he really wanted to look at everything else.

'I just want to do a few more lengths,' she said and glided off like a streamlined water nymph, slowing down as she approached Jerry to give him ten minutes' notice of their departure. Mark just gazed after her. Now he had a burning desire to see the full length Sandy exit the pool, which she did a few minutes later. Her long slender, but shapely legs, seemed to take forever to leave the water and she had a small, but perfectly shaped bottom to complete the picture. It was as well that the cool water was keeping Mark's ardour in check. Any doubts he had about this long distance relationship were now dispelled. But he craved more intimate surroundings.

Even back in the car, Mark still found it difficult to enter into any meaningful conversation. This wasn't helped by the presence of Jerry in the back seat.

Angela greeted them with the offer of a cup of tea to warm them up after the swim and the news that their meal would be ready soon. She certainly wanted to talk. 'Are you a keen swimmer, Mark?'

'I enjoy swimming, but I'm not very good. It's because I've got a footballer's build.'

'How does that stop you being a good swimmer?'

'According to my old P.E. teacher, it's something to do with the angle of your instep. I thought he was talking rubbish at first, but then I noticed that very few of the better footballers were strong swimmers and very few of the better swimmers got into the football teams. So there must be something in it.'

'That probably explains why Sandra and I can't play football!' Angela replied.

'No I don't think either of you have a footballer's build.'

'I haven't been swimming for a few years,' she added.

'You could come with us, if we go again,' Mark said.

'You don't want me tagging along with you young people. And I'm not letting you see me in a swimming costume.'

'Spoilsport!' said Mark, with a smile. Then realised that he really shouldn't be flirting with his girlfriend's mother, but he really would quite like to see Angela in a swimsuit. So he added 'Seriously, you would be most welcome if you did want to come. I'm sure there's no need to feel self-conscious. Everyone is too busy swimming to look at each other.' Mark didn't include himself in that statement!

'Well thank you for the offer,' Angela said. At least she didn't appear to have taken offence. 'I'll go and check on your meal. I hope you like hotpot, Mark. Take a seat at the table. I've got some home-made soup first and that's ready.'

Mark couldn't help noticing that Angela gave a delightful little wiggle of her shapely hips as she walked towards the kitchen. And she had great legs as well.

While they ate, Angela and Mark did most of the talking. 'How did you get into soul music?' Mark asked Angela.

'It was when they had the Motown Special on Ready Steady Go. After seeing all those scruffy pop groups in the early sixties, it was a revelation to see groups wearing smart suits and singing with strings and brass and performing all those slick dance moves. And I fell in love with Marvin Gaye. He just looked so cool. I got rid of all my old pop records and started buying as many Motown records as I could afford.'

'And that rubbed off on Sandy?' Mark asked.

'I always prefer the flipsides,' said Sandy, joining in at long last.

'Do you know, so do I,' said Mark. 'My favourite group is the Impressions and their flipsides are always at least as good as the 'A' sides – just less commercial.'

They carried on talking about music for a while longer, until it was time to leave for the pictures, by which time, Sandy had changed into a pretty green dress.

'That looks pretty, Sandy,' Mark said. 'You always dress nicely – and so quickly, too.' Angela gave him a questioning look, so he quickly said 'Sorry! That's just a little joke. We'd better go before I get into trouble.' But Angela just smiled.

After the film, Mark took Sandy for a quiet drink. He was determined to introduce a little more intimacy into their relationship, so he felt he had to get her to communicate more. 'Did you feel upset when the otter was killed?' he asked.

'No, it's just a film,' Sandy replied. Mark thought most people would have felt something at that particularly emotive scene. Was she really that hard-hearted or was it just an act?

'Do you mind if we talk about your father?'

'In what way?'

'Well, do you ever see him?'

'About once a year, but I don't really want anything to do with him.'

'Are your parents divorced?'

'I don't know. I know mother was trying to get a divorce, but it got complicated. Don't ask me why.'

'Did your mother take it badly?'

'Yes she did. When he left, it all happened out of the blue.'

'Did he go off with another woman?'

'I believe so. We never talk about it. My mother didn't do anything to deserve that. She's dedicated herself to bringing us up as best she can. She's always made sure we've been fed and clothed. I hate my father for what he did to her.'

'I think your mother is a lovely person. I'm surprised your father would want to go off with someone else.'

'Do you think she's attractive?' Sandy asked, looking intently at Mark.

'Yes. You both look quite similar, so, of course she's attractive. You take after her.'

'Do you think she's more attractive than me?'

'No. You're both about the same. She's just a bit older.'

'You seem to talk to her more than you do to me.'

'You're surely not jealous of your mother? I talk to her because she talks to me. Do you want me to be rude and ignore her?'

'No, I just want you to pay more attention to me. Why did you have to invite her to come swimming with us?' Sandy was starting to get cross and not for the first time that day.

'Look! I just want to be with you, like we are now. But in the swimming pool, we're not alone, anyway.' Mark was going to mention the fact that Sandy had virtually ignored Mark in the pool, but he didn't want this silly argument to continue.

'If you'd rather she didn't come, I won't mention it again. What's more, after seeing you in your swimming costume, I've been waiting for hours to get you alone. I thought you looked fantastic. I've been having indecent thoughts about you ever since.'

'You naughty person,' Sandy said with a grin, but then spoke seriously. 'Look, I realise that you're older than me and have probably been out with lots of girls. But if you're just going out with me for sex, you can forget it.'

'I'm not going out with you for sex! I was just trying to make you realise how much I do want to go out with you. But only if you want to go out with me.'

'I do want to go out with you.'

'Right then,' said Mark. 'Do you want to go out tomorrow night?'

'Not Sunday nights. I like to wash my hair on a Sunday.' Mark let out a big sigh.

'We could go bowling again in the afternoon,' she added, realising Mark's frustration. 'We enjoyed that, didn't we?'

'Yes. I would like to try and do better next time. Perhaps we can play three games this time.'

As they walked back to Mark's car, Mark put his arm around Sandy's shoulder and she yielded to him. Then he held her hand and they walked along like that until they reached his car. Before Mark unlocked the passenger door, he turned Sandy to face him and kissed her. This time, he hadn't taken her by surprise, but it still wasn't the best kiss he had ever experienced. Somehow, their mouths didn't seem compatible. That didn't make sense. He let her go and opened the door for her.

When he was seated next to her, he leaned over and tried again – still much the same. He let his hand wander over her shapely thighs. That was nice, but his attempt to address her breasts met with resistance, so he returned to her thighs. When he ventured further up, she again stopped him, at which point, he gave up and started the engine.

CHAPTER 10

What does it Take (To win Your Love for Me)?

Sandy was pleased with herself for getting only her second proper boyfriend. Her first had been a big disappointment. Lenny had been more interested in getting drunk with his mates and had never treated her with any degree of tenderness or respect. He didn't have a car and he could be very coarse at times. But Mark, by contrast, seemed like a genuine and considerate person. Moreover, he must have serious intentions; otherwise he wouldn't be prepared to travel over from Sanford just to see her. Mark also seemed to have gained her mother's approval, unlike Lenny, whom Angela had repeatedly criticised, mainly for his general attitude, dismissing him as a 'disaster waiting to happen.' It was out of consideration for her mother that Sandy had terminated her relationship with Lenny, who didn't seem particularly upset about that. And Sandy hadn't lost any sleep either.

Sandy began looking forward to seeing Mark each time and her one regret was that she didn't see him more frequently. However, that didn't mean she was ready to relinquish her virginity just yet. She had been brought up to view it as a valuable asset.

Mark was also starting to feel much more content with the direction his life was taking and he was particularly gratified that the improvements had been very much of his own making. He had been successful in chatting up the lovely Sandy, whom he now considered to be his girlfriend – in fact, only his second ever girlfriend, because he had never considered Maggie to be such, despite using her to increase his sexual experiences.

Mark was the one who had successfully applied for a new position at work and he was the one who was making a success of it. But he had suffered one minor disappointment in this respect. He was hoping that when Tommy moved on, Mark would inherit a position as the Senior Work Study Engineer or perhaps Team Leader, because he felt he was so much more capable than David. He didn't expect a managerial position because he knew his age was against him, but with only two engineers and one Bonus Clerk, there was no need for a manager. But Tommy announced that a new Work Study Manager was to be appointed. This was to be a chap named Eddie Hudson. Eddie had many years' experience as a production manager and had a thorough grounding in Work Study practices. His appointment would overlap with Tommy's to facilitate a smooth handover of responsibilities, two weeks after the incentive scheme had been introduced and one week before the new bonus Clerk was due to arrive; meaning Mark and David would have to do their own payment calculations for one week.

It soon became clear to Mark that Eddie had got the job because of his 'gift of the gab.' He seemed to have a little anecdote to match every conversation – mostly involving great exaggerations, if not out and out lies. And many of his yarns included tales of his sexual prowess – although he hardly looked the part. He was about fifty years old, with a grey beard to match his thick head of grey hair and was barely five foot four inches tall and nearly as wide. As an instance of his anecdotal endeavours he told of the time when, whilst doing some work for Trinity House, he found himself being seduced by an attractive widow in the top of a lighthouse. He boasted of their silhouette being plastered across the countryside, giving all the locals a free porn show. Yeah! That was totally believable!

Another example of his exploits was when he bet a voluptuous young lady a ten bob note that he could fondle her lovely breasts without her feeling a thing. When she said she could feel everything he had done, he said 'Here's your ten bob. It were worth every penny!'

The Bonus Clerk was Della Adams. On her first day, she was introduced to Mark and David by Eddie Hudson who had already met her because he was staying at the same hotel as Della and her husband, who were both Geordies and still in the process of relocating to Norfolk. Mark struggled to understand a lot of what she was saying. Every sentence seemed to end with 'like', 'pet' or a word that sounded like 'but'. Being a northerner himself, Eddie acted as interpreter, but since he also had a thick accent – in his case, a Yorkshire accent – that wasn't always successful, especially as Eddie was frequently chewing on an old pipe, which he also used as a pointer to emphasise his statements.

Della was a pretty young lady with a great mass of reddish hair cascading down her shoulders, but she seemed to do a lot of scowling, probably as a defence mechanism against her own inability to understand Mark's accent! She had obviously married at a young age because she could only have been a year or two older than Mark. Eddie seemed very familiar with her, despite the fact that he had only known her himself for little over a week, but he was soon telling of an escapade in the hotel involving Della, her husband, himself and a well-built barmaid. Della seemed uncomfortable with this tale and didn't contribute in any way. But at least she was pretty. What a pity she was wearing one of those horrible maxi-skirts!

She was asked to sit at a desk at a right angle to Mark who would show her how to calculate the workers' bonuses. To start with, this was hard work, but eventually they both got used to each other's accents and they soon formed a good working partnership, but with, at first, little in the way of chit-chat. His new responsibility of teaching Della confirmed to Mark that he was the more accomplished of the two male colleagues.

Meanwhile Mark continued to drive over to Peterborough to see Sandy, mostly at weekends with the occasional mid-week excursion. Because the Lido was an outdoor pool, they only had one more swimming session together. Jerry joined them again, but Angela did not, much to Mark's disappointment. Mark made a point of interrupting Sandy's lengths a couple of times. The first time was away from the shallow end, so that when she stopped and stood up, he was able to put his arms around her and give her a discrete underwater cuddle and a quick kiss on the lips. He said 'I've been waiting all week to do that.'

His hands went down to the small of her back and he held her close, just as he had wanted to do a few weeks earlier when they had danced together. 'I don't think we should be doing this, here,' Sandy said. 'We might get thrown out.'

'Surely a chap can cuddle his girlfriend, can't he?' And just to reinforce the point, his hands ventured down to her small, but perfectly formed bottom. With that, she pushed him away and resumed her swimming. Yet again, Sandy had demonstrated a total lack of passion. But he wouldn't give up.

Fifteen minutes later, he interrupted her swimming again. Mark wasn't going to let her get away with continually ignoring him. 'I will be playing football most Saturday afternoons, so this may be the last chance we will have to swim together.'

As he spoke, he couldn't help just putting his arm round her slender waist. This time she didn't resist, but she replied 'Would you rather play football than come out with me?'

Mark replied 'It's not as simple as that. If I miss a game, I will be dropped and they'll get another goalie, so I wouldn't be able to play again. So I have to turn up to every game. I also play on Sunday mornings, but at least that will leave Sunday afternoons free. I just thought I'd warn you. I have a friendly tomorrow morning and probably a mid-week friendly for my Saturday team. But the Friday evening tennis will end soon, so I could get over Friday evenings, if you want.'

'That will be nice,' she replied, but without conviction and then swam off again. Mark was finding this all very frustrating.

Angela provided another delicious tea and again she and Mark dominated the conversation, but whenever possible, Mark did his best to involve Sandy. Each time he did this, Sandy responded with a little smile, thus recording her recognition that Mark had reacted to her concerns. Mark would actually have preferred to just sit and talk to Angela. She was looking very attractive that evening and he found her smile quite disarming, but he knew that Sandy was his main objective.

The film that evening was 'The Pride of Miss Jean Brodie.' As they walked back to the car after the film, Mark stopped Sandy and held her in his arms to kiss her. He was expecting her to say 'not here' again, but she didn't. So he felt emboldened to let his hands wander down to her lovely firm bottom and pulled her closer trying to generate some passion. For some reason, she returned the gesture by grabbing his buttocks, remarking that they were very muscular. At least she was making some kind of effort, but to Mark it seemed a little contrived, especially when she said 'You're cute!' He didn't know how to respond to this. He'd never been called 'cute' before. But as she seemed to be trying to further their relationship, he hurried her into the car where he continued to kiss her and explore her lovely shapely body. This time, she did allow him a little fondle of her breasts, but stopped him when his hand went 'down below.' Well that was some kind of progress, but there still wasn't any real passion on her part and there certainly wasn't any sign of encouragement that Mark might proceed to the next step – not even a bit of heavy petting.

On a whim, Mark took her hand and directed it to his member. She instantly pulled her hand back with disgust. 'I just wanted you to know what effect you're having on me,' Mark said.

'You'll have to learn to control yourself, Mark!' she exclaimed, as though he was some kind of pervert, instead of a normal red-blooded male – quite a contrast to Maggie who would, by now, be insisting he couldn't go home in this condition!

At this point, Mark decided it was time to take Sandy home, but the car didn't want to start. The starter wouldn't engage. He got out and looked under the bonnet, although he'd no idea what he was looking for. He jiggled all the leads and tried again. This time it did fire. 'I really must get a new car,' he told Sandy who was probably wondering if this was some sort of ploy to leave them stranded until Mark had had his way with her. At her house, he decided to leave the engine running in case it wouldn't start again and he leaned over to give her a one-sided kiss. 'See you next week,' he said.

'You do still want to see me, then,' she says wistfully.

'Of course I want to see you. I hope my car wants to see you again. Would you rather I didn't come?'

'No, of course not!'

So Mark drove home again with all sorts of mixed feelings. In so many ways, Sandy was close to the ideal girlfriend for him. She was very attractive and had a great figure, even though Mark would have preferred a little more shape; and, of course, what had initiated his interest in her, she had great taste in music. Sandy was giving some indications that she wanted to continue the relationship, but there was just this lack of passion and even though he had made a little progress in breaking down her resistance, there were still some barriers to overcome. It wasn't that he had to have sex for the affair to flourish, but he needed to see more warmth in her rejections.

Perhaps if she was more of a tease like Blodwyn – that might make for an interesting challenge, but Mark didn't think that Sandy was deliberately being a tease.

He wondered if he would have more success with her mother, but that really wasn't an option and he had to stop thinking about Angela in that way.

To make matters worse, his car was misbehaving; making him fear that he might, one day, get stranded in Peterborough. He had to change it soon. It wasn't worth spending money on.

The next day, Mark turned up for the first football friendly to be played on Greshams' new pitch. Even during the warm-up, it soon became apparent that the turf was not ready for football. As soon as players started running around and tackling, clods of turf were coming away revealing a badly prepared surface beneath. To make matters worse, the pitch was littered with stones and every time Mark had to dive to make a save, he injured himself. By the end of the game, he was covered in cuts and was in considerable pain from a gash in his knee. At least two people seemed to be hobbling, probably with twisted ankles.

Mark approached the new manager who had taken over from Nobby during the summer. 'Look Charlie,' he said, 'we can't possibly play our home matches on this pitch. I'm covered in cuts.'

'I can see that, Mark,' Charlie replied, looking at the drying blood down Mark's leg and socks. 'But we're committed now. The council pitches will have already been allocated. The pitch will improve once it's been watered.' Mark didn't think so. Even if the turf did establish itself, there was still the problem of all the loose stones. He had visions of getting injured every time they played at home.

On Monday, he telephoned Dougie who had often tried to persuade Mark to play for his Sunday team, the Reds. Mark had always declined out of loyalty to Greshams and because he was always kept busy playing for Greshams, giving him ample scope to shine (as well as more opportunities to make mistakes, of course). But he was fed up with losing nearly every week. He explained the situation to Dougie.

'I'm sure I can get you into the Reds' first Team,' said Dougie. 'Several of the team have seen you play on Saturdays, so they know what you can do.'

So Mark agreed to follow it through and the following Sunday, he played in goal for the Reds in the first league fixture of the new season and Greshams had to find a new goalkeeper. The Reds, like Northfleet in the Saturday league, regularly won their league, but the Sunday league was always a lot closer and Mark was called upon to make several saves in their 3-1 victory. This was against the Ship Inn which was close to the Northfleet Estate and three of their players also played for Mark's Saturday team, so they would know of Mark's weaknesses. Because Mark had to play in glasses, he avoided diving at attackers' feet, but he made up for this by being very swift off his line and being expert at 'narrowing the angle' and 'making himself look big.'

Rain was another big weakness for Mark. Everyone joked about needing wipers, but Mark never felt like laughing when it rained. Fortunately, it hadn't rained in this first fixture, so Mark felt confident of securing his place with his new team. Mark was very good at crosses; always preferring to catch the ball when possible rather than punching. Mark felt that if you are going to punch the ball, you need to get a good distance, and for that you need good impetus. And if you've got good impetus, you might just as well catch it. He even perfected a one-handed catch like Pat Jennings, which he only used when absolutely necessary. Dominating the penalty area gave the rest of the defence confidence in his ability and that confidence filtered through the whole team. One mistake could undo all that confidence and a goalkeeper's mistake was usually punished – and remembered long after the successes.

* * * * * *

On Monday, as soon as he walked into his office, Mark was summoned to see Paul O'Connor. He was accompanied by Eddie Hudson. As they both walked towards the office, Mark asked Eddie if he knew what this was about. 'All I know,' said Eddie 'is that it has summit t' do with the Paint Shop.'

Mark was immediately filled with trepidation when he saw Red Miller sat opposite Paul O'Connor, loudly saying 'We 'in't gonna hev it!', thus betraying both his Norfolk background and his prejudices. Paul just moved his hand gently up and down to calm him down. Red turned to glower at Mark. Mark remembered that look from their previous unfortunate encounter.

Red was the Union representative for the small number of workers in the Paint Shop, but that department had never been particularly militant. The average age of the Paint Shop workers was about fifty-five and they had always struck Mark as being quite laid back. So much so, that Mark had found it difficult to set accurate targets for their various tasks, since none of them performed with any great zeal. As a consequence, whenever a new task needed to be studied, the Paint Shop Foreman, Greg Stanley, would volunteer to perform the task; just until Mark was happy that he had a representative time. So far, very little bonus had been paid out for that area; and nobody was surprised. Mark had enjoyed doing his studies in the Paint Shop. The work didn't just consist of painting. They performed French polishing; waxing and wiring with bees' wax; staining; as well as the obvious priming, undercoating and glossing. He had learnt quite a lot about the techniques employed for each task and how the nature of the surface dictated the effort required. All the people in that area had been particularly friendly and helpful, so this confrontation had come out of the blue. Mark wondered if Red still had an axe to grind after their encounter at the darts match.

Paul didn't invite either Mark or Eddie to sit down. He just calmly asked Mark how the targets for the Paint Shop had been established, so Mark explained what had happened and mentioned that the foreman had always considered the times had been fair and reasonable.

Again, Red said 'We 'in't gonna hev it!'

Eddie spoke next. Mark assumed that Eddie would back him up, but the tone of his voice was more conciliatory. 'The best thing is for me to do a few more studies. You can volunteer anyone you like for me to study – probably the person who has raised the issue. Who's that?' he asked of Red.

'They've all raised it. The targets are far too tight. I'm told the targets in the Metal Shop are tight, as well.'

Mark chipped in at that. 'Most people in the Metal shop are earning decent bonus – obviously, some more than others, but you would expect that.' Mark was confident in his targets, but he suspected that the workers had been comparing their bonuses with the Joiners' Shop, where the targets were, in his humble opinion, mostly too loose.

Paul wanted to bring matters to a close, so he said 'The matter in hand is the Paint Shop. So we'll do what Eddie says. I'll check the figures and so can you.' He directed his last remark to Red, who just grunted reluctantly.

Paul had a reputation of being very firm with any Union activists. Mark had heard of the time when two outside Union representatives had met with Paul. Paul asked Anne to bring in three coffees and then proceeded to drink all three in front of the activists.

Eddie and Mark went to see Greg Stanley to see who and what Eddie could study that day. Greg suggested he should study Harry Drew who was going to wax and wire a batch of doors that afternoon. Then later, Cyril Stapleton was due to undercoat some door frames. Cyril's real name was Ben. He'd been given his nickname after the well-known band leader. Very few people knew his true name, but Mark did, as he had seen Cyril's National Insurance card when Mark had worked in the Payroll office. As they walked back to the Work Study office, Mark tried to warn Eddie that he had previously tried to study both of these individuals and had thrown away the results as they were both so slow, it was impossible to come up with accurate times. Eddie insisted that all you had to do was assess the rate at which someone was working and apply the appropriate percentage. Mark said he knew all that, but it only works within a certain scale. Eddie ignored him.

That afternoon, Eddie returned from his first study and slammed his clipboard on his desk. 'That man will never earn bonus as long as he's got a hole in his arse! I've never seen so much dithering and farting around. You can't time him. It's impossible.'

Mark resisted the urge to say 'I told you.' But he did have a smug look on his face when he asked 'Can't you just apply the appropriate percentage to his times?'

'You can only apply a percentage if the person you've studied has got a clue about what he's doing. I was tempted to tell him to let me have a go.'

'Are you going back to study Cyril?'

'You bet your life, I am. And if I get the same sort of reaction, I will tell bloody Red to bloody-well whistle.'

When Eddie returned from studying Cyril, he just sank into his chair and uttered a giant sigh. Without either of them speaking, Mark felt vindicated. Eddie decided it was time to light his old pipe. Mark turned to Della and said, 'I don't think we need to change the targets for the Paint Shop.'

This was a little disappointing, because it robbed Mark of the opportunity to visit the Typing Pool to see the lovely Stella who had recently taken over the role of Supervisor. Stella was about seven or eight years older than Mark and in a steady relationship, so he had no aspirations there. But that didn't stop him from lusting after her. She was blonde and of Amazonian proportions. Mark found that when she stood up next to him, his knees turned to jelly and she had this effect on all the men in the office. She was said to be a champion swimmer and she had the build to go with it. Mark had seen her with her boyfriend at a company function. He played rugby and was six inches taller than she was, so they made a very impressive pair. Mark had wanted to engage Stella in a gentle waltz, but didn't have the nerve to risk a rejection, especially as nobody else sought to separate the pair.

Apart from looking absolutely gorgeous, she was always friendly and efficient in her job, but she had such an effect on Mark when he was in her company that he feared that in his efforts to engage her in friendly conversation, he would, one day, be lost for sensible words and embarrass himself by saying something really stupid like 'What's your favourite stroke?' or 'If I said you had a great figure, would you hold it against me?' But so far, all he had done was to look like an idiot when he had been lost for words.

CHAPTER 11

Getting Mighty Crowded

One evening, Mark and Sandy were having a quiet drink in a pub in Werrington. As usual, Mark was finding the conversation hard going. The one thing the two of them had in common was their love of music, but enjoying the same music and actually sharing it were two different matters. Occasionally, they found a pub with a juke box, but the choices on offer were very limited and were mostly chart music, so weren't usually worth wasting a bob of anyone's money. Mark's previous attempts to converse on the subject had been rather one-sided, so he tried a different tack this time.

'One of the main reasons I wanted to go out with you is your taste in music. And yet, we never have the opportunity to listen to music together. Have you got any ideas how we could do this? Do you know of any clubs or anything in Peterborough for instance?'

Sandy sat back as though she was really thinking hard and after a minute said 'I'm not really up on clubs. You could come over our house one night and bring some of your records. I'd like to hear some of them.'

'Do your family ever go out, so we could listen alone?' asked Mark. Mark remembered the time he and Jenny had babysat for his sister and how some relaxing music and soft lights had helped his seduction technique.

'Not the two of them together,' Sandy replied. 'I must admit that Jerry wouldn't be too happy about us playing records all night. He doesn't like our music and I don't like his, but mum wouldn't mind. Perhaps we could find a night when he wants to go round his friend's. Why don't we talk about it with them when you drop me off?'

'That sounds like an enjoyable evening – as long as we can spend some time alone together – even if it's only a quick drink afterwards.'

Sandy just smiled and then they encountered another one of those silent moments when neither could think what to say next, so Mark tried a couple of jokes. Sandy's resultant little laugh seemed to Mark to be half-hearted. 'Do you know any jokes?' he asked.

'I'm not very good at jokes. I've got a funny little anecdote, though. When Jerry was much younger, he went to the dentists to have a tooth extracted. He made a lot of fuss about it and didn't want to go. Mum said he wouldn't feel anything, because he could have gas. He said '"*I don't want gas. And I don't want electricity either!*"

Mark laughed. Then Sandy added 'You mustn't say anything to Jerry about that. He still finds it embarrassing.'

And then another period of silence engulfed them.

When they got back to Sandy's house and discussed the idea about a musical evening, Jerry said he would be happy to go round his friend's house on the following Saturday. He couldn't go any other evening as he and his friend always had homework to do.

Angela said she would cook them all a nice tea. Mark pointed out that he had an away match that afternoon and by the time he had gone home and cleaned up, he wouldn't be able to get to Werrington before seven o'clock. But everyone was happy about that.

'Will you bring that Jerry Butler record?' asked Sandy.

'I'll bring a couple of his records,' Mark replied.

As Mark drove home, he bemoaned the fact that he'd just spent another evening with his girlfriend without much of a kiss and cuddle again, let alone a good fondle and a grope. But he was looking forward to his next visit. If only he didn't have an hour's drive each way. He told himself he had to remember those lonely years when he couldn't get a date of any description. He'd hate to go back to those days. And now he had the pleasure of working with the lovely Della. Their relationship was improving all the time, now that Mark realised that Della usually only scowled when she had to put up with Eddie Hudson's bullshit. And Della had also started to understand Mark's sense of humour, which enabled them both to form an alliance as protection against David's stern attitude towards work. Mark had explained to her that he and David shared the same sense of humour.

'I thought you meant it,' she had said. 'You're always so dead-pan, like, I never know when you're being serious.'

'Shall I say "*boom, boom!*" at the end of every joke?' he had replied. 'Or you can just assume I'm trying to be funny all the time.'

'I think "*boom, boom*" would get on my nerves,' she had said.

When David was in the office, conversation was usually restricted to matters concerned with work. But as soon as he left the room, the atmosphere lightened considerably, even when the manager was still there.

Mark was particularly proud of the time he made Della laugh at Eddie's expense. He had said 'Did you know there are three types of orgasm?'

Eddie had to butt in. 'There's more than that where I'm concerned, tha' knows,' he said. Della scowled.

'For the purposes of my joke, there are three,' said Mark firmly. 'There's the positive orgasm, where the woman says *"Oh, yes! Yes"* Then there's the religious orgasm, where the woman says *"Oh my God."* And finally there's the faked orgasm, where the woman says *"Oh Eddie! Eddie'*

Mark was pleased with the reaction he got from Della who giggled, with just a touch of embarrassment. Mark wasn't sure whether she was a little embarrassed at the ribald nature of the joke or because the joke was at the expense of their manager. Eddie didn't laugh, but he gave a polite smile. At least he was a good sport. Mark knew he couldn't have told that joke in front of David without receiving a very hard stare. He also knew he couldn't use that joke with Sandy. She didn't approve of anything sordid.

The next day, Mark had another little joke lined up at Eddie's expense and, this time, he didn't bother whether David was there or not.

'Eddie,' he said. 'You've been around a lot up north. Have you ever made love to a woman in Keighley?'

Eddie suspected another gag coming, but he went along with it anyway. 'I believe I have, you know.' He couldn't resist a chance to boost his glorious image as a sex god.

'And have you ever done it in Skipton?'

'Mebbe.'

'What about Upper Ramsbottom?'

The rest of the office burst into laughter, but David carried on pretending to work, with a look on his face that resembled Queen Victoria at her most solemn. Mark wasn't sure if there was a place called Upper Ramsbottom, but he heard someone else telling the joke, so it served its purpose.

'I can confidently say I've never managed that one – not really my neck of the woods,' Eddie replied, sucking on his pipe.

During the week, Mark experienced another problem with his starter motor. Again, looking under the bonnet and fiddling with the leads seemed to cure it, but he knew it was only a matter of time before the car really let him down. He spent Saturday morning driving around all the local car dealers, but he still didn't find his ideal replacement.

That evening, after a quiet afternoon in goal, followed by a lot of rushing around to clean himself up and get ready, he headed off towards Peterborough with a good selection of singles in a cardboard box. He had decided that it would be too time-consuming to listen to LP's and it was only quite recently that he had invested in a record player that could play stereo records, so nearly all his best LP's were in mono. He had bought the record player from his sister's mail-order catalogue and was paying for it at 10/6 per week. Even his mono records now sounded so fresh, that he was listening to all his collection as though he were hearing them for the very first time.

When he arrived, Angela told him to make himself comfortable while she prepared their meal. Sandy was looking through the records he had brought and sorting them into some sort of playing sequence. Mark soon felt bored of just sitting there, so he ventured into the kitchen to ask if he could be of any assistance.

Angela suggested he could lay out the plates and cutlery. 'I hope you like dumplings, Mark' she said.

'I'm sure I'll enjoy your dumplings,' he said with a grin.

'Mark! Are you flirting with me?' Mark had become so used to flirting with the various married women in the factory and making suggestive comments, that he was now doing it with his girlfriend's mother.

'I'm so sorry,' he said. 'I hope I haven't offended you.'

'No, I'm not offended,' she said with that little grin that often disconcerted him. He knew he had coloured up, but, if he was not mistaken, she had actually enjoyed his flirting, but it wasn't right; and he should have known better. He hoped Sandy hadn't heard any of this conversation. Fortunately, when he returned to the living room with the plates and cutlery, she was showing signs of excitement and anticipation at the prospect of hearing all these wonderful records Mark had selected.

When Angela came in to place some condiments on the table, she deliberately smiled at Mark and he was sure she gave a little wiggle as she disappeared back into the kitchen – or was it his imagination?

After a delicious meal, Mark asked Angela if she would like him to help with the washing up. 'Sandy and I can do it together,' he said making assumptions on Sandy's behalf.

But before Sandy could confirm or refute this offer, Angela said 'Oh, no. We'll leave that for now. Are you sure you wouldn't like another helping of apple pie?'

'No, thank you. It was delicious, but I'm absolutely full up.'

'Oh, good,' Angela replied. 'We like our men to be well fed.'

'What's this *"we"* and *"our men"* business?' thought Mark. Was he suddenly their joint property? He could think of worse things, because he realised that he really was starting to be much more attracted to Angela than he was to Sandy.

Sandy stood up and said 'Can we listen to some music, now?' and without waiting for a reply, she stood up from the table and sat on the settee. 'Are you going to be the D.J., Mark?' she asked. 'We haven't got an auto-stacker, so you'll have to put them on one at a time. Don't be afraid to play some flipsides if you think they're any good.'

Mark ignored the sequence into which Sandy had already sorted the records. 'This is the Jerry Butler record that Sandy and I danced to when I first asked her out,' He said as he placed the record on the turntable. He turned to sit beside Sandy only to find that Angela was also taking a place on the settee and invited Mark to sit between the two of them. It was a three-seater settee, but it wasn't particularly big and Mark only just fitted. He was aware that his thighs were tight against both ladies and there was nowhere to put his hands other than on his own lap. As the music started, he couldn't help comparing the physiques beside him. Angela definitely felt 'more comfortable'. Her hips were just slightly wider, but softer and her thighs felt fuller – and more to Mark's taste.

'I love his voice,' said Sandy. 'I'm surprised he isn't better known.'

'It is very nice,' responded Angela. 'I'm not surprised you enjoyed dancing to this. His voice is quite seductive. Do you use this record to sweep all the girls off their feet?'

'Not yet; but thanks for the tip,' he replied.

As the record climaxed, Mark extricated himself from his wonderful position to ready the next disc.

'See if you recognise this song,' he said, as he squeezed back into position.

After a few bars, Angela said 'Yes. I used to have this by The Swinging Bluejeans. It's called *'You're No Good.'* Who's this then?'

'It's Betty Everett,' Mark replied.

'Is this the original version?'

'I used to think it was, but I recently found out that Dee Dee Warwick had the original, but I've never heard her version.'

'Is she related to Dionne Warwick?' asked Sandy, doing her best to ensure Angela and Mark didn't exclude her from the conversation.

'Yes, she's her sister. What do you both think of this?'

'It's so different to the version I had,' said Angela. 'There's none of that twangy guitar. There's a lot more feeling to it.'

And so the evening continued like that for a while, with Mark impressing his ladies with his selection; sometimes playing original versions of songs that had been covered by British artists; sometimes playing flipsides; other times just playing some of his all-time favourites. Each time he got up, he had to squeeze himself back between these two attractive ladies and he was getting warmer and warmer. He wasn't used to central heating and eventually he had to remove his sweater. The gap between Sandy and Angela seemed to be reducing each time he returned to his position. Was Angela deliberately edging slightly closer?

The evening seemed to fly past and when Jerry re-appeared, Mark had only played about half of the records he had brought. As Jerry pulled a face to indicate his dislike of the music, it was the cue to bring the musical soiree to an end. Mark turned to Sandy and asked 'Are we going for a quick drink?'

Before Sandy could reply, Angela said 'I'm sorry. I've been so busy enjoying your records, I forgot to offer you a drink, Mark. I've got some beer in the fridge. I'm sure you'd like one.'

After spending a pleasant evening squashed up against her, Mark thought it would be rude to turn around and say 'No, I really just wanted an excuse to go out and snog your daughter.' And Sandy didn't make any attempt to solve his dilemma,

So he just said 'Yes, please. What have you got?'

'Come and have a look. I got a selection, because I didn't know what you prefer.' It sounded as though she had made a point of buying some drinks just for his benefit, so it would certainly have been rude to have declined.

Mark followed her into the kitchen and, from the 'fridge, she took her selection of drinks and placed them on a small worktop situated in the corner of the small kitchen. There was pale ale, brown ale, stout, lager and cider. There wasn't a lot of room up this corner and Angela stood her ground, so as Mark moved forward to pick up a couple of bottles to read the labels, he once again, found himself in close proximity to her. She made no attempt to move out of his way and he found her left breast was brushing against his arm. He carried on reading the labels for a few more seconds and neither of them was in a hurry to move. Eventually, Mark said 'I'm quite thirsty, so I think a lager would be best.' He then moved out of the corner to allow Angela room to open the bottle and pour his drink.

Angela opened the cider for herself and said 'Sandy and Jerry can help themselves.'

Back in the living room, Sandy asked 'Are you going to leave me some records to play?'

This was a major test of their relationship. Mark's records were very precious to him and many of those he had brought were now deleted and therefore irreplaceable. No, he wasn't going to do it. But how was he going to handle the situation? He couldn't afford to hesitate for too long or Sandy would be grossly offended to think that Mark didn't trust her with his precious discs.

'I tell you what,' he said. 'I've got a few songs that are duplicated on singles and LPs. I'll dig those out and bring them next time I come and then they are yours to keep.'

'Thank you. But you're not going to leave any now?' Sandy asked.

'I'll have a good sort out when I get home and see which ones I can afford to be without for a while to lend you. And I'll bring some you can keep. Do you realise', he said, trying to quickly change the subject and turning towards Angela, 'we didn't play any of your records tonight? I've been so busy showing off mine. I'd have liked to have heard some of yours – perhaps another time. Look at the time. I'd better make a move. I've got another football match tomorrow morning. Angela, thank you for a lovely meal again.'

'I hope you enjoyed my dumplings,' she said with that lovely disconcerting smile.

'Your dumplings are just the way I like them,' he replied, not caring whether or not she had spotted his double meaning, because he assumed she hadn't bothered either.

'Are we going bowling tomorrow?' asked Sandy.

'Er… yes, all right.' Mark hesitated because he wasn't looking forward to the journey so soon. 'Will you be washing your hair again afterwards?'

'Oh, yes. I have to do my hair on a Sunday.'

At the doorstep, Mark gave Sandy a quick kiss. It still wasn't a very satisfactory kiss. He knew whom he would rather kiss, but that wasn't going to happen. He loaded his box of records into the car and hoped his car would start. It did.

The next day, he saw very little of Angela. He decided that was a good thing. He enjoyed the bowling, but got chastised because he hadn't found time to sort out some records for Sandy. He promised he would have them ready for Wednesday evening when they were next due to meet.

Except that Wednesday didn't happen. He was all ready to leave, but his car wouldn't start. This time, fiddling with the leads had no effect. He kept trying the starter; then he fiddled with the leads; then tried the starter. But it just wouldn't engage and he could tell the battery wouldn't take much more of this. So he abandoned it and headed down the road towards the public telephone box to tell Sandy he couldn't make it and he would call her later in the week.

He had never gotten around to joining a motoring organisation. And in any case, they wouldn't come round his house. There was no such thing as 'home start' in the sixties. Just as he had resigned himself to taking the next day off work to get his car sorted, he remembered Dougie's father was a mechanic. Tim lived just a short walk away, so Mark didn't think it would do any harm to consult him.

Tim was still at work, but his wife said he was due about eight o'clock and she would speak to him when he returned. So Mark walked home to make himself a cup of tea and change out of his suit.

At 8.45, Tim knocked on Mark's door. He was still in his overalls and hadn't yet had his evening meal. Mark thanked him profusely for coming round so quickly and explained the problem.

Tim got under the bonnet with a torch and his toolkit. After a few minutes, he said 'Try it, now.'

Sure enough, it started this time. 'It's your starter motor,' said Tim. 'It's badly worn and needs replacing. You might get a second hand one from a breaker's yard, but the chances are that will be worn as well. I wouldn't have thought it's worth forking out for a new one.'

'I've been trying to find a new car, but I haven't found one in good condition.' replied Mark. 'I really fancy a Wolseley 1500 or Riley 1.5.'

'They're nice motors, but prone to rust in the wheel arches and sills. I'll keep an eye out for you. I've got a few contacts in the trade. Meanwhile, if this plays up again – which it will – what you want to do is bounce it up and down. That will free the motor…hopefully! Or if you've got someone with you, you could try a push-start.

'When it played up before, I found fiddling with the leads helped.'

'I don't think so. Did you slam the bonnet down?'

'Yes.'

'That may have freed the motor. But it's only going to get worse. So don't rely on the bouncing technique forever. I'll let you know if I find a good vehicle for you'

'Thanks ever so much, Tim. I'll buy you a pint next time I see you in the Bricklayer's'

'I'll probably accept it,' Tim replied.

CHAPTER 12

Hello Stranger

The next day, Mark's car started first time, but he knew it would continue to give him problems. He had spent the night fretting about the possibility of getting stranded in Peterborough. To minimise the risk, he would have to reduce his visits to see Sandy; at least until he had found a replacement vehicle. But the more he thought about this, the less it bothered him. He seldom enjoyed his time with Sandy as much as he had done with Jenny and Maggie. The truth of the matter was that he had still not developed any strong feelings for her.

It was true that he had entered into lustful thoughts when he had first seen her in a swimming costume, but then Mark would probably have felt like that for most young girls of her age if they had presented themselves in front of him in a tight fitting costume. Moreover, he would still rather see her mother in a bathing suit and that couldn't be good for their relationship. The more he thought about the matter, the more he realised that if he broke it off with Sandy, he would miss her mother more than her. But she was nearly twice Mark's age and could never be interested in someone just turned twenty-one. Even if she could actually be attracted to Mark, he knew that neither of them would do anything to hurt Sandy. And, in any case, there was still the travelling problem. Mark had to break it off and the sooner the better.

Mark called Sandy that evening to arrange to meet on Friday. He explained the problems with his car and said he would probably only see her once that weekend as he didn't want to risk the car not starting. Now all he had to do was find the best way of breaking the bad news. He wondered how she would take it. She had never expressed her feelings to him, but did always seem keen to see him again – except for Sunday evenings when her hair was more important. When he split from Maggie, she had more or less solved the problem for him by her perception of Mark's demeanour that evening. Somehow, he didn't think Sandy would be so helpful.

Mark was also concerned that Angela would not be impressed by his treatment of her daughter, but Mark's experience of upsetting factory operatives with his tight targets was making him realise that he couldn't always seek the popular route in life.

Mark hardly slept Thursday night. He even considered continuing to see Sandy. After all, he didn't relish the prospect of not having a girlfriend again. So by the time he turned up at her house, he had no clear plan and decided to play it by ear.

Mark had set off early in case his car hadn't started, but it did. Consequently, Sandy wasn't ready when he arrived, so Angela invited him in. 'How are you, Mark?' she enquired, with that lovely smile.

'All the better for seeing you,' he replied. 'Stop flirting!' he told himself, but he did feel a little better for seeing her, albeit tinged with a degree of guilt at what he was about to do to her daughter.

'How's the car?' Angela asked.

'It's a bit poorly. I desperately need to change it. I want to spend this weekend having a really good look around for a replacement. I can't go on like this.'

'What are you both doing, this evening?' was Angela's next question.

'I think we're just going for a quiet drink. There's nothing we want to see at the pictures.'

Sandy appeared, looking lovely in her nice green dress. She didn't have an extensive wardrobe, but she always looked smart. She gave Mark a quick kiss. It was the first time she had ever kissed him, rather than him kissing her. And it was the first time they had kissed in front of her mother. Did she actually have inkling as to what he was planning?

As they got in the car, Sandy noticed a bag on the back seat. 'Are they my records?' she enquired.

'Yes. There aren't as many as I had hoped. A lot of the songs I've got duplicated have got nice 'B' sides which aren't on any LPs, so I have to keep those, I'm afraid. But these are all records you can keep.'

Sandy fingered through them. 'Oh, I like this one,' she said.

'I hope you like all of them. Where are we going?'

'I don't mind. I don't know that many pubs.'

'I know,' said Mark in a flash of inspiration. 'There's a place I've passed on the way to Leicester about a year or two ago. It's on the A47. I've always thought it looked nice. It's at Castor & Ailsworth.'

'That's two separate villages,' Sandy pointed out.

'Well, the sign outside the village said Castor & Ailsworth.'

'Yes, if you approach from the other direction, it says 'Ailsworth & Castor,' Sandy replied.

They found the pub, which was called the Fitzwilliam Arms. It looked very "olde worlde" from the outside, with its lovely thatched roof. The two villages themselves looked attractive with their stone cottages, but were right on the busy A47.

As they sat down with their drinks, Mark said 'I'm sorry about Wednesday.'

'It can't be helped,' Sandy replied.

'I was just telling your mum that I'm going to really try hard this weekend to find a replacement.'

Then it went quiet for a minute and Mark started to feel nervous about what he had to do.

Eventually, he spoke again. 'This problem with the car has made me stop and think about you and me.'

'In what respect?' Sandy asked.

Mark was hoping that Sandy might have also questioned their relationship, but he knew he had to force the issue. 'Oh, I don't know. We only see each other a couple of times a week and I seem to spend as much time travelling as I do being with you.' She still wasn't helping him. 'Do you think it's worth pursuing?'

Sandy sat there blinking for a few seconds before she answered. 'Don't you, then?'

Mark sighed. 'It should be. I think you're lovely. You've got a great figure and we like doing the same things together. But there's no real... *spark* for want of a better word.'

Sandy just stared at her drink. Mark wasn't sure if she was angry, upset or just not bothered. Then she spoke. 'It's because I won't let you have sex with me, isn't it?'

'No! It isn't. It really isn't. Of course, I would like to have sex with you, but that's never been my reason for going out with you.'

After a minute's silence, Sandy just shrugged and said 'Okay, if that's the way you feel.'

Mark wanted to know how she felt, but he didn't want to precipitate an argument or an outpouring of feelings, so he left it. But then Sandy asked 'Are you seeing someone else?'

'No, I'm not. I wouldn't do that to you. I hope you know me better than that.'

'No,' she said. 'I didn't think you would, but I don't know what you get up to the rest of the week.'

'I don't know what you get up to, but I've never for one minute thought you might be seeing someone else. Anyway, let's not get into negative thoughts. I have enjoyed going out with you, so let's leave on good terms. Do you want another drink?'

Much to Mark's surprise, Sandy said 'yes'. He remembered when Jenny broke up with him, he had just wanted to go straight home, but then Jenny had been dishonest with him and he had been particularly annoyed with her.

Mark and Sandy spent the next half hour talking about the records that Mark had brought that evening. In fact, they enjoyed each other's company at least as much as any previous occasion.

Mark made a point of visiting the toilet facilities before they left the pub because he had no intention of facing Angela. But in a strange way, he didn't want the evening to end. He would have liked to have parked the car in a secluded spot and have one last kiss and cuddle, but he didn't think that was good form.

As they drove back to Werrington, he suddenly asked 'Do you fancy some fish and chips? I only had a sandwich before I dashed out.'

'Oh, I love fish and chips. Why don't we take some back for mum and Jerry?'

'I don't think I can face your mum tonight. She'll be angry at me for breaking up.'

'No she won't. She would probably be more annoyed if you disappeared without saying goodbye.'

'Are you sure about that?'

'I know mum better than you.'

As Mark tried to re-start the car outside the chip shop, it played up again. He stood on the door sill and bounced up and down. He heard a clunk and tried to start it again. This time the starter engaged and they were off again. That was a big relief. He didn't know whether Sandy was strong enough to give him a push start.

It was with some trepidation that he entered Sandy's home with a large bag of fish and chips, but the smile on Angela's face made him feel a little better. 'I shouldn't eat them really,' she said. 'I have to watch my figure, you know.'

'I'll happily volunteer to do that for you,' thought Mark, but he resisted saying it this time.

'Sandra seems to be able to eat anything she likes and never puts on weight,' Angela added.

'You've both got great figures,' Mark said, figuring that by complimenting both of them, it didn't sound quite so much like flirting. And he wanted to say something nice before Angela learned what was happening.

'You must let me pay for this,' Angela said.

'Certainly not! I've had enough free meals off you.'

As they all sat down and passed the salt and vinegar to each other, Sandy said 'Mark and I have decided to split up.' Mark was amazed at the way she had phrased this, as though it really was a joint decision.

Angela stopped eating and just said 'Oh!' She looked across at both of them, eyes darting from one to the other. Then she asked the one question Mark didn't want to hear. 'Why?'

It was all going so well. Mark had found breaking off with Sandy had been a little easier than he expected, but now he had to tackle the issue all over again with her mother. But before he could say anything, Sandy spoke first.

'We didn't think there was any future in it.'

'She's brilliant!' thought Mark. Perhaps Sandy didn't want Angela and Jerry to know that she had been ditched and so had made it sound like a mutual decision, but whatever, he had a renewed admiration for her maturity.

'Oh, well,' said Angela. 'You both know what you're doing. I suppose you've done well to give it a good go, considering all the travelling. I'm sure we'll all miss you, Mark. You've been like a breath of fresh air to this household.'

'That's very nice of you to say so. And I will certainly miss all of you.'

When they'd all finished their supper, Mark stood up and said 'I think I ought to be on my way. I've probably outstayed my welcome. Thank you for your hospitality and lovely meals over the last few weeks.'

'You're very welcome, Mark' said Angela. 'Come here and give me a hug.'

Mark didn't need asking twice. Angela gave him a whole-hearted hug and he returned the gesture, feeling very tempted to let his hands wander over her delicious warm body. God, she felt good. He could feel her thighs pressing into his and then she gave him a delightful kiss on the cheek before he could develop a pyramid.

Mark turned to Jerry and shook his hand. Jerry looked a little embarrassed at all this sloppy stuff.

'I'll see you to the door,' said Sandy. At the door, she, too, gave him a big hug, but her kiss was on the mouth. Neither the hug nor the kiss felt as good as her mother's, but it was still with regret that Mark had to leave.

'Thank you for taking this all so well,' Mark said. 'I will miss you, you know, but I do think it's best to end it now. I'm glad we ended on good terms.'

'It's been good fun,' Sandy replied. 'And thanks for the records. I'll think of you when I'm playing them.'

'With fond memories, I hope,' he said.

'Of course.'

The next day, Mark was up bright and early to trawl around some car dealers. He widened his net a little further than before and found himself on the outskirts of Tilney St. Lawrence, where he saw a batch of old cars in what looked like a former farmyard. Amongst these, was a grey Wolseley 1500 and in the grey drizzle, it didn't look that attractive. But he'd set his sights on a 1500, so he parked his car and went for a closer look. The car was filthy and one of the tyres was flat, but it looked solid enough. All the cars in the compound were in a similar state. None of them had a tax disc. Mark decided it wasn't a car dealer at all, so he ought to leave. Just then, a red-faced middle-aged man appeared. 'Can I help you at all?' Mark decided he was a farmer – or even an ex-farmer.

'Are you selling these cars?' Mark asked.

'If you're buying, I'm selling.'

'How much is the Wolseley?'

'That one's £175.'

'Does it have an M.O.T.?'

'It will have if you buy it.'

'But not at the moment?'

'No, there's no point in getting it tested and then it sits there for a few months.'

'Has it been serviced?'

'No. It will be, if and when you buy it. Again, I'm not going to service a car and then leave it in the field. Don't make sense, that.'

'Can I look inside and start it?'

'If it'll start. I'll get the key.'

'Do they do courses at the Tech. on how to sell used cars?' thought Mark.

The man returned with a handful of keys. 'I think it's one of these,' he said looking at each of them and trying them one at a time. The third set fitted and he tried to start the car. The battery was completely flat. 'Hold on. I've got a fully charged battery in the house. I'll fit that.'

Mark didn't want to spend all morning getting wet, so he said 'Can you sort out the back tyre and get it ready for me to come back and have a test drive?'

'Only if you're going to buy it.'

'I can't buy it unless I take it for a test drive.'

'I'm not going to do any work on it unless you're going to buy it.'

Mark couldn't imagine this chap was going to make a living, selling cars. He was applying a tight-fisted farmer's mentality to the buying and selling of cars which just wouldn't work. This car could probably be just what Mark needed, but he couldn't do business like this.

'Sorry,' said Mark. 'I'll have to pass on this.'

'Please yourself!'

Mark had had another frustrating morning and still no car to show for it. He might have to lower his sights and buy a mini. Earlier models of the mini were in plentiful supply, but he really didn't want a smaller car. He wanted something bigger and with four doors. And he didn't think he could cope with all that double de-clutching business.

He headed for the Bricklayers' where he had arranged to meet Dougie. The first team didn't have a football match that afternoon, so they were both going to watch the reserves play at home – after a beer and a turn on the pinball machine.

Mark was pleased to see Dougie's father Tim was there as well, so he offered to buy him the beer he had promised during the week.

'I'm glad you're here, Mark' said Tim. 'I think I've found your new car. You wanted a 1500 didn't you? I've got a mate who works at Mann Egerton and someone has just traded one in. They won't be putting it on their forecourt, so if you get round there straight away, you can do a deal. I haven't seen it, yet.'

'I'll go just as soon as I've finished my beer and had one of Mike's dried up ham rolls.'

'I heard that,' said Mike, the landlord.

'Just joking, Mike,' Mark replied.

'Well don't make jokes about my dried up ham rolls.'

The car was nearly perfect. It was registered in 1964, but Mark was slightly disappointed to see that it didn't have the 'B' suffix. The salesman was very reluctant to take Mark's Anglia in part exchange, but after a little haggling, he agreed to give him £5 for it, leaving Mark £220 to pay. The part exchange wasn't enough for a deposit, so Mark ended up signing an HP agreement for £200, spread over two years and he signed a cheque for the remainder. The car would be ready to collect the following Saturday morning with a full MOT and six months' warranty on parts (but not labour).

So now he had a new car lined up, but he no longer had a girlfriend. Perhaps the new car would help resolve that matter. Women would be throwing themselves at him when they saw this new beast.

He headed off to watch the Reserves' match which had already started. Dougie and Tim were already there and Mark had missed two goals scored by the home team. Mark told Tim he was pleased with the car and he owed him another pint. He asked Tim if, in view of what he had said about possible rust, whether he thought Mark ought to get it undersealed.

'I wouldn't bother myself. If you're going to underseal a car, you need to do it when it's new. Unless you really strip it down and do a thorough job, you may be sealing in a problem and you won't be able to see it. The first you'll know about it is when the metal gets so thin with rot that it just disintegrates one day. So just keep an eye on it. That would be my advice.'

After the match, Mark was driving away from the pitch along Compton Drive when he spotted Blodwyn, standing at the bus stop at the end of her road. He had often thought about her as he passed her house on the way to and from his home football pitch, but this was the first time he had seen her since that night when she had abandoned him at the Maid's head. His first instinct was to ignore her, even though he could see she was wearing a short skirt under her short coat. For some reason, he stopped his car thirty yards past the bus stop and reversed back. Mark never liked driving past anyone he knew without offering a lift. It was a habit he had picked up when he had first got a car and was always desperate to get a girlfriend. And it was now getting dark, so it was the gentlemanly thing to do. That was his only motive, he told himself.

'Do you want a lift somewhere?' he asked through his open passenger window.

'Are you going over to Lynn?' Blodwyn asked with that lovely Welsh accent.

'No, I'm going home, but I go near the bus station if that helps.'

'Oh, well. That will save me a little money,' she replied getting into the car, while Mark had a quick glimpse of those gorgeous legs lowering themselves into his passenger seat. They exchanged a few pleasantries about each other's health and the weather and then Mark asked 'Are you off to see Terry?'

'Oh, no. We finished a long while ago, see. What are you doing down my road? Were you hoping to see me?'

'Of course not. I've just been to watch a football match down the road. I told you I play for Northfleet, didn't I?'

'You might have done. I don't remember.'

'No, you were probably more concerned about meeting your precious Terry, weren't you?'

'Oh dear, yes, I'm sorry we parted like that. I didn't know Terry was going to be there that night.'

Mark didn't like being lied to, but he didn't want to get into an argument, so he bit his tongue. He wasn't really sure why he had stopped to give her a lift. And then he remembered. He had always fancied Blodwyn; ever since the very first time he looked into those lovely green eyes, but he wasn't going to be tempted to ask her out – even if she begged him to. However, Blodwyn always had the knack of making Mark's heart race, which she did with her next question.

'I'm not seeing anyone at all at the moment. Were you going to ask me out again?' Her lovely lilting Welsh tones sounded so seductive when she said this. How could anyone possibly resist.

Mark hesitated. 'Umm… no. I just thought you might want a lift. Offering you a lift doesn't mean I have an ulterior motive.' He'd done it. He'd resisted her many charms. Well done, Mark.

'Have you already got a girlfriend, then?' She asked, thinking there must be a reason for Mark's response.

'No – not at the moment.' Mark didn't need to tell her that he's just split up with someone.

'I thought you'd always wanted to go out with me?'

'Oh, yes. I dearly wanted to go out with you when I first met you in 1965. Then I wanted to go out with you last year when I saw you again. But at the moment, I've got other things going on in my life, so I won't be asking you out today. But thanks for the offer.' Mark was turning the tables on her and being a bit of a tease himself. He was torn between the desire to go out with her and the desire to tell her what he thought of someone who would do what she did to him at the Maid's Head (not forgetting the other poor idiot who had received the same treatment). But who knows, one day, he might be glad of a date with her, so a little intrigue might put him in an interesting light.

'I don't believe I had made any kind of offer,' Blodwyn answered.

'Oh, sorry, Blodwyn. I never know when you're teasing me or being serious.' By then, they were near the bus station. 'Can I just drop you here, so I don't have to fight my way back through the buses? It was nice to see you again.' He'd left her a fifty yard walk. Had it been anyone other than Blodwyn, Mark would have probably driven all the way into the bus station, but he was making a point – at least to himself, if not Blodwyn.

'Aren't you going to open the door for me? You were always such a gentleman.'

'How rude of me! Of course I'll open the door for you.' But he wasn't going to get out and wait on her. Instead, he leaned across, taking great care not to touch her in any way and then opened the passenger door.' But as he did so, she leant forward a little so that her bosom was just resting on his shoulder. Mark pretended not to notice. In any case, she was wearing a coat, so he gained no pleasure from this.

As Blodwyn exited the vehicle, Mark said 'Goodbye then. See you around.'

'Bye,' she said, but it wasn't with any grace and she didn't thank him for the ride.

But she had left her scent behind and Mark spent the journey home preparing a fantasy for later; probably involving being surrounded by her wonderful thighs. He'd probably had more fantasies about Blodwyn than anyone else he'd ever known. However, he was pleased with himself for resisting her charms. Knowing how frequently, Mark drove down Compton Avenue, he had often considered how he might react if he did encounter her, so the conversation and the outcome did have a little forethought to it.

It was the first time they'd met when neither of them had mentioned her legs, otherwise the result may have been different.

Blodwyn was puzzled by what had just happened. When she first met Mark she had found his shyness and his susceptibility to embarrassment to be a great source of fun. She knew she could use her charms to great effect and she liked having that power over a man. Terry and Gareth had been the dominating partners in her previous relationships and were not so easily influenced. She might welcome a change in personality type, particularly someone who wasn't so possessive. Mark wasn't a 'sweep-you-off-your-feet' sort of person, but he seemed honest and reliable. He was no longer the gauche teenager he once was. He could do with a new car, but at least he had a car. Why had he just resisted her charms? Was she losing her allure? Perhaps it was because it was getting dark. Or perhaps she had upset him at the Maid's Head, but if so, why did he stop to give her a lift? And how did he know Terry's name?

CHAPTER 13

I Can't Help Myself

'The other night, I was followed home by some creepy looking chap,' said Della.

'I'm sorry about that. It won't happen again,' said Mark with a deadpan look on his face.

Della stared at him for a moment.

'Boom, boom,' he added quietly.

'Hadaway man. It's no joking ma'er,' Della said, indignantly. 'Tha's twice that's happened on my way home.'

Mark wondered why Geordies always struggled to sound some of their "Ts". The word is *matter* not *ma'er*. And what does *Hadaway* mean? But realising Della was really concerned, he asked 'Where was this?'

'On the foo'path, at the back of the estate.'

Mark used to make use of that path when he biked home and he wouldn't have fancied walking along there in the dark. He said 'I never realised you have to walk home. Were you on your own?'

'Apar' from this creepy bloke, aye.'

'Where do you live, then?'

'Drummond Green.'

'Where's that?'

'Off Fletcher Lane, on the council estate.'

'That's a fair old walk. Do you walk home every night?'

'It's no' that far round the back of the industrial estate. It's abou' four times the distance if you go by road. I canna catch a bus the whole journey, so if I'm gonna walk a lo' of the way, I migh' as well walk all the way.' Della was doing a lot of scowling as she said all this. And missing out a lot of her "Ts".

'Well, I go roughly in that direction. I'll give you a lift,' Mark said.

'Noo. I don't wanna take you out of your way. I'll be all righ', pet.'

'Look. I'll be glad of the company,' said Mark. 'If anything happens to you, I haven't got time to train up another Bonus Clerk. The next one might be some ugly old hag.'

'I'll take tha' as a compliment,' Della replied. 'Thanks, pet.'

'Is your husband not able to pick you up?'

'He doesn't drive. He likes his beer too much to bother, like. In any case, he works the other side of town. He gets a lift 'imself.'

'Well, I'll be glad to help you out. You'll have to put up with my old Anglia, though. I don't change it 'til Saturday. If the Anglia doesn't start, you won't mind giving me a push, will you?'

'Did you just say "boom, boom"?'

'Umm... no.'

Mark was really starting to like Della. They worked very well together as a team. Della always calculated the bonus for Mark's areas before she did David's. Mark didn't know if this was some kind of favouritism or whether it was because that's the way she had always worked from the first time Mark had shown her how to calculate the bonus. He liked to think it was favouritism. Now, however, Eddie was advertising for a new Bonus Clerk as Della's workload was getting too much for her on her own. Mark was hoping the new girl would be assigned to work with David so that Mark continued to work with Della – unless, of course, the new girl was particularly stunning and single.

When Mark saw Eddie lighting his old pipe, he asked 'Do you have problems getting a good shag in Norfolk, Eddie?'

'Mark Barker!' exclaimed Della.

'What's the matter? Shag is just a type of tobacco.'

Eddie just said 'I don't have problems with getting a good shag, anywhere.'

That evening, Mark's car wouldn't start again, but as Della was starting to get concerned about having to push his grubby car, Mark solved the problem by bouncing the car. 'Will it get us home?' Della enquired.

'Yes, it will be fine – as long as I don't stall it.'

It was a four mile journey to Della's flat and the time passed very quickly as they both enjoyed each other's company. Della wanted Mark to drop her at the edge of the estate, but he insisted on taking her all the way. Drummond Green was a small development of three-storey flats in a circle around a large circular piece of land laid to grass – very useful for the locals who didn't want to walk too far with their messy dogs..

As Mark stopped the car, he asked if Della would like him to pick her up in the morning, but Della replied 'Noo, I'll be all righ' walking to work in the daylight. It's no' that far. But I am gra'eful for the ride home. I'll let you get home to your wife.'

'What wife? I'm not married. What made you think I was married?'

'I don't know. I just assumed you had a pretty little wife at home. You've got a girl though, haven't you?'

'I did have. We've just decided to split up. It was never that serious, so it's no big deal.'

'Well, we'll talk some more tomorrow, pet. Thanks for the ride.'

Mark felt a warm glow as he drove home. Pleasant female company always had that effect on him. When he had first met Della, he wasn't sure if they would get on together, but there was no fear of that now. He always seemed to enjoy the company of married women. It was something to do with the fact that he never felt the need to make a good impression, so he was able to be more relaxed. But he still had a desire for Della to like him.

That evening, Mark watched a play on television in which a young girl was jilted by her lover and she took it so badly that she committed suicide. It made him start thinking about Sandy. He still couldn't believe how well she had accepted his decision to split up and he started to wonder if she had just put on an act rather than show her emotions. No, Sandy was far too level-headed to do anything silly.

But the thought still nagged him. He woke up in the middle of the night with the thought still troubling him like a bad nightmare. He had to know that she was all right. He couldn't live with himself if she was in any danger. He could telephone her the next evening, but it might sound like he was missing her and would give out the wrong message. Maybe, with a bit of luck, Angela would answer the 'phone. It would be easier to talk to her. That's what he would do.

So after another pleasant journey home from work in Della's company and soon after tea, Mark wandered down to the telephone box. Sure enough, Angela answered the phone. 'Hello Angela. It's Mark.'

'Hello Mark. How are you, dear?' She sounded genuinely pleased to hear from him. And he was definitely pleased to hear her voice again. It had only been a few days since they last saw each other, but Mark had really missed her. He still remembered the lovely hug she had given him.

'I'm fine, thank you. I know this sounds strange, but I just wanted to make sure Sandy was all right.'

'Of course she's fine. Why wouldn't she be?' Angela sounded very puzzled.

Mark answered 'It's just that we broke up quite suddenly and there was no great show of emotion. I just wanted to make sure she was still all right about it.'

Angela gave a little laugh. 'Sorry, Mark. I'm not laughing at you, but it is all rather amusing. It seems that there is this chap she knows at work, who has previously asked her out, but she had told him she was going out with you. Well, when she went to work yesterday, she told one of her mates about you both splitting up and it got back to this chap, so he asked her again. And that's where she is tonight. She told me she'd always wanted to go out with him, but she didn't want to break it off with you – especially when you were prepared to keep driving over to Peterborough to see her. So it's all worked out for the best.

What about you, Mark? Have you got your sights on someone else?'

Mark wanted to say "You", but he didn't. Instead he said 'No. But I'm getting a new car this weekend, so once all the girls see that, they'll be throwing themselves at me... or maybe not. What about you? Are you seeing anyone?'

'Oh, I think my romancing days are over. If I wanted someone, I wouldn't know how to go about it. A girl can't chat up someone in a pub like a fellow can do. If I go out with Sandra and Jerry, everyone assumes I'm a happily married woman – and I'm not going out on my own. That looks even worse.'

Just then the pips went, so Mark said 'Hold on. I've got some more change. Are you still there? Good. I never trust these payphones. No – I see your dilemma, but speaking as a bloke, I couldn't chat up someone in a pub anyway. I have to find other ways; and, so far, not with a great deal of success. I met one of my old girlfriends at a Badminton club. Do you belong to any clubs, like that?'

'No. Why are you suddenly trying to get me fixed up?' Angela asked.

Mark didn't know how to answer that. He had no intention of trying to get a date, but it seemed such a waste of a good looking woman that she wasn't seeing someone.

'I'm sorry if I've spoken out of turn,' he eventually replied.

'It's all right, Mark. I always go on the defensive when anyone questions my situation. Perhaps I ought to get out more.'

'The truth of the matter is...' began Mark and then he stopped. He shouldn't have started this sentence and was now feeling a little nervous again.

'Yes, Mark. What were you going to say?'

'I was going to say… that if I were a few years older, I would definitely throw my hat in the ring. I think you're a very attractive woman.' There! He's said it. He'd wanted to tell her that for weeks.

'Why, thank you, Mark. If you were a few years older, I might accept, but we have to consider that when you're forty years old, I will be sixty. And you wouldn't be waiting around that long. No, if I were to find someone else, he would have to be nearer to my own age. People would see us together and think you're my son.'

'I know,' he replied. 'But I just wanted to say it. I hope you just accept it as a compliment. I wasn't trying to get off with you.'

And then the pips went again. It didn't seem as though you got much time when you 'phoned Peterborough from Sanford, so he inserted some more money. He didn't really have anything else to say, accept he still secretly hoped Angela might suggest another meeting. 'That's my last bit of change,' he said. 'And there's a woman outside waiting to use the 'phone.'

'Thank you for the compliment, Mark. 'I'll think about your idea of joining a club. You must do the same… and stop flirting with older women! Get someone your own age.'

'Yes,' Mark replied. 'Would you mind not telling Sandy that I rang? She doesn't need to know about my silly fears; nor about the rest of our conversation. I'd better let this lady use the 'phone. She's staring daggers at me.'

As Mark strolled back home, he felt pleased with himself for his half-hearted attempt to explore the possibility that Angela might consider Mark as a possible suitor. Of course, it was never going to happen and he could see all the drawbacks, but she was lovely and he was sure it could have been fun. But his exploratory conversation at least confirmed he hadn't really been in with a chance and he'd got the matter off his chest, otherwise he would always have wondered.

In any case, he had the benefit of Della's company, now. If he didn't have a girlfriend, that was some kind of consolation. In fact, it "wor' just champion," as she would say.

The next morning, at work, Della asked Mark if he was going to the Sports and Social Club dance on Saturday. He had previously decided not to bother, but after Della brought up the subject, he had second thoughts. 'I wasn't sure whether to go or not,' he lied. 'Especially now that I've broken up with Sandy.

'We were thinking of goin',' Della said.' I thought it might be a good way to meet a few more people at Greshams. Phil wants to go. Mind you, I think that's 'cos he heard the beer is cheap.'

'I'll go if you go,' Mark said. 'I'd like to meet your hubby. He sounds like an interesting character.' Mark didn't really want to meet Phil, but the main reason he wasn't going to attend originally was because he had no one to go with and, now, who better than the lovely Della (albeit with her 'interesting' husband). 'I'll give you both a lift if you like,' he suggested.

'Oh, noo. We'll get a taxi. You don' wanna be waiting around for us.'

'I don't mind.'

'Noo. I think it's be'er we make our own way, pet.'

So Mark turned up at the clubhouse at 8.35 Saturday evening in his lovely new Wolseley 1500. Unfortunately, it was dark so he couldn't show it off to anyone. By the time he arrived, the evening was in full swing and Della and her husband were standing at the bar with Eddie Hudson, who took it upon himself to introduce Mark to Phil. Phil immediately offered to buy Mark a drink, but pulled a face when Mark only wanted a half pint. Mark explained that he was driving and would have to pace himself throughout the evening, but being a non-driver, Phil still didn't appreciate Mark's refusal to have a pint.

Phil was only about five foot six inches tall, but what he lacked in height, he made up for in girth. He was wearing a three-piece suit which seemed ready to explode and his shirt was struggling to contain his thick neck. Mark tried to engage him in conversation. 'What do you do for a living?' he asked.

'Accoun'ant,' Phil spat out between mouthfuls of beer.

'Whereabouts?'

'Shadbolts,' followed by another gulp of beer. Phil couldn't be bothered with verbs and adjectives. They only got in the way of his drinking. After another gulp, Phil's glass was empty. Mark asked him if he'd like another.

'Pint of heavy, please, pal.'

Mark turned to Della and Eddie to see if they wanted a drink as well, but they both had half-full glasses. Eddie didn't appear to have a wife with him, although Mark knew he was married.

As Mark handed Phil his pint, little Jenny from the Metal Shop came up to Mark and dragged him onto the dance floor. This was a quite a relief to Mark who wasn't enjoying his scintillating conversation with Della's husband.

After some vigorous "shaking it all about" (as Jenny described it), Mark returned for a welcome gulp of his beer, only for Della to insist he danced with her as well. Phil was now talking (and drinking) with someone else. After a couple of up-tempo numbers, the band started to play a slow number. Mark suggested to Della that she might prefer to dance with Phil, but she just said 'He'll not be dancin' tonigh'. Not when there's drinkin' to be done.'

So Mark was quite happy to hold Della closely in his arms as they jostled with the other folk on the small dance floor. Up until that point, Mark had never paid any great attention to Della's figure as she mostly wore those dreaded maxi-skirts and loose fitting blouses, but now he had the chance to appreciate it at close quarters. Mark didn't think she was quite in the same league as Angela, nor even Sandy, but she still felt good to hold and the scent from her thick hair wafted around Mark's senses.

During the second slow number, Mark was busy telling her about his nice new car with its wood veneer dash and door cappings and how he was looking forward to the weekend to drive around Norfolkshire.

'Norfolkshire?' queried Della. 'Isn't it just Norfolk?'

'One of my old colleagues in the surveyors' team always called it *Norfolkshire* so it became a running joke.'

'Very funny, I'm sure,' Della said sarcastically.

She suddenly pushed him to one side and rushed towards the bar.

Mark was facing the other direction at the time, so he hadn't noticed that a fight had broken out. There in the thick of it, Phil was being restrained by Woody, while flailing around trying ineffectually to land blows on another thickset chap, whom Mark did not recognise. Eventually, Phil gave up struggling and Della took him outside to finish calming him down. That was the last that Mark saw of both of them that evening, but Eddie told him that this wasn't the first time that he had seen Phil in a scuffle after a few beers.

Mark asked Eddie if he knew why the fight had started, because Mark was wondering if Phil had got upset about him and Della dancing closely together.

'Probably nowt. It don't take much to set him off. He'd already drunk about ten pints and was still going. I like a pint, but I can't keep up with him.'

Mark said 'If I'd have wanted to see a lot of fussing and fighting, I could have stayed at home.'

'Happen we ought to go 'round your home next time,' Eddie added.

Mark was pleased now that he hadn't transported the couple to the dance. He wouldn't have fancied having a drunken Geordie in the back of his car.

He didn't stay much longer. He now felt like a spare part standing at the bar on his own. It was all going so well when he was dancing with Della, but when she pushed him to one side, it made him feel somewhat insignificant. Of course, her husband was always going to be more of a priority than dancing with some four-eyed colleague. It felt like some kind of rejection, which Mark hadn't had to experience for a little while and it brought back bad memories. He'd have to get a girlfriend of his own.

On Sunday afternoon, Mark took his mother out for a drive to Manningford to see Aunt Louise. Mark would have liked to have ventured further afield to enjoy his new transport, and show it off to some nice person of the female persuasion, but after a game of football in the morning and a late lunch, there wasn't much daylight left in the day. Never mind, he would be taking Della home the next evening.

Except that she didn't turn up for work the next day. Mark and David had to do their own bonus calculations, but Mark was disappointed with more than just the fact that he had to do a little extra work. He missed her company that evening. The journey home seemed that much longer, although it was actually shorter than the previous few evenings.

But she was back at work the next day. She was very quiet, but that wasn't particularly unusual, especially as she had some work to catch up on. When asked why she hadn't turned up for work on Monday, she just muttered that she hadn't felt very well. Mark waited until the two of them were alone in the office and enquired what the fight was about.

'Nothing. It never is.'

'It wasn't anything to do with you dancing with me?'

'Noo, of course not. We were just dancin', like. Wha's wrong with tha'?' Della asked, scowling as she often did when someone said something stupid.

'Nothing, I suppose, but you've been very quiet all day.'

'I'm just tired. I haven't been well over the weekend. And I've got a lot of work to do, so just leave me to get on with it, will you?'

'Will you still want a lift home, tonight?' Mark asked.

Della hesitated before answering 'Yes, please... unless you'd rather not?'

'I'd rather not if you're going be grumpy all the way.' Mark was hoping she would call his bluff, because he did want to her to join him, but he also wanted their friendship back.

Because that was how he viewed their relationship now. They were friends. Not matey, going-out-for-a-pint type friends; but friends that could discuss the price of sprouts and share little details of their lives together; friends that could build an office alliance against the other members of the team.

Mark had never had great success with friendships since leaving school and his periods between girlfriends (which were usually much longer than periods with girlfriends) exposed him to times of loneliness, which only his music could alleviate to any degree.

Again she hesitated, before replying 'Noo. I won't be grumpy all the way. Jus' the last bit as I get nearer to home.' That last sentence said an awful lot.

Mark decided there were two Dellas. There was the moody, scowling Della whom he had first encountered at their introduction and who re-appeared from time to time – a somewhat dowdy individual who took less care of her appearance. Then there was the bubbly attractive Della who could light up his life with her attractive smile and a hand passed enticingly through her thick tresses.

★ ★ ★ ★ ★ ★

'This is nicer than your old car,' Della said, as she settled into the passenger seat. She was obviously making an effort not to be grumpy. 'Wha's this wire, here?' She picked at a wire that was hanging beneath the glove compartment.

'I think it's for the aerial.' The car had an aerial fitted to the front wing, but there was no radio in the car.

'So could you plug a transistor into that and get a signal?'

'Possibly, but my radio hasn't got an aerial socket, so I haven't been able to prove that.'

'I've got a good transistor. If that works, we can have some music as we drive along.'

'I'd rather sit and talk,' Mark said. 'And we probably won't like the same music. I won't enjoy Radio One. It's not a very good signal 'round here, anyway.'

And then they had a conversation about their relative tastes in music. Mark discovered that Della was nearly as narrow-minded about music as he was, but she enjoyed Folk music and had no interest in soul music. She insisted he would like Bob Dylan and Simon and Garfunkel, so she would lend some of their LPs to him. Mark didn't offer to return the compliment. He didn't want his precious music anyway near someone prone to violent outbursts.

As he stopped the car outside Della's flat, he said 'You know if you need someone to talk to, I'm always available.'

Della just sat there for a few more seconds, but didn't say anything before opening the door to leave. She didn't even wish Mark 'goodnight.'

Mark wasn't going to push his offer, but he did want to be her friend, and friends were meant to lend a sympathetic ear to each other, weren't they?

★ ★ ★ ★ ★ ★

After a few days, Della seemed to cheer up considerably and things got back to normal. Mark did borrow some of Della's LPs, and he quite liked one or two Simon and Garfunkel songs, particularly 'Bookends' but most of it sounded a little bland to Mark's ear. He couldn't come to terms with Bob Dylan at all.

A new bonus clerk arrived and was duly assigned to David's area of responsibility, leaving Mark and Della to reinforce their close working relationship. The new clerk, whose name was Eileen, was a very pleasant young lady, but was of no interest to Mark, for three reasons; the first being that she was already in a steady relationship; the second that she wasn't really to Mark's taste, being a little on the thin side; the third reason was that she wasn't Della. To Mark, Eileen was another colleague; Della was his friend. Their relationship wasn't just confined to work, because Mark did occasionally venture down the clubhouse with Della and her husband, discovering that Phil could actually be pleasant company when he wasn't trying to drink himself stupid. In fact, he was able to add a few jokes to Mark's repertoire – always a big plus as far as Mark was concerned. Without a girlfriend, Mark knew his only chance of meeting someone new was to get out and about, but even when he did get out, he had no success in that respect. He considered calling Jane, but decided it wasn't worth the risk of being rejected. Christmas was fast approaching and it was the time of year when Mark most felt in need of a girlfriend, but a new decade was also on the horizon and perhaps then, his luck would change for the better.

CHAPTER 14

You've Really Got a Hold on Me

During January, the Work Study team were greeted with the news that Eddie had been promoted to Works Manager. Paul O'Connor had only ever intended to do the job for a limited period and now after a few years, he was to return to a position as Chief Contracts Manager, leaving his old position to be filled by Eddie.

The team were all wondering how Eddie would be replaced. Would they bring in another Manager or would they promote from within? Mark felt sure that if it were the latter, he would be the favourite.

A few days after Eddie received his promotion, he invited each member of the team for a one to one private meeting to inform them of his decision for a replacement Manager. David Ross was first to be told, followed by Mark. When Eddie told Mark of his decision that David Ross was to be the new Work Study Manager, Mark couldn't believe his ears. The popular decision amongst the rest of the team was Mark was the more able of the two.

Eddie could see the obvious disappointment on Mark's face. 'It had to be David,' Eddie said. 'He's older and more mature than you – and he doesn't have the history that you have with Red Miller. I'm sure you'll give David your whole-hearted support.'

'It's going to be unbearable in the office,' Mark said. 'The fellow's got no sense of humour and he pulls a face every time any of us tries to talk.'

'I've already had a word with him about that,' Eddie replied. 'He knows of his shortcomings and has assured me that he will make every effort to be a fair leader. I don't think you'll find it a problem. But you'll have to do your part, as well.'

Mark reluctantly promised to try. He wondered how much his little spat with Red Miller had affected his future career.

Della wasn't so co-operative. She expressed her anger to Eddie and gave no undertaking to make any special effort. As far as she was concerned, the onus was on David to change his attitude, not her. Moreover, she told Eddie that in her opinion, Mark should have been given the position.

The atmosphere in the office for the rest of the day was very icy. Very few words were spoken by anyone and Della wore a permanent scowl.

During the journey home, she asked 'How're ya feelin', pet?

Mark said 'I'm not too happy, pet. Not only did I not get the job, but old Misery Guts did. We'll just have to see how it goes. I don't intend to change my behaviour. If he doesn't like us having a laugh, he can whistle – except that I've never heard him whistle.'

After a few weeks of taking Della home each evening, Mark was now also picking her up in the mornings. This was seldom so enjoyable, because Della was not at her best first thing in the morning, so the journey to work was usually a quiet affair. She was also inclined to keep Mark waiting, as well as, on a few occasions, claiming to be unfit to go to work, thus taking him out of his way for nothing. Mark regretted that he had insisted upon picking her up in the mornings, but he still enjoyed her company for the trip home. And now with David's promotion, the two of them were even more united in their alliance against the rest of the world. Mark and Della had a slogan – *United we stand, together we fall.*

One morning when Mark picked her up, she was even more surly than usual and snapped at Mark a couple of times. He saw no reason why he should put up with that, so he said 'Look, don't keep taking it out on me. I don't know what your problem is, but I'm sure it's not my fault.'

Della went quiet for a few minutes. Then she said 'I'm going back home. I'll be handing in my notice today.'

Mark felt as though someone had just punched him. 'Why?' When Della didn't respond immediately, he probed further 'Has Phil got a transfer?' Shadbolts were an American company who felt they could move people around the country whenever they wanted, which was one reason why Della and Phil were renting a council flat rather than buying their own property. So Mark had jumped to conclusions.

'Noo. I'm leaving him. I've had enough of the constant arguments and abuse.'

'Does he hit you?'

'Noo. He's never actually hit me, but when he comes home drunk, I do start fearing that he might. And he comes home drunk several times a week. He often goes for a drink with his boss after work and once Phil has a drink, he doesn't know when to stop. He says that if his boss invites you out for a drink, you have to go. I've just had enough.'

Mark didn't know what to say next. He certainly didn't want Della to leave, but neither did he want her to live a miserable existence with Phil.

After another quiet period, Mark said. 'If there's anything I can do to help, just ask.'

'Thanks, pet,' she replied.

Mark added 'At least there's no chance of our boss inviting us out for a drink every evening.'

'Not that we'd go,' said Della.

On the way home, Mark asked if she had handed in her notice.

'Noo. I need to 'phone me mom to make sure I've somewhere to stay and she wasn't around. I'll try again tomorrow.'

So Mark still didn't know whether to feel totally devastated or not. But he had spent the day fretting about how much he would miss Della if she did leave. He said very little on the way home, so after a while Della asked 'Are you feelin' all righ', pet? You're very quiet.'

'No, I'm not too good. The truth is I don't want you to leave. I've grown very fond of you – probably much more than I should have done.'

Della said nothing. She already had a suspicion that this might have happened.

As they got nearer to Della's home, she said 'You know we can only ever be friends, don't you?'

'*Friends* is fine with me,' Mark replied. 'But *friends* is no good to me if you leave.' After a further pause, he added 'But you have to do what's right for you. Whatever that is, I hope it works out for the best.'

Mark wondered if telling her about his feelings for her was a good move. He remembered the time when he was infatuated with Karen and having confessed his feelings to Karen meant he was forever under her power. It was a particularly miserable time for him. And now it was starting over again. He ought to get out and find a girlfriend of his own, but that wasn't going to be easy when anyone else was going to be second best to Della.

During the middle of the next morning, Della and Mark found themselves alone for a while. Della said 'I 'phoned me mom and she told me I had to try to work things out. I still call her me mom, but she's really my grandmother. She brought me up as me mom. Then, when I wan'ed to get married, I needed to see me birth certificate. That's when she told me that me sister Edie was really me mom. Edie wasn't married, see and were too young to raise me on her own. It's like I've got two moms, now.'

'That must have come as quite a shock.'

'Yeah, it were a shock at the time. And now, like, me Nan is really me great grandmother. I still call me real Nan, *mom*, though.'

'Well, I'm just glad you're staying,' said Mark. And he really was happy about it. He also gained some satisfaction from the fact that Della had taken him into her confidence about this very personal matter.

The next day, in another confidential discussion, Della informed Mark that she and Phil had had a heart to heart conversation about things and Phil had promised to cut down on his excessive drinking.

A social evening had been planned at the clubhouse the following Saturday. There was going to be some inter-department competitions with darts, dominoes, table tennis and cribbage. Eddie had already recruited Mark and Phil to play dominoes for the Works Management team, having given his assurance to the Social Club that Phil would not cause trouble. According to Della, after Phil's previous spot of bother, they had threatened to 'damn him for sewages.' She assured Mark that Phil would be well behaved.

And sure enough, the evening passed off without incident. Phil only drank four pints all evening, which was three more than Mark who was driving. He hadn't offered a lift to Phil and Della.

So things seemed to be back to normal, with Della and Phil reconciled, and Mark totally besotted, but consoled by spending most of each weekday in Della's company; albeit at arms' length. Mark had thought he had grown out of these silly adolescent feelings. What made it so much worse this time, was that he had no desire to steal another man's wife, so even if Della had returned his feelings, he would never aspire to anything other than friendship. He had never set out with any designs on her and if she had been single, Mark wouldn't necessarily have pursued her, but a certain biological chemistry had attacked his nervous system. That's how he viewed it.

In some ways, he regretted ever offering to give her a lift home, but there was no way he could have let her walk home in the dark. Mark had many faults, but he was always going to be a gentleman.

A new trainee Work Study Engineer was enlisted to take the load off David who needed to spend more time with 'management issues'. In Mark's eyes 'management issues' involved interfering with Mark's work David insisted on re-visiting several of Mark's targets which David considered to be too loose. This was a result of employees earning high bonuses, but Mark had pointed out to both David and the Metal Shop Foreman that operatives were taking short cuts to beat targets. For instance, the targets for drilling aluminium posts involved letting the drill do the work and applying copious lubricant, but Mark had seen people punching holes with the drills and without applying lubricant. This meant drill bits lasted a fraction of their intended life and the drilled holes often had jagged edges.

Mark was annoyed that such happenings were permitted and his targets, which he considered to be accurate, were being brought into question through bad supervision.

The new trainee was a chap of Mark's age named Ray Pointer. Mark knew him from primary school, but hadn't seen him for several years, as he hadn't attended the same Grammar School as Mark. Ray was a laid-back, easy going sort of fellow, who didn't seem to suffer the same ill will towards David as Mark and Della, but he was quite capable of pulling faces behind David's back. Mark welcomed Ray as a valuable ally in their efforts to make the office environment more tolerable. He had a very dry sense of humour, so he and Mark were soon swapping jokes.

Della joined in with one of her own. 'What's brown and sticky?' she asked.

'A stick,' answered Mark.

'Oh, you're horrible. You spoilt my joke!'

'Sorry,' replied Mark, 'but you did ask.' And he did feel sorry for spoiling it for her, so he added 'I never like people spoiling my jokes and that's just what I've done to you. I really am sorry.'

'It's all right, pet.'

Mark loved it when Della called him 'pet.' He knew she called everyone that, but it felt special when she said it to him.

Soon after Ray joined, David felt it necessary to draw a *Reporting Hierarchical Chart* as he called it and pinned it to the office door, so that all visitors could tell who in the department was responsible for each particular area of the factory. Except that all visitors already knew all this and it just caused a certain amount of mirth. For additional entertainment, Mark pinned a map of the London Underground beneath the *Reporting Hierarchical Chart.*

Everyone thought this was most amusing – except David, who marched Mark out of the office and into a quiet corner – at least David marched. Mark just shuffled in his own good time. David asked if Mark knew who had done such a thing.

'Oh, yes. I know who did it.'

'Who was it?'

'It was me.'

'What's the meaning of it?'

'I was just having a laugh.'

David's face turned to thunder. Mark had never seen David lose his temper before, but it just made Mark more determined to make light of the situation.

'I don't understand why you think that's funny.'

'Well, it is funny. You stuck a silly little chart on the door which made everyone laugh. So I just joined in with the fun.'

'It's not a silly little chart. It's a very important document. You will cease from treating this office as a source of your infantile amusement.'

Mark said nothing.

'Do you understand?' David asked through gritted teeth.

'No, not really. If you think we're all going to sit in silence all day because you haven't got a sense of humour, you can forget it.'

'Right! I'm taking this to the Works Manager.'

'Good idea. He likes a laugh.'

They both returned to the office, with Mark smiling as he entered and David's face a colourful mixture of red and purple. Everyone returned a secret smile to Mark when David wasn't looking.

As soon as David left the office, everyone asked what had happened. Mark said 'I think he's just gone to see Eddie to get me put on a charge. Don't be surprised if I have to go and peel spuds in the canteen. He repeated their conversation as best as he could remember it to his appreciative colleagues.

But Mark wasn't put on a charge and he didn't have to peel spuds. Moreover, both charts mysteriously disappeared and were never seen again. From that point on, the strained relationship between David and Mark became even icier, and both parties were guilty of only speaking to the other when absolutely necessary.

Fortunately for Mark, he was spending more and more time on the shop floor, establishing targets for several new products. This included the much vaunted aluminium windows, which were being manufactured and assembled in the Metal Shop. It was taking longer than expected to time these operations, because the design team was still ironing out design flaws during the manufacturing process. One chap, in particular, was proving to be problematic, because he would insist on stopping regularly to take a swig of the adhesive cleaning solution. His name was Bob Goodyear, who was a known alcoholic and according to his charge-hand, he was using the solution as a substitute for booze. The rubber beading was also causing delays, because it needed warming to soften it before it could be hammered into the aluminium frame, and the amount of warming was still by trial and error – not very good for establishing accurate bonus targets.

Ray and Mark soon struck up a friendship and began socialising together at the Clubhouse, both enjoying a game of darts or cribbage. However, Ray would be no use in Mark's search for a female companion as Ray was already courting a jolly young lady called Valerie, who often joined them at the Social Club.

Seeing this young couple enjoying such a close relationship filled Mark with envy. Why couldn't he just enter into an uncomplicated arrangement like theirs? All his previous liaisons had been fraught with unnecessary baggage – a single mother; women who conducted affairs with married men; girls who lived a long way away (with attractive mothers); girls who accepted a lift off you so they can meet an old boyfriend – and now a married woman. What chance did a chap have of finding the girl of his dreams?

Della knew of Mark's desire to find a girlfriend and she offered one bit of advice. 'Do you remember, I thought you were already married? That was because you never bother to look fashionable. Get yourself some flares and some brigh'er colours. And some different specs migh' help.'

'Anything else?' Mark asked sarcastically.

'Well, you could let your hair grow a bit longer.'

Mark had to admit that he had never bothered about keeping up with fashions. At school, he had resisted drainpipe trousers and winkle pickers. Although his mother did allow him to have a pair of chisel toes and, after all, for most of his teenage years, he was dependent upon her for buying his clothes.

He knew it was time to buy some new clothes, so he ventured into Fosters Menswear to see what they had. Up until that point, he had resisted the new fashion for brightly coloured shirts and floral ties, feeling they didn't present a particularly masculine appearance. But with the advent of colour television (which Mark's family had yet to enjoy), more and more people could be seen embracing the new fashion. In fact, as he looked around the menswear shop, there seemed to be little choice for the less adventurous like Mark. So he bit the bullet and bought a bright yellow shirt and a pair of olive-green and black checked trousers with mildly flared bottoms.

Mark's sister had recently bought him a hand-painted tie, which she had brought back from her holiday in Spain, so that would match the outfit. Mark didn't enjoy wearing these things, but if it meant getting a girlfriend, he would have to make that sacrifice. It had only been a few months earlier that he had changed his spectacles, so he decided not to pursue that option to make himself irresistible to the opposite sex. At least it wouldn't cost anything to let his hair grow, but he wasn't going to let it grow over his shoulders; perhaps he could let his sideburns grow a little.

So this was the new seventies style Mark Barker – a new decade and a whole new image; except that Mark wasn't sure of the most appropriate time and place to launch himself upon the world. He couldn't wear these clothes for work as he often had to go onto the shop floor where there was grease and swarf everywhere just waiting to contaminate his clothes. Not only that, but Mark also felt he would have to fend off lots of wolf whistles – and not necessarily from the female workers.

Mark's social life was not so full as to present him with too many opportunities to parade himself in all his fashionable glory, but the one person he wanted to impress was Della. Why he would want to impress her, he didn't know, but that was his main aim.

So he asked if she and Phil would join him on the following Saturday night at the Clubhouse. But Della said that they had a prior arrangement. Ray and Valerie were also otherwise engaged that weekend.

When Mark woke up on the Saturday, it was a fine Spring morning, so he thought he would wear his new clothes to go shopping, but decided against Sanford, in case he met someone he might recognise. Instead, he drove over to King's Lynn, knowing there were a couple of record stores where he occasionally picked up the odd bargain in their sales. As he walked down Tower Street, he felt very self-conscious and in Bayes Record

Shop, he was sure everyone was staring at him. Not only that, but his trousers were very tight around his crotch and he felt very uncomfortable.

He couldn't wait to get home and change back into his old jeans, ready to drive down to the football pitch. There was no way he would have turned up for football looking like Quentin Crisp.

After this experience, Mark was very selective about when he would wear his new clothes – at least until he felt his new fashionable image was more run-of-the-mill in sleepy West Norfolkshire.

Life in the Work Study department was becoming intolerable for Mark, only alleviated by the jokes which Mark and Ray took turns at telling, but usually when David wasn't around. The ladies toilet was situated right next to the Work Study office and on one occasion when Eileen returned from a visit to see them all laughing, Ray asked her if she had heard them next door.

'No,' replied Eileen, looking intrigued.

'Well, we could hear you,' said Ray.

Della said 'You're funny. Where d'you get your jokes from?'

Della had never told Mark he was funny, so he felt a little jealous that Ray was getting this attention. He couldn't help butting in. 'That's an old Ted Ray gag. Ted was on stage once when a chap in the audience got up to go to the toilet. Ted used that joke to thoroughly embarrass him.'

Ray didn't appear to take offence at Mark's need to be number one in Della's affection.

When David Ross was in the office, he and Mark barely spoke to each other and Mark was no longer prepared to put in extra hours. He was effectively 'working to rule'. All his hopes of a bright new career had come to nothing. He wasn't even a proper Work Study Engineer, since Work Study involved an awful lot more than just setting targets for an incentive scheme and there seemed to be little prospect of this changing.

Ray had become David's favourite. Mark did not hold this against Ray. In fact, he was pleased that Ray was an object for all David's little madcap projects, leaving Mark to pursue his normal work routine of ensuring all operations in the Metal Shop and the Paint Shop had targets. But it had all become a little too 'routine' for Mark; only made bearable by his alliance with Della. When they found the atmosphere in the office was too quiet, the two of them would often pass little notes to each other.

Della would write 'Have you upset your boss again?'

Mark would scribble back 'No, I think it's your turn.'

Or perhaps he would write a silly little rhyme.

Roses are red,

Violets are blue.

What about yours?

Sometimes, Della would give a little squeal of muffled laughter and she would get a dirty look from David, who, in turn, would give Mark a dirty look of his own.

Even so, Mark was finding his feelings for Della difficult to deal with. It was good that he spent a great deal of time in her company, but it wasn't enough. If he should chance to touch her in the course of their working day, such as the briefest touch of hands while pointing to an item on her desk, it felt like an electric current coursing through his body. This situation was becoming unbearable, but there was nothing he could do. She had never given any indication that she returned his feelings and it wouldn't have changed things if she had. Mark often wondered how this was going to end. As long as they worked together, he couldn't see his feelings changing.

As he had feared, this situation had become similar to the time when he had an unrequited infatuation with Karen. But there were differences. Karen walked all over Mark and often treated him with utter disdain, mainly because of his age, but Della treated him as an equal – in fact mostly as a friend. And she was a great support in his battles with David, often openly siding with Mark over contentious issues. Mark's feelings for Karen were only brought under control after she left Greshams to be replaced by the lovely Debbie.

The answer to Mark's current problems was to find another job, but where?

CHAPTER 15

Breaking Down the Walls of Heartache

As Spring turned into Summer and the football season came to a close, Mark found he had more time on his hands at weekends. He decided it was time he bought himself a camera and whenever the sun came out, he would drive around the Norfolk countryside looking for photo opportunities. He opted for an Instamatic which used the 126 format film cartridges. It was a simple point and click camera that had no facility for focusing or altering the exposure. Results on a cloudy day were less than satisfactory, but Mark decided to use Kodachrome slide film. This had a better ISO rating to cope with duller conditions and variation in contrast, but in addition to that, the price of the film included developing. The developed slides came back mounted in either stiff cardboard or plastic, depending upon the make of film used. He also bought a little hand-held slide viewer so that he could show off his results to his family and colleagues.

After a few trial films, Mark developed a good eye for framing interesting sights, mostly of landscapes, with a few historical buildings thrown in. The camera was of less use for filming wildlife, but the duck-ponds in places like South Wootton and Docking produced some good results. Sometimes, he ventured out with a definite objective in mind, such as Castle Acre Priory or Oxburgh Hall; other times he would just see where the road would take him, but avoiding the busy coastal road between King's Lynn and Hunstanton. Occasionally, he would find unexpected treasures such as the picturesque Bintree Mill; other times he just enjoyed driving his car. But the main thing was that these visits occupied his time over the weekends when he was unable to spend time with Della.

However, none of these activities helped him in his quest to find a girlfriend.

Mark was entitled to three weeks annual holiday each year, but he seldom used his full allocation, because he never actually had a holiday. When Della asked his advice as to how she could entertain her two nieces who were due to stay with her for a week, he made several suggestions, but they mostly required transport of some description. So he volunteered to use one of his days holiday to take them all out for a day. Phil was working that week, but the nieces could act as chaperones, allowing Mark to spend an enjoyable day with Della. They decided upon the area around Colchester and Constable Country – or as Mark called it – Essexshire!

This was further than Mark had ever ventured before in his car, but they had all day.

The two nieces were nine and eleven years old and were noisy and energetic. By the time they reached Colchester, Mark was pleased to get out of the car to give his ears a rest. Della hadn't helped by spending the whole journey trying unsuccessfully to get a signal from her radio, into which she had plugged Mark's aerial.

After a quick visit to the castle, they had a picnic in the castle grounds, provided by Della. When a swarm of ants invaded, Della started trying to kill them all. Mark said 'Don't do that. The ants are my friends.'

'Wha' on Earth are you talkin' abou'?' asked Della.

'I thought you were a Bob Dylan fan. The ants are my friends – blowing in the wind!'

'Oh, very funny.'

The nieces looked at them both as though they were mad. They'd never heard of Bob Dylan.

After the picnic, they headed off with the intention of finding Flatford Mill, but Della wasn't the best navigator in the world and when they eventually found themselves driving past a mill, Della said 'There it is!'

Mark parked the car and could see a small expanse of water with a mill in the background. It didn't look anything like the pictures Mark had seen of Flatford Mill.

'It's changed since Constable painted it!' said Mark with a hint of sarcasm. He had seen recent photos of Flatford and he knew this wasn't it, but he thought it might be worth a photograph, so he got out of the car and wandered around. Then he saw a sign that said 'Dedham.' They were in the right vicinity, because Mark knew that Constable had also painted Dedham Mill and Dedham Vale, but if this was Dedham Mill, it had changed since Constable's days.

On the other side of the road, he saw some rowing boats and a sign pointing down the river to Flatford.

'How about hiring a boat and rowing down?' he suggested.

'Champion!' the three Geordies all said.

Mark paid a deposit for the boat, with the understanding that he would receive a refund when they returned the boat and at which time the owner would know for how long they had hired it.

This was Mark's first experience of rowing a boat and as they all gingerly found their places in the boat, Mark began to realise that it wasn't as easy as it looked. His first pull resulted in him losing his grip and very nearly losing an oar. After five minutes of going round in circles and hitting the bank three times, they eventually started making some headway. Della acted as cox and kept barking orders at Mark. 'You're goin' into the trees, man!' and 'There's another boa' coming!'

Mark didn't like going backwards and relying on someone else to be his eyes. When Della told him to go left or right, he had to remember which oar to pull on and by the time he had worked it out, it was usually too late.

After half an hour of this, he was tired and he felt he was in danger of getting blisters. He had no idea how far they had come, nor how far they had to go to reach Flatford. He didn't want to appear to be a wimp by complaining, so he asked Della if she wanted to try rowing. The nieces both said 'I want to try', but Mark said he didn't think that was a good idea.

As Mark and Della changed places, he put his hands on her shoulders to steady them both and he felt the old surge of electricity coursing through his veins, but he had to concentrate on the task in hand or they would all end up in the water.

Now the tables were turned and Della was the one who was struggling to understand Mark's instructions. She also went through a period of hitting the bank or getting entangled in trees.

Della's progress down the river was even slower than Mark's and after another half hour, she too was exhausted and worried about blisters. There was still no sign of Flatford, so Mark suggested it was time to turn around since it would be harder to row back upstream.

Again, he had the pleasure of holding her shoulders as they swapped places. The journey back did take much longer and, sure enough, Mark had blisters by the time they arrived back at the landing. At least no one had received a soaking and they all agreed it had been an enjoyable afternoon, but it was now time to drive home.

But first, Mark wanted a couple of photographs as a memento of his day out. He took one of Della standing next to the two nieces. Then he found a spot beneath a willow tree where there was just enough afternoon sunlight diffusing through the foliage, where he positioned Della on her own. There was a glow on her cheeks and forehead where she had been mildly perspiring that just caught the sun. Mark was pleased with the setting and would eagerly await the developed slide which, he imagined, he would treasure long after she had left his life, because it was inevitable that she would one day leave his life.

He really wanted a photograph of the two of them together, but decided that it was not appropriate.

The journey home was much quieter than the trip down. It seemed that the activity on the river had exhausted the two nieces. Mark was in pain and was struggling to grip the steering wheel and change gear, but he had enjoyed being in Della's company in such relaxed surroundings. His one regret was that he didn't really feel that he had seen the best of the wonderful Constable countryside – no sweeping views of Dedham Vale; no sign of Willie Lott's cottage; not even Flatford Mill. But the weather had been kind to them.

Mark wondered about Della's relationship with her nieces. As her sister was really her mother, did that mean the 'nieces' were really her cousins? Or even her sisters? He decided they could even be her grandnieces. He thought about enquiring, but decided he couldn't do it in front of the nieces – or whatever they were.

That evening, after he had deposited his passengers back home and they had thanked him profusely, it was a return of the old feelings of frustration that there was not a better way of rounding off the day; perhaps with a kiss and a cuddle – or even something more passionate. He knew the following day he would be back at work, while Della continued her week's holiday without him. He had been merely the chauffeur, but what else did he expect?

He couldn't go on like this. His job was now purgatory and he slept very badly at night. The irony was that just a few months ago, he had an attractive girlfriend, but he had to let her go as there was none of that magic chemistry that had now invaded his system. As well as that, a few months earlier, he was enthusiastic about his job and was optimistic for the future, but now, it had all gone pear-shaped.

Or as Ray would have said, 'It was a ball of chalk.'

There was one bright area on Mark's horizon and that was that he had struck up a new friendship with Ray and Valerie. Of course, it could have been so much better if Mark had a girlfriend so that they could all go out more regularly as a foursome. And because Ray was in a steady relationship with Valerie, Mark and Ray could not go 'out on the pull,' so Mark had to find another way of tackling this problem, but he was able to join Ray and Valerie for the occasional game of darts or cribbage at the Social Club. As Mark and Ray shared a similar sense of humour, they became a bit of a double act, which usually resulted in Valerie accusing them both of being a couple of fools.

On Monday morning, Mark had wanted to know if Della had enjoyed their day out, but she was in one of her early morning grumpy moods, so neither of them said much in the car on the way to work. However, during the day she gradually cheered up, so Mark was able to talk to her.

'What did your nieces make of Norfolkshire?'

'They weren' very complimen'ry. It's too quiet for them. But they enjoyed their day with us. They said you're a grea' bloke.'

'Really! I hardly spoke to them.'

'Noo, but it were good of you to take us all out and wouldn't let us pay for anything.'

Mark replied 'It was the only way I'm ever going to be able to spend a day out with you. You enjoyed it as well, did you?'

'It wor champion. Phil never takes me out like that.'

This left Mark with very mixed emotions. It was gratifying to hear Della say she had enjoyed their day out, but so frustrating that nothing could come of it. He wanted to ask Della if she also considered him to be a *grea' bloke*, but it wouldn't make any difference to his happiness.

The next day, everyone in the office was laughing about a recent episode of 'The Benny Hill Show' and a particular sketch involving Nicholas Parsons. Ray said 'I know a lady who likes Nicholas Parsons.'

So Mark responded 'That's ironic, because I know a parson who likes…' and he paused for everyone to mentally finish his sentence. It was obvious to everyone that they had been rehearsing this one.

Then he said 'I understand that Benny Hill is responsible for selling thousands of television sets.'

'Yes,' said Ray. 'My Aunt Alice has sold hers. So has the lady next door.'

Then Mark added 'The young girl chased me in a well-known farmyard vehicle.'

'A tractor?' asked Ray.

'Well, I supposed I must have done.'

'Who was that lady I see'd you with last night?' asked Ray.

'You mean "*I saw*"' came the response.

'All right, then. Who was that eyesore I see'd you with, last night?'

Then it was Mark's turn again. 'My wife's going on holiday to the West Indies.'

'Jakarta?'

'No, you fool! Jamaica. Jakarta's in the East Indies!'

'We're never going to make a living doing this. We'd better cancel the booking.'

Eileen said they both had an infectious sense of humour. Their jokes were making her sick!

During July, Mark saw a job advertised on the internal notice board that sparked his interest. It was for a Computer Programmer – a position he would not normally have considered, imagining that it was for clever geeks. But he knew the current incumbents of that position and neither could be described as exceptional beings. In any case, he had nothing to lose by applying. After all, the notice stated that full training would be given. He decided to go and see James McDougall who was the Senior Programmer.

James explained that Tim Peart, the other programmer was changing jobs, thus creating a vacancy. He also pointed out that all applicants were required to sit an aptitude test. This test was designed to assess whether the candidate had the right sort of logical brain. A failure in this test automatically ruled you out. There would be no formal interviews until all the applicants had sat the tests, so Mark asked if he could put his name down for the test.

Two days later, Mark found himself seated in a quiet room while James explained the tests to him. 'Are you sure you understand?' James asked.

'Yes, it all seems straightforward,' Mark replied, wondering why James was being so pedantic.

'Once you start, you can't ask any questions – and you must complete the test in thirty minutes. Are you sure you're ready?'

Mark completed the test in twenty minutes. It was so straightforward that he wondered if there was a hidden catch.

'I'll get these marked and I'll be in touch by the end of the week,' said James. 'There are two more applicants.'

Mark hadn't told anyone else about this job, apart from Della, who kept asking if he'd heard anything yet. When Friday came around and Mark still hadn't been contacted by James, he began to suspect that he had failed the tests, but just after lunch James rang him to ask if he could join him for a chat.

As Mark got up, Della said 'Good luck.'

David looked across at them both and asked 'What's this?'

It had been a few weeks since Mark and David had last argued about anything, so David probably thought they were back on speaking terms, but Mark just said 'I've got to see a man about a dog.'

'You're getting a dog?'

'No, I'm not getting a dog,' said Mark as he left the office, giving David no further chance to interrogate him.

But David pursued the matter with Della. 'I'm not saying anything,' she replied, deliberately arousing his curiosity.

James McDougall always struck Mark as a very pleasant amenable chap, despite having a rather monotonic Edinburgh accent, and he warmly welcomed Mark into his office, which he shared with Tim Peart and a young punch girl named Mary, of whom Mark knew very little, except that he had seen her mounting a motor bike driven, presumably, by her leather-clad boyfriend.

'So how were my test results?' asked Mark impatiently.

'Not bad,' came the reply. 'You scored eleven.'

'Out of how many?' Mark remembered there were only eleven questions.

'Out of eleven, Mark.'

'The maximum?'

'Yes, the maximum.'

James had a very strange sense of humour if he thought this was amusing. Still, that was better than the sense of humour of his current boss – not that Mark ever acknowledged David as his boss.

'What about the other candidates?' Mark asked.

'They got five and seven.'

'And what's the pass mark?'

'Eight is the minimum that we would accept.'

'I'm going to smack him in a minute,' thought Mark. Instead, he asked 'Am I in with a chance then?'

Just then, Tim, who had been listening to this annoying conversation, chipped in 'I only got eight, when I did the test…and James got nine!'

'So, on that basis,' continued James, 'I would like to offer you a position as a Computer Programmer.' Mark had expected there to have been a formal interview, but there didn't seem to be a lot of point if it was all down to the test results and the other candidates had already failed.

'Thank you,' said Mark. 'I would like to accept, but I think I need to find out a bit more about the job – such as what the training involves and my terms and conditions.'

'In terms of *terms and conditions* – that's funny – in terms of *terms and conditions*' and then James gave a funny little laugh, while Mark was thinking that it wasn't funny at all, and James' laugh was going to get on his nerves.

'Seriously, your terms and conditions,' James continued, 'will be exactly the same as what you're on at the moment and you would get an annual pay review at the usual time in April, by which time we will know how well you've come through the training.

'The training would involve, in the first instance, attending a three-week course with NCR. Their next course starts in the second week of September at Greenford. We would therefore like you to start on the first to give you the best part of a week to get your feet under the desk, in here.'

'Where's Greenford?' asked Mark.

'It's in London. You'd be put up in a hotel and all your meals and travelling would be paid for. You come home for the weekends, of course. Tim and I did the same course and we enjoyed it. So do you have any other questions?'

'Not at the moment,' Mark replied.

'So are you going to accept?' James asked.

'Can I have a couple of days to think about it?'

'Yes, but don't be too long. We have to arrange a place on the course and you will have to give notice for your current job.'

'I'll let you know on Monday, if that's all right?'

'Well?' asked Della, as he returned to his desk.

'I've got it, if I want it.'

'And do you want it?'

'Yes. I told them I'd let them know on Monday, but I'm sure I'm going to accept. I'm fed up with this.'

Mark was aware that David was listening to their conversation, but neither spoke to the other about it. Ray, in his usual mischievous manner said 'So you're getting a new dog, are you? Congratulations!'

Later, when David had left the office, Mark confirmed to the others that he would, indeed, be moving on and gave them all details of the 'interview.'

Della said 'If you're off, so am I. I'm not staying to put up with him on my own.'

'What are you going to do?' asked Mark.

'I've been thinking of goin' into nursin'. I saw this thing in the paper about takin' on some trainees. I think the trainin' starts in September.'

Mark felt touched that his departure had caused Della to take this step and from his point of view, it would make the break from her so much cleaner. If Della remained, Mark would probably continue to give her a lift home and that would just prolong his agony.

Ray had to chip in with one of his little quips. 'So it's all change round here. As one door closes, another door shuts!'

That evening, on the way home, Della said 'I hope we'll still be friends?'

'Of course,' said Mark, but he knew this wasn't possible, although he knew it was going to be tough to make a clean break of it.

CHAPTER 16

Things Get Better

Mark was in a good mood when he arrived for work on the following Monday, ready to hand in his notice for one position and accept the other.

Ray always liked to start a Monday with a little whimsy or words of wisdom ready to set them all up for the day.

On one occasion, it was 'Did you realise that the word "verb" is a noun – that's strange, isn't it?' On another occasion he poured forth on the mystery of belly-button fluff. 'Where does it come from? Is there a belly-button fairy that creeps into your bed at night and deposits it there?'

This day it was 'Never trust a fart!'

'Is that from personal experience?' Eileen asked.

Ray ignored her, but added 'A chap goes into a bar and says to the barman *"I've just come from the hospital. Give me a triple whiskey and a pint of stout."* He downed them both quickly and asked for a repeat order, which he again drank very quickly. After a third order, he said *"I'm not sure I should be drinking this with what I've got"*

"Why? What have you got?" asked the barman.

"One and sixpence" he replied.

For some reason, which Mark didn't understand, David always seemed more tolerant of Ray having a laugh and a joke than he was with Mark. Mark noticed that David actually smiled when he saw everyone laughing at Ray's joke. Mark had also observed that he and Della had been greeted with an unusually friendly 'Good morning' when they had both arrived together. Perhaps David had wind of what was happening and was hoping that being nice might dissuade Mark from leaving – or maybe he was just pleased that Mark was leaving!

Whatever the explanation, it wasn't going to make any difference to Mark's decision to move on, although he knew he would miss the company of Ray and Della, because James McDougall didn't look like he was going to be a lot of fun. Mark didn't know much about Mary the punch girl, but she always seemed cheerful enough.

After informing James of his acceptance, Mark went to see Eddie to tell him the news. Eddie made no attempt to persuade him to stay, but, ironically, later in the day, David did, but to no avail. Mark didn't say too much, but he made his point that he needed to move on and look to the future. David wished him every success, which would have been touching, except that Mark felt that David Ross was to blame for the failure of his current position.

Although Mark knew he had to embrace his opportunity, he felt apprehensive about his new role. What if he turned out to be a useless programmer? And he had to spend three weeks in London. Mark had only ever been to London twice before. The first time was on a school trip to the Tower of London, which had been very enjoyable. The second time however, was for an unsuccessful interview with the Civil Service and that had been a traumatic experience for a young teenager. On that occasion, he had found London to be noisy and overwhelming – not an experience he was seeking to repeat, and his next visit wasn't for a day trip. It was for three weeks and he would be totally alone. To him, London was a place filled with murderers, prostitutes, pickpockets, pimps, sleazy nightclubs and gangsters; well, that's how it looked on television, anyway.

What he was looking forward to though, was to be working back in the office block rather than the Factory. He could wear smarter clothes, see more young ladies and enjoy cleaner toilet facilities.

Meanwhile, he had to serve out his notice period, enjoy the rest of the summer and make the most of Della's company for a few more weeks – and there was still no prospect of any young girl whisking him away from his life of celibacy.

One Sunday afternoon in late August, Mark was out with his camera, in the quiet and pretty little village of South Walton. The sun was catching the crenulated tower of the quaint little parish church and he tried to position himself so that the peaceful little duck pond could act as a picturesque foreground. Try as he might, he couldn't quite get the position he required. There was only one thing for it. He would have to lie down to get the best angle. He looked round to make sure no one was going to see him in this undignified position, but there was someone approaching, so Mark decided to wait, looking nonchalantly across the pond.

As the person got nearer, he could see that it was a young woman in a track suit and she was running. Why on Earth was anyone in their right mind running on a hot August afternoon?

Mark knew that most people who live in a village would say a friendly 'hello' as they passed – even complete strangers, whereas in a town like Sanford, they were more likely to totally avoid eye-contact. He decided that when she got nearer, he would turn and exchange a greeting. This was something he would never have dreamed of doing a few years earlier, but he had learnt that, rather than being considered too forward, it would have been rude not to at least acknowledge the lady's presence. It was always possible that she might ignore him, but then that was her problem.

He tried to time it so that he turned just as she reached speaking distance, which he did and much to his satisfaction, she smiled and returned his 'hello'. She was very pretty and despite panting a little, gave him a lovely smile. If only he had the courage to stop her and exchange further pleasantries, but he doubted whether she would appreciate such a forward approach. In any case, she was fully occupied with her endeavours.

Just as she drew level, her foot slipped against the grass verge. She let out a little feminine squeal of pain and fell over clutching her ankle. Mark rushed across to see if he could help. 'Are you all right?' he asked. He knew it was an obvious question, but what else was he to say?

'I twisted my ankle,' she said. 'What a stupid thing to do. I should be watching what I'm doing.'

'It's probably my fault for distracting you,' Mark said. 'Take your shoe off. I'll be back in a minute.'

Mark rushed to his car to get rid of the camera and to pick up an old cloth that he used for wiping his windows. He took the cloth down to the pond and soaked it.

He then wrapped the cloth around her ankle. 'It's important to keep it cool to lessen the swelling,' he said.

'Are you a medical person?' she asked.

'No. I twisted my ankle last year, playing football. Our trainer told me all this when he gave me the wet sponge treatment. I still had to go to the hospital, but the doctor said the trainer's action probably quickened the recovery. Just leave that there for a few minutes and try to keep your ankle raised a little. I don't think you'll be doing any more running today. How far have you got to go?'

'I live in North Walton. I was doing a circular run to get fit for the hockey season.'

Mark said 'That's about two miles away. You need to stay off your ankle or it will just get worse. Is there anyone who you can call to pick you up?'

'No. I live on my own.'

'Just give it a few minutes and we'll see if you can stand on it. Where do you play hockey?'

'I play for the High School O.G.s…Old Girls. We play at the High School itself on Sunday afternoons. I had glandular fever at the end of last season, so I felt I needed to get fit again – not such a good idea as it turned out. Where do you play football?'

'I play for Northfleet – on the Northfleet Estate. We play on Saturday afternoons.' After a few more minutes, he added 'Are you ready to try standing up?'

'I'll give it a try,' she said.

'Let me support you,' said Mark as she manoeuvred herself into position to try to stand. As soon as she tried to put her weight on her swollen ankle, she winced with pain.

'No, I can't,' she said and dropped down again.

'I think you ought to get it checked out.' Mark knew he couldn't leave her there on her own, but he wasn't sure if she would want to get in the car of a complete stranger. 'I doubt whether the ambulance service would view this as an emergency. Would you like me to take you to Casualty to get it looked at?'

'I can't ask you to do that,' she replied.

'Well, I can't leave you here – and you can't move. Do you have another idea?'

'I'll just have to hobble home as best I can.'

'You don't want to get in the car of a complete stranger, do you?'

'No, it's not that. I don't want to drag you out of your way.'

'I've got to go back to Sanford, anyway, so it's not much out of my way. I do think you should get your leg looked at. It might be broken.'

'Well, I didn't hear a crack, but you're probably right. Are you sure you don't mind?'

'I would mind more if I had to leave you here to get home on your own. Let's get you into the car. I'll bring it a bit nearer.' Mark had deliberately parked his car a few yards away from the pond so that it didn't spoil his picture. He brought it closer and opened the back door. 'I think you'll be better in the back seat, so that you can put your leg up. By the way, my name's Mark – just so you know whose car you're getting into.'

'I'm Melody,' she said.

'What a lovely name.'

'Yes, everyone says that. Most people call me Mel, though. This is really kind of you. You must let me pay for your petrol.'

'I said I'm going in that direction, so it's not costing me anything. Just put your arm 'round me, while we get you into position.' Mark was trying not to enjoy touching a woman again, but she felt lovely. It had been so long. 'That's it. Now, just slide along the seat. That's it. Are you comfortable like that?'

'My leg is throbbing, but I'll be all right, like this.'

'Let me just wet the cloth again. It's important to keep your ankle cold.'

It only took just over ten minutes to get to the Hospital. It was an old red-brick Victorian building and Mark asked Melody to stay in the car while he sought a wheel chair and thus was able to wheel her into Casualty. A friendly round-faced nurse came with him to assist Melody into the chair and to open the doors while Mark pushed.

'So what have you been up to, young lady?' the nurse asked.

'I was jogging and I slipped and twisted my ankle. It's probably nothing, but I can't put any weight on it at the moment.'

'What's *jogging*?' asked the nurse.

'It's an American idea. It's really just another term for running, but it's a new craze in America. People jog around a park to get fit.

By now, they were in the Waiting Room and after transferring Melody to a chair, the nurse said 'Right! The first thing is to get some of your details. What's your name?'

'Melody Morris.'

'What a lovely name,' said the nurse.

'Everyone says that,' said Mark, before Melody could say it.

'Is this your young man?' the nurse asked.

'No, he's my knight in shining armour who came to my rescue when I fell over.'

'Do you know,' replied Mark, 'I've always wanted to be a knight in shining armour and come to the rescue of a damsel in distress. It was hardly that heroic, though, was it?'

The nurse carried on taking down Melody's details and then had a look at the ankle. 'You're going to have a nice bruise there in a day or so, but I don't think anything's broken. Best to get you X-rayed though and then I'll get the doctor to look at it. I see your sock is wet. Did you try to keep it cool?'

'Yes, that was Mark's idea. He said it would lessen the swelling and help it recover quicker.'

'Well he did the right thing.'

Melody turned to Mark and said 'You'd best get off, now. You don't want to be hanging around here the rest of the afternoon.'

'How were you intending to get home?' Mark asked.

'I can get a taxi. Please – I've taken up enough of your time. I'll be all right, now.'

The nurse intervened. 'Before you go, you can help me take Melody down to the X-Ray department. You support her on that side and I'll take this. That's it. Now just use your good leg and stay off the other one. It's not too far.'

Mark was only too pleased to be able to support Melody and put his arm around her lovely firm hips.

There was another person waiting outside the X-Ray room, with his arm in a temporary sling, so Melody took a seat, while the nurse disappeared back to Casualty. Mark sat down beside her and said 'I might as well hang on to see what the results are.'

The chap who was waiting said 'I'm just waiting for my results, so you shouldn't be too long. I bet you'll be quicker than I was. They don't like football injuries, here. They view them as self-inflicted. We shouldn't be playing dangerous games like football.' Mark recognised that to be true from his one and only visit to Casualty.

'Who do you play for?' asked Mark.

'Manningford… we had our first friendly this morning and I think I've broken my arm.'

'We don't play Manningford,' said Mark. 'You're in Division two of the Saturday League aren't you?'

'We were. We got promoted last season.'

'Oh, you'll be playing our reserves, then – Northfleet.'

'So you play in the first Division, then?' the chap enquired.

'Yes.'

A young lady came out of the X-Ray room and handed the chap a large envelope. 'Here you are Mr Davidson. Take that back with you and let the doctor see it. Would you like to come in Miss Morris?'

Five minutes later, Melody re-appeared hopping to her seat.

'Is it getting any easier?' Mark asked.

'I think it is a little, but I daren't put any weight on it. Are you sure you don't need to get off?'

'I'm all right, as long as you don't mind. I might as well see you home safely. You don't want to be messing around with taxis.'

'You're very kind,' she replied. But Mark had ulterior motives. He wouldn't come straight out and ask for a date...but if he waited for the right opportunity. He also had to ensure she was totally unattached and that would need some very careful probing.

While they were waiting for the X-Ray, they continued to exchange small talk and the time flew by. As the round-faced nurse had returned to Casualty, it was left to Mark to support Melody all the way back while she clutched the X-Ray envelope. He enjoyed every minute of it, but he could tell that it wasn't much fun for Melody and she was very relieved to reach the waiting area and take a seat again.

It was several minutes before the nurse attended them again. She had a quick look at the X-Ray and said she thought it looked like a mild sprain, but she needed a doctor to confirm that. This took another fifteen minutes before the doctor arrived and had a little feel of the sore area before confirming that Melody needed to rest the ankle for a few days. Meanwhile the nurse would apply a bandage to contain the swelling, and Melody would have to remove this each night before retiring. There was no need to return to the Hospital unless the injury didn't start to improve after a few days.

Again, there were a few more minutes waiting while the nurse went to fetch a bandage, so they carried on talking.

'What do you do for a living, Mark?'

'I'm a computer programmer,' he lied. He thought that would sound impressive.

'Coo, you must be clever. How long have you been doing that?'

'Oh, I wish you hadn't asked that,' thought Mark, so he thought he'd better tell the truth. 'I don't actually start until September. I'm serving out my notice as a Work Study Engineer.'

'What's one of those?'

'It's effectively *time and motion,* but there is a bit more to it than that. Both jobs are at Greshams. What do you do?'

'I'm a Payroll Clerk at Sanfoods.'

'No! I used to be a payroll clerk. I used to really enjoy that. Is it computerised?'

'No, we use the Kalamazoo sheets, so it's all done manually.'

'We used to use Kalamazoo,' said Mark, 'but then they introduced the Sumlock Comptometers and took some of my work away, so I moved on. I'm expecting to be involved in writing or maintaining a payroll program on our computer among other things. I'll probably have to code the changes for the decimalisation next year.'

By then, the nurse had returned with the bandage so Mark wasn't able to bore Melody with any more details. The nurse said 'I don't think you'll be doing any trotting for a few weeks, young lady.'

'Jogging,' corrected Melody.

After the nurse had tied up the bandage, she went to fetch the wheelchair again and Mark pushed it out to his car. This time Melody insisted on sitting in the front of the car and they were soon off towards North Walton.

'This is a nice car,' Melody said. 'I've got a Wolseley as well – mine is a Hornet. I like the standard mini, but the Hornet is just a bit more distinctive.'

Mark agreed, but in the short time available, he wanted to find out a bit more about Melody. He knew she lived alone, so he asked 'How long have you lived in Walton?'

'Only about six months. I'm originally from Northamptonshire. We used to visit Norfolk regularly as a family and I've always liked the area. It's so peaceful and I love all those little places on the North Norfolk coast – Blakeney, Wells, Cromer, Brancaster. They're all different. The funny thing is that since moving here, I never seem to have the time to visit them. There's always so much to do when you live alone.'

Mark said 'My favourite place is Thornham. There's a nice little pub called the Lifeboat where I used to do some courting. Do you know it?'

'I don't think I do. Don't you use it for courting now?'

'Not at the moment,' Mark replied. He nearly said 'Not anymore,' but that might have given her the impression that he had settled down with someone and he was pleased with the opportunity to let her know he was not currently courting.

He dearly wanted to ask Melody if she was seeing anyone, but she was very talkative, so before he could ask her that one important question, she said 'Anyway, when I saw the payroll job advertised in Sanford, I jumped at the chance to move here. I rent a little carstone cottage on the edge of the village.'

'I like carstone,' said Mark. 'I don't know if it's unique to this area, but I've only ever seen it in West Norfolk.'

Melody pointed out her cottage on the edge of the village. It certainly was a quiet position. She had the last of a terrace of three carstone cottages, with a small front garden enclosed within a white picket fence. The fence contrasted nicely with the dark rustiness of the stone building and tall hollyhocks filled her small garden. All three properties in the terrace had neat little cottage gardens and together would have made a pretty little photograph.

'Stay there a minute, while I open the passenger door,' he said. He gently helped her to her feet and she winced with pain. 'Have you got your keys?' he asked.

'The door's not locked. I didn't think I would be this long.'

As they hobbled along together with Mark supporting her wonderful firm body as best he could, a neighbour appeared from next-door.

'What've you been up to, Mel?' the neighbour asked – a middle-aged fussy looking woman with a cigarette in her mouth.

'I twisted my ankle while out running.'

The neighbour helped support Melody on the other side, and at the door, she urged Mark to let her take over, saying to Mel 'Let's get you lying down. I bet you want a cup of tea.'

Mark fancied a cup of tea, but he was left standing at the door. He hadn't been invited in and he felt it rude to invite himself, so after waiting a minute to receive such an invitation, he turned away, disappointed. He should have walked in straight away, but now he'd left it too late.

When he got to the car, he spotted Melody's running shoe on the back seat, so, hoping he might still get the chance for a cup of tea, he returned to the front door and knocked. The neighbour answered and Mark said 'Mel left her shoe in the car.'

'I'll see she gets it m'duck. I don't think she'll be in a hurry to use it again,' and she left Mark just standing there again, cursing his luck – or was it luck? Should he have been a little bolder and seized the chance earlier? But if he had done that, he wouldn't have been Mark Barker.

CHAPTER 17

Only the Strong Survive

'Why is *abbreviation* such a long word,' said Ray as his opening words of philosophy on Mark's last day in the Work Study department.

Mark decided to join in with his own words of whimsy. 'And why do moths come out only at night and then fly towards the light? If they like the light so much, why don't they come out in the daytime?'

None of these questions actually required an answer, but this type of banter was one of the things Mark was going to miss in his new job.

'So, Mark,' continued Ray, 'have you got any last thoughts on your time working with us?'

'Yes… I think it's been an honour and a privilege.'

'Well, it's been an honour and a privilege for us,' Ray responded.

'That's what I meant,' said Mark. 'Did you know that six out of seven dwarves are not happy?'

A minute later, Ray said 'Did you know that in the latest edition of the Oxford English dictionary, they omitted the word *gullible*?'

'Is that right?' asked Della, innocently.

'What do you think?'

Then the penny dropped. 'Oh, you're horrible!'

Mark's successor had been appointed and was due to start the following week. He was a labourer from the Despatch area, which at first had seemed a strange choice for such a technical role, but it turned out that Vic Riley was a semi-professional footballer with King's Lynn and he subsidised his meagre football earnings by working at Greshams. He was reported to be quite an intelligent chap – at least by footballers' standards. And he had a little joke. When asked about his second job, he said he worked in boots.

Della had been successful in applying for the Student Nurse position, but she still had four weeks of her notice period to serve. Mark had agreed to continue transporting her to and from work for one more week, but then he would be in London for the rest of her notice period. So it was unlikely that he would see her after the next week, since neither of them was in a position to continue their friendship. Mark naturally had mixed feelings about this, but he hoped he would still see Ray and his girlfriend on a regular basis.

Meanwhile, Mark was still thinking about Melody. In fact, ever since he had met her, he had been thinking about her. He joked to himself that she was a haunting Melody. He kept remembering those little details that he hadn't had chance to take in at the time. Because she had worn a track-suit during their encounter, he didn't have a full appreciation of her figure, but he knew she had nice firm hips. When he had seen her running, she seemed to move with an elegant fluid action without looking like an out-and-out athlete. Despite being hot and slightly dishevelled, she was very attractive with a lovely smile enhanced by a slight gap in her front teeth and he remembered that she had a dimple in one cheek only. She was only a few inches shorter than Mark himself. He always liked a woman who held herself upright, but for most of their encounter, she was unable to stand up straight, but Mark assumed, because of her involvement in hockey that she would be reasonably fit. All of these facts meant that as far as he was concerned she was ideal as his next girlfriend. He also liked to think that he had been able to make a good impression on her, such that if he were in a position to ask her out, he could be reasonably confident of success – provided, of course, she didn't already have a companion.

But how could he hope to see her again? He could just drive over to North Walton in the hope of bumping into her, but her cottage was on the edge of the village, so his presence there would indicate a deliberate attempt to seek her out – and Mark wasn't comfortable with that. Maybe he would run into her in town one day. He certainly hoped so. He ventured into town on Saturday morning and, as he had nothing better to do with himself, he returned after lunch as well, but without success.

The following week found him working in the Computer Department, although 'working' is the wrong term because until he had received his training, he was unable to contribute anything. Instead, he was given a manual to read – a manual that meant nothing to him without at least some grounding in the subject. Mark also had to put up with James' strange sense of humour. It wasn't so much that his jokes were poor; it was more the way he reacted to his own jokes – laughing as though he had just told the funniest joke ever and when no one else joined in, he was determined to explain the joke so that everyone could enjoy it as much as him. One such joke was when he couldn't get the Costing Ledger to balance and he was twenty four hours out on the Labour Analysis. After a while, he announced that he wouldn't bother finding the twenty four hours – he would call it a day!

'All right,' thought Mark, 'it was reasonably funny, but don't keep going on about it!' He and Mary kept looking at each other with a degree of mutual understanding that unless they gave at least a grin, James would never let it lie.

During the week, James discussed the arrangements for the course. Mark was booked into an hotel in Maida Vale, where the majority of the attendees would also be based. A coach would collect them each morning and transport them to Greenford where the actual course was being conducted. Mark could eat at the hotel each evening if he wished and the bill would be taken care of by Greshams. If he chose to eat elsewhere, he had to obtain a receipt for later reimbursement. Mark imagined it highly likely that he would stay in the safety of the hotel. James pointed out that he and Tim had enjoyed trying lots of local restaurants, but there was a big difference here – Mark was going to be on his own. 'You'll soon make friends with other people on the course,' said James, but Mark wasn't very good at making friends with strangers, so he thought that was highly unlikely.

James made it sound as though Mark was going to have fun for three weeks, but Mark didn't see it like that. However, he knew this was something he had to do if he wanted to turn his life around and start a new career.

James suggested that Mark should travel down on Sunday to avoid a very early start on the Monday morning. As Sanford railway station was now closed, Mark would have to drive to King's Lynn and leave his car parked at the station all week.

Such was the tedium of this first week in the computer room that Mark decided three weeks in London might be an improvement, despite his fears of visiting the capital. At least the football season was due to start that coming weekend, with, unfortunately, an away match to start with, so there was very little time to wander around town in the morning, but he went anyway and there was still no sign of Melody. He resigned himself to the fact that it wasn't going to happen. He wasn't even sure he would recognise her again. Yet another woman had escaped his clutches.

* * * * * *

Mark had never stayed in an hotel before, so after lugging his suitcase from the Maida Vale tube station along the Edgeware Road, it was with trepidation that he entered the foyer of the large building. The swarthy looking male receptionist was in no hurry to attend to him, but after a short while, he turned towards Mark without speaking. Mark said, 'I'm booked in for five nights. The name is Barker.'

Still the receptionist did not speak, but he picked up the registry book and scanned down the page with his finger. When he turned a page and shook his head, Mark started to worry. The man went back to the original page and this time, he did find the entry. He fetched a key from a pigeon-hole and said 'You want dinner?' in an accent Mark didn't recognise.

'Dinner?' asked Mark back.

'A table for dinner?'

'Oh, yes, please.'

'Time?'

'It's nearly five-thirty,' replied Mark.

'What time you want dinner?'

'Oh, sorry. Six-thirty, please.'

'We start at seven.'

'Seven, then.'

'Seven?'

'Yes, seven – if that's all right.'

'Table for one,' the man muttered as though disapproving the waste of a whole table just for one person, while writing something down. 'Room 305,' he added, pointing to the lift. 'Third floor. You need help with luggage?'

'No thank you. I've managed the Edgeware Road. I'm sure I can cope with the last bit.' Mark's nervousness was now replaced with annoyance at this rude person. Did he look like someone who needed help with his luggage? Not only was this the first time Mark had stayed at an hotel, it was going to be the first time he had used a lift, but he'd seen people on television, so how hard could it be. He found a button to press, but nothing seemed to happen. After a few minutes the doors to an adjoining lift opened. That wasn't the lift that Mark had summoned, but it was empty, so he decided to use this one, instead.

'What floor, did he say?' Mark thought to himself. He looked at the key. That didn't tell him, but was the number 305 a clue? He pressed the button for the third floor, the doors closed and the lift clunked into action, startling Mark. Shortly afterwards, the lift came to a sudden halt and the doors opened again, revealing an elderly lady with too much make-up, who stood in his way as he went to leave.

'Is this going down?' she asked in a rich upper-class accent.

'I don't know,' replied Mark. 'Is this the third floor?'

'It's the second!' came the abrupt reply.

'I'm going up to the third,' Mark added.

The lady huffed impatiently and stood back. Mark wondered if he had pinched her lift, but he wasn't going to get out now. He waited for something to happen, but it didn't, so he pressed the button for the third floor again. The doors started closing, and then opened again. So he pressed the button again. Eventually, the stern looking woman disappeared behind the closing doors and the lift shuddered into action again. This time when the doors opened, Mark could see a sign that pointed towards rooms 301 to 325, so he followed the arrow and found his room.

His first impression of the room was not encouraging. The smell of tobacco hit him first, so he immediately opened the window, but that let in the overpowering noise of the traffic below. Somehow, Mark didn't think he would be getting much sleep that week. His father smoked and he had worked in offices where other people smoked, so Mark was used to the smell of tobacco, but never in a bedroom before. At least he had a desk and a chair, so he could sit and read his book. On the desk, was a pen and a notepad, together with a selection of envelopes; each had the hotel's logo on them. There was a washbasin, but no toilet, so Mark ventured down the corridor to find one. It seemed he had to share a solitary toilet with the rest of the floor's occupants – or perhaps some of the other rooms did have their own toilets?

After the tension of the underground and the receptionist, Mark was grateful for a period of relaxation. He felt a little more confident about facing the restaurant – and by seven o'clock, he was extremely hungry. But as he entered the restaurant area, he felt all at sea again. There was no one in sight, so he checked his watch. Yes, it was after seven o'clock. He waited a little longer and then another foreign looking chap appeared. 'Can I 'elp you?' he asked in what Mark took for a French accent.

'Yes. Mr. Barker. I have a table booked for seven o'clock.'

'Your room number?'

'Oh, er… 305,' Mark said after checking his key.

'Can I see your key, plis?'

'Don't you believe me,' Mark thought to himself, while flashing the key.

'This way, plis.'

Mark was directed to a table right in the very middle of the large room and a leather-bound menu thrust in his hand. Mark understood very little of the contents. He had been taught French at school, but had never learnt expressions such as '*a la carte*' and '*entrée*', so he looked for things he did recognise, but while he was deliberating, another waiter appeared with another menu. It was the Wine List. Mark couldn't understand why it took two waiters to attend to him when there was no one else in the restaurant.

The first waiter returned. 'Are you ready to order?'

'What's the soup?' Mark asked. There was no way he was going to say '*de jour.*' He was in England after all. Why should he have to speak French in England?

'Ees consommé,' came the reply.

Mark was about to say 'What the Hell's that?' but decided that he didn't want to look a complete fool, so he said 'I'll try that, please... and the Chicken Chasseur.' He liked chicken, so he assumed he would be safe with that. His mother has never ventured beyond straightforward English cuisine, although she had recently starting buying chilli con carne in a tin for Mark to cook when he was on his own.

When Mark saw the prices of the wine he asked for a glass of the house red.

'Red? With chicken?' questioned the haughty wine waiter.

'Oh, no. I'd better have white,' Mark said, as though he knew what he was talking about – which he obviously didn't!

The consommé that was served up turned out to be similar to a vegetable soup. 'Why couldn't they just call it vegetable soup?' he thought to himself, whilst also thinking it wasn't as good as the Campbell's soup that was made down the road from him in King's Lynn. The chicken dish though, was delicious and gave Mark encouragement for the rest of the week. He really didn't want to venture out elsewhere on his own. The hotel's restaurant made him feel uncomfortable enough and he was pleased to get back to his room to read his book which was 'The Mayor of Casterbridge.'

This reminded Mark of two of Ray's little jokes when they had been discussing literature in the office. Ray had announced that he had always wanted to be a writer and he had just finished his first novel. It had taken him two years and he was so pleased with himself that he was going back to the library to borrow another one. The book he'd read apparently, was about a young girl who goes off in a campervan for adventures in Dorset. It was called 'Tess of the Dormobiles.'

The next morning, after a decent cooked breakfast, Mark presented himself outside the hotel to wait for the coach to take him to Greenford. He was feeling very tired as the traffic noise and the strange surroundings meant he hardly slept at all. The Edgeware Road must have been a favourite route for police and ambulance drivers as it seemed to Mark that a siren was blasting past his window every ten minutes or so.

He remembered several of the Londoners at Greshams complaining that Norfolk was too quiet for them and many had felt the need to return to *civilisation* as they called it. Mark couldn't understand why anyone would rather live in this noisy dangerous place and still think it was more civilised than the peace and quiet of Norfolkshire.

Outside the hotel, there were about a dozen people waiting. They were mostly people of a similar age to Mark, except for one man with a droopy moustache and thick side whiskers. He looked about thirty. More to the point, there were two young females, one of whom was very attractive and convinced Mark that the next three weeks might be more interesting than he had thought. She probably had a boyfriend or lived the other end of the country, but for three weeks, she would be nice to look at, if nothing else and might help take his mind off Della. The second young lady wore glasses, was a little overweight and looked a bit 'frumpy', but Mark had learnt from experience that one should not make rash judgements about people.

The thirty-year old man approached Mark and asked 'Is everyone waiting for the NCR coach?'

'Well, I am, so at least you're not on your own.' Mark had assumed the chap was trying to break the ice, but he just moved away again.

When the coach arrived, they all piled on board. Mark was hoping he might find himself next to the attractive young lady, but she sat next to the other young girl. Mark found a vacant seat further down the coach and gazed out of the window while the final few people boarded. Some of the people had already 'paired up', so Mark found himself sitting alone. Perhaps the pairs were from the same organisation, he thought. Or maybe they had met over dinner. The thirty-year old also ignored Mark and sat alone. It didn't matter. Mark had resigned himself to a lonely week, anyway.

When they all entered the training room, Mark noticed a few people already seated – presumably local attendees who didn't need overnight accommodation. The tutor welcomed them all and introduced himself. 'My name is Michael O'Brien. As you can tell, I'm from Ireland – a little place called Ballybutton. It's a navel base.'

'That was a good start,' thought Mark, joining in the laughter. 'If he's got a sense of humour, it might make the experience more enjoyable.'

'Here's a little joke for you,' said Michael. 'See if anyone gets it. There are only ten people in the world – those that understand binary and those that don't.'

Everyone sat there in stilled silence, except the thirty-year old, who did smile.

'So you know about binary, do you, Paul?' Michael had the advantage over everyone else with names because each attendee had their name on a piece of card in front of them, but Michael was the only one who could see these.

'I touched on it when I did 'A' level Pure Maths,' Paul replied, looking pleased with himself.

'Right,' said Michael, 'at the end of today, I'll repeat the joke and see if everyone gets it.'

He then proceeded to the principals of binary numbers, which led on to hexadecimal values. Some people seem to struggle with the concept, but Mark found it very interesting. By the end of the day, he understood binary, hexadecimal, bytes and bits, and even the function of the parity bit.

And everyone did now understand Michael's repeated binary joke, but no one actually laughed.

As they all filed out of the Training room to catch the coach back to the hotel, Mark deliberately walked past the attractive young lady's desk to see her name card. It said 'Tracey.' He was tempted to swap some name cards around so that he could be sitting next to her the next day, but the tutor was still gathering up his notes, so he couldn't. His hopes of sitting next to her on the coach were dashed when she again sat next to the other lady, so Mark sat in the same seat as before. Still, with three weeks to go, there would surely be a chance to talk to her. Perhaps she would be eating in the hotel that evening... but she wasn't.

It was Friday morning before Mark got a chance to talk to her over coffee. He still found it difficult to initiate conversation with single females. He asked 'How are you finding it?'

'All right, I think. Ask me again in two weeks.'

'Do you already have some applications written back home?'

She hesitated for a moment while she realised what Mark meant by *applications*. 'No, we've only just got the computer installed, so we're starting from scratch. I think we need the Nominal Ledger first.'

'Does that mean you will cater for decimalisation from the start?'

'No, they're expecting the system in January.'

'Surely, that means you will have to re-write chunks of it?'

'That's a good point. I don't think anyone thought of that.'

Mark was aware that he was asking all the questions, but he continued with the next important enquiry. 'Where are you based?'

'Witham, in Essex.'

'We're in Sanford, in Norfolk. We've had our NCR for a couple of years, but my manager wants all the software re-written for various reasons – and it needs the decimalisation.'

As they returned to their seats, Mark considered that if she lived in Essex, he wasn't going to even contemplate asking her out – not after the problems with his long-distance relationship with Sandy. But that didn't stop him trying to share her company over the next two weeks – if he got chance. Of course, if she asked him out, that would be a different matter.

Over the next two weeks, he didn't get any further chance to enjoy Tracey's company. She didn't seem to dine in the Hotel. Mark never even saw her at breakfast, so by the time he boarded the train from Liverpool Street back to Kings' Lynn on the last Friday afternoon, he felt rather frustrated, but at last he could get back to normality – and good old-fashioned meals and home comforts; no more surly hotel staff; no more confusing underground journeys and no more noisy police sirens in the middle of the night. He had survived three weeks in London without witnessing any murders, prostitutes or gangsters. He had come through unscathed and it made him think of that Jerry Butler song – *Only the Strong Survive* – perhaps a little exaggeration, but that's how he felt about it.

CHAPTER 18

Out of Left Field

The Saturday after the completion of Mark's course saw him playing football at Northfleet. This was the team's first home fixture of the season as they had so far played two away games and having received a bye in the local cup competition, had one free week.

As Mark drove down Compton Avenue towards the football pitch, he kept an eye out for Blodwyn. Having been without a girlfriend for several months, he was re-considering her as an option. He knew she would mess him about, but he sorely missed female company and she often entered his daydreams. If he had to describe the perfect physical form, she would probably fit the bill, but he had never developed anything other than a physical attraction for her. So maybe if he could just go out with her a few times until she started playing her silly games, that would satisfy some of his lustful feelings. Of course, she might not want to go out with him, but she did give off positive signals last time they met.

But he never saw her.

The football match was one of those one-sided games that he had come to expect while playing for Northfleet, although their recent form had not reached the standards of previous seasons. They had lost a couple of key players at the end of the last season and some of the other teams were much improved.

Towards the end of the match, he was leaning against the goalpost, having only touched the ball four times all afternoon. His team was 8-0 up against the weakest team in the league and it was drizzling, so he was feeling quite fed up, when he heard a female voice behind him say 'Hello Mark.'

His first thoughts were that it might be Blodwyn who only lived a few yards away, but it wasn't a Welsh accent. He turned to see a bedraggled Melody standing behind the goal.

'Melody!' he said. 'What are you doing, here?'

'I've just been in town and I was passing close by. I never got the chance to thank you properly for all the help with my twisted ankle. I remembered you said you played at Northfleet, so I thought I might find you here on a Saturday afternoon. You left so suddenly, I never thanked you for all your help.'

'Well, your neighbour took over and made me feel redundant. How is the ankle?'

'It's fine, now. It was a funny colour for a few days, but once the swelling went down, I was soon out and about again. I'm actually playing hockey tomorrow. I went to a practice session on Wednesday and it didn't cause me a problem. Look, I bought a little something to show my appreciation.'

It was a small square parcel and Mark thanked her and placed it in the corner of the goal, hoping it wouldn't suffer for getting wet.

'The ball's coming this way,' she said and Mark turned to see if he was going to be called into action, but after the opposition made a few unproductive passes on the halfway line, the defence dealt with the attack and the final whistle was blown

Mark turned to speak to Melody, but she was already leaving the ground and he had to stay to shake hands with the opposition. Why did she leave so quickly? He was going to ask her out, but if she was in such a hurry to leave, she probably didn't want him to. Or was that his old lack of self-confidence appearing again?

As he walked off towards the changing rooms, one of the regular supporters approached Mark. 'Hey, Mark. I see your young lady found you. She was here last week, looking for you. She asked if someone called Mark played here and I told her you'd probably be here this week. She's nice, isn't she? If you don't want her, can I have a go?'

Brian used to play for Northfleet when he was younger. He lived locally and came to all the home games, whether it was the first team or the reserves.

Mark looked at the small package and wondered what it could be. He would open it when he got back to the car. He didn't want to risk some ribbing from his colleagues in the changing room. It might be something soppy and footballers had a strange sense of humour he found. Nevertheless, there were still some unfortunate ribald comments flying around the changing rooms, much to Mark's embarrassment. Didn't these people ever talk to females, themselves?

When he got back to his car, Mark ripped off the soggy wrapping paper and found Melody's gift was a box of chocolates. Instead of the conventional Milk Tray, Black Magic or Dairy milk, these chocolates were made in Belgium. Mark felt disappointed.

After tea, he offered them round to the rest of his family. 'Belgian chocolates!' exclaimed his mother. 'Someone likes you.'

'What do you mean?' asked Mark.

'Belgian chocolates are the best you can buy.'

'I thought they were just a cheap foreign make,' said Mark. 'In that case, you can only have one each.' When he tried one himself, he agreed that they were special – in fact, the best chocolate he had ever tasted.

He re-appraised his gift. Melody had gone out of her way to find him two weeks running and bought him expensive Belgian chocolates. Was that just gratitude for his assistance at the hospital? Or was it more than that? Now, he really was determined to seek her out. He still didn't know if she had a boyfriend, but he would have to find out for himself. If Melody could visit him when he was playing football, why couldn't he visit her when she was playing hockey? So that was his plan for the next day. What a good thing that she had told Mark where she played; and for that matter, a good thing that he had told her where he played football.

This was the first time that Mark had ventured anywhere near the Girls' High School. In many ways, the building reminded him of his days at the Boys' Grammar School, with its high Edwardian stonework and tall windows. It brought back as many happy memories as bad ones.

He assumed the playing fields would be somewhere around the back of the main building and after passing the bike-shed, he could hear some girlie cries, which he followed. The voices came from the netball court where a match was in progress between what appeared to be two teams of teenagers. As Mark wasn't sure of their ages, he thought he ought not to linger, despite the appealing vision of several short skirts. So he hurried past towards the back of the buildings and there he could see some green fields where two hockey matches were in progress.

He scanned the nearest match, but he couldn't see Melody among the players, so he edged around that pitch whilst surreptitiously looking at all the glorious array of female legs on show, pretending that he was interested in the actual game. The truth was that he didn't really understand hockey. He had played it once while at the Grammar School, but he was useless and had been more concerned about being hit by the dangerous hard ball and the flailing sticks. He couldn't understand why there were not several casualties at the end of every game. He also resented the elitism that existed with hockey as it was at Parkside Grammar. No one was allowed on the hallowed turf unless you were actually playing. If a stray football went onto the pitch, it had to stay there until an authorised person returned it. There were eight football pitches at Parkside and only one hockey pitch.

At last, Mark could see Melody. That was a relief, because he could not have been sure that she had a home match that week and he didn't want to repeat this exercise every week. She was wearing a very fetching green top and skirt. She seemed to be playing in what Mark considered to be a right-half position, if there was such a thing in hockey. This meant she had to cover defence as well as supporting the attack, so no wonder she wanted to get fit before the start of the season. Mark just stood on the touchline and watched. He still didn't understand the rules and he didn't understand the various infringements that were penalised, but he knew he wanted Melody to win and to play well, so he naturally supported her team and cheered when they scored.

Ten minutes after Mark arrived, it was half-time and Melody walked off with her colleagues for a drink and a slice of orange. She hadn't noticed Mark standing there – or certainly hadn't acknowledged his presence, so he would have to stay and watch the rest of the game if he wanted to talk to her at the end. And he certainly did want to talk to her. She was every bit as attractive as he remembered. What was more, he had managed the occasional glimpse of her legs despite her wearing a knee length skirt – and he liked what he saw.

After a five minute break, play resumed with a bully-off and Melody still hadn't noticed Mark standing there, but, in fairness, there were quite a few people on the touchline; many of them men of a similar age to Mark; so probably boyfriends of some of the players, Mark imagined. He hoped there wasn't one with a special interest in Melody. That would ruin all his plans.

About mid-way through the second half, Melody found herself in space well inside the opposition's half of the pitch with the ball at her mercy. 'Shoot, Mel!' cried Mark, but several of the supporters and one or two players looked at him as though he were some kind of idiot who knew nothing about hockey. Then he remembered that you can't score from outside the goal area.

When the attack broke down and Melody ran back towards her own half, she glanced over to identify the idiot on the touchline. 'Oh, it's you, Mark,' she said as she ran past, not giving him a chance to reply – nor a chance to defend his ignorance.

Mark felt dreadful. This was not a very good start if he wanted to create a good impression and win her favour. However, when the match ended, Melody did make a point of walking towards Mark. 'What are you doing here?' she asked.

'Oh, I'm a big fan of hockey – as you can tell by my intimate knowledge of the rules.'

'Yes, I did notice,' she replied.

Just then a voice said 'Hello Mark.'

He turned to see the lovely Janice whom he had once admired during his time at school and she looked as lovely as ever. At any other time, he would have been very pleased to have seen her, but this wasn't the time.

'Hello Janice. How are you?'

'I'm fine, thank you – and you?'

'Yes, I'm very well. It's nice to see you again.' He turned back to Melody, hoping that Janice would take the hint to leave them alone and Janice duly obliged. Mark hoped he hadn't offended Janice.

He continued his conversation with Melody but felt he needed to explain his relationship with Janice. 'Janice lives near me and she used to go the High School. No, I wanted a better chance to thank you for the chocolates. They were delicious.'

'Were? Have you finished them all already?'

'Not quite, but I don't think they'll last very long. You seem to be running around on your ankle all right.'

'Yes, it's almost as good as new. There is still a slight twinge, but nothing to worry about.'

'I'm very glad to hear it.' Now there was a lull in the conversation and Mark was starting to feel anxious. He'd made this visit with the sole purpose of trying to get a date, but he suddenly felt all tongue-tied.

Melody broke the ice. 'I need to go and get changed. It was nice of you to come and see me again'

'Wait a minute! Before you go… Would you like to go out for a drink sometime?'

'Yes, of course I would.'

Mark was taken aback by her swift response, so he decided not to hang about either. 'How about tonight?'

'Gosh! You're keen. Let me think. Today is Sunday. I've got to iron a dress ready for work tomorrow… but, yes. I think I'll have enough time. Not until eight o'clock, though – and I mustn't be too late home.'

'Eight o'clock is fine. I'll come and pick you up at your house, if that's all right.'

'Yes, that will be nice. I'll see you at eight, then. I must go. Time flies like an arrow. Fruit flies like a banana.'

Mark smiled at her little joke. That was a lot easier than he thought it would be. There was none of this 'playing hard to get' business with Melody. He was sure that didn't mean she was easy. He considered that their previous encounters had already paved the way to a successful outcome to his invitation.

★ ★ ★ ★ ★ ★

Mark felt as excited as he had done when he had achieved his very first date. He still didn't know very much about Melody, but so far, he liked everything he did know about her. She was bright; had a sense of humour; was attractive, fit and shapely; had her own house and transport. What was there not to like? Well, he would find that out once he got to know her better, starting that evening.

Usually, when he went out on a date, he wore his favourite suit, but as it was a Sunday, he opted for his most fashionable attire, which consisted of a bright yellow shirt and his colourful hand-painted Spanish tie; a brown corduroy sports jacket; his olive-green and black checked flares (with the tight crotch!) and a pair of black leather shoes.

It was dark when he arrived outside Melody's cottage and there were no street lights down her lane, but there was a little light emanating from her windows so that Mark could find her door knocker. As she opened her door, she said 'Hello, Mark. I'm all ready, but I'm going to ask you a little favour, please. Can you help me take my dustbin through the house?' I keep it out the back, but the dustmen don't have access round the back, so I have to drag it through the house every week ready for the Monday collection.'

Mark was glad to help, but he was a little concerned about getting his clothes dirty. He followed Melody through her small house, which seemed to consist of a cosy little sitting room which opened directly onto the front garden and a kitchen at the rear, with what appeared to be a larder and a back entrance to the rear garden. There was no sign of a staircase, so Mark guessed this was hidden behind the small door in the corner of the sitting room. 'This is a cosy little cottage,' he said, looking around.

'Yes, it used to be a farmworker's cottage owned by the local squire. It's not much more than a one-up and one-down. There's only one bedroom and an upstairs bathroom. It would have been very crowded if the farmworker had a family, but it's just right for my needs. I only rent it, of course.'

She opened the back door and pointed to the small galvanised dustbin. Mark lifted it by the handles, trying very hard to make sure it didn't touch his clothes, and carried it from the back garden to the front.

'Do you have to do this every week?' he asked.

'Yes. I used to keep it out the front, but it looked so untidy.'

'Our binmen are quite happy to come around the back – as long as they get their Christmas box each year.'

'I'm sure mine would, but, as I say, there's no access to the back. Anyway, thanks for that. You'd better wash your hands before we go. I'm all ready. Where are you taking me?'

'Do you have a favourite pub?'

'I've hardly been to any of the pubs 'round here. What about that one where you said you used to do some courting?'

'The Lifeboat? It's up on the coast at Thornham. It's a bit of a drive if you don't mind that.'

'I don't mind if you don't mind taking us there. We can have a good chat on the way.'

The journey took them up through quiet country roads through villages such as Great Bircham and Docking, but there was no need to hurry since they did, indeed, have a good chat on the way. This included Mark describing his three weeks in London, the snooty hotel staff and a very brief overview of the things he'd learnt on the course.

'Once you get experience as a computer programmer, you'll be able to get a good job with some big companies, won't you?' Melody asked.

'No,' Mark replied, 'it doesn't work that way, unfortunately. I've only learnt how to program an NCR500 machine, which has its own unique language. If I want to move on, I've either got to find another company with an NCR500 or learn another language. I didn't realise that until I got on the course. Most big companies use IBM or ICL computers and they all use different languages. The only good thing is that I'm told most of the other languages are easier to learn than NCR500.

Still, it's a big challenge and I'm looking forward to a new position.'

As they got near to Thornham, Mark's mind was filled with memories of his previous visits to The Lifeboat. He hoped that Jenny wasn't going to be there. The Lifeboat was her favourite pub as well, so there was every likelihood that she still frequented it. If she was there, Mark didn't know how he would handle the situation. The truth was that he still had feelings for Jenny – more so than even Della. But that didn't mean he necessarily wanted to see Jenny again – especially in their favourite old haunt. More importantly, he didn't want anything to interfere with his ability to give his complete attention to Melody.

He blamed himself for the failure of all his previous relationships, going right back to Karen. In each case, he considered he might have done something different to achieve a better result. This evening could be the start of something special, so he had to get it right. Unfortunately, this made Mark feel tentative, if not actually nervous. So he decided that in order to keep the mood light-hearted, the first thing he would do when they got in the pub was to invite Melody to a game of 'penny-in-the-hole' but there were a few people sitting in that area of the bar and he had to abandon this idea.

Melody wanted to buy the first round of drinks, but Mark said 'Certainly not! I invited you out for a drink.' He wondered if she was still trying to show her appreciation for his kindness with her ankle, but he wanted a relationship built on mutuality, not out of gratitude.

They sat down and continued conversing. The conversation did not flow as freely as it would have done with Jenny, but was so much better than with Sandy. Mark felt he wanted to introduce a little more humour, but he didn't want to tell jokes, since this might detract them from getting to know each other better, but his usual quick-fire quips just weren't happening. When their glasses were empty, he did allow Melody to buy the next round. As it was a Sunday and the pub therefore closed at 10.30, it was soon time to leave. Throughout this time, Mark was becoming more and more attracted to her, and he was constantly thinking about how he could move the relationship onto a higher phase. Should he attempt a kiss on their first date? Should he try putting his arms around her as they walked to the car or just try to hold her hand?

In the end, he did none of these things and he waited until they arrived back at her house before he asked 'Can I see you again?'

'Yes, I'd like that,' she replied. 'Can we go to the pictures? *Love Story* is on at the Odeon.'

'Oh, good!' said Mark sarcastically.

'Don't you want to see it?' Melody asked.

'Of course I do,' he lied. 'Do you want to go tomorrow?'

'Cor, slow down, Mark. Can we make it later in the week? I've got jobs to do in the house and I'm usually busy at work at the start of the week until we get the payroll out. How about Thursday?'

'It sounds like it will have to be Thursday.' He didn't see any reason to hide his disappointment.

'Sorry, Mark, but when you live on your own, there are always little jobs to do around the house and garden. I'm sure you'll enjoy the film. I'm flattered that you seem disappointed to have to wait.'

'I can wait 'til Thursday comes around, but I'll be counting every day. Do you know what time the film starts?'

'I don't. Shall we assume it's early and if it's not we can have a quick drink beforehand. Do you want to meet in town?'

'I'd rather we went together. Shall I pick you up at say 6.30?'

'All right,' and she moved to get out of the car before Mark could make any attempt at a goodnight kiss. She leaned back into the car and said 'Thanks for a very nice evening. I'll see you on Thursday.'

'Goodnight, Mel,' he replied.

CHAPTER 19

Take Me In Your Arms And Love Me

So Monday found Mark back in the Computer Office for the first time since the week before his course in London. A lot seemed to have happened in his life during that time, but for now he would have to concentrate on his new role and put into practice all the things he had learnt on his course. Della had left Greshams and Mark hoped that with his interest in Melody and his new job, he could move on and forget her.

He kept wondering if he had appeared to be too eager with Melody. In the past, he had been guilty of being backward at coming forward, but in his eagerness, to rectify this, had he gone too far in the other direction? He still didn't understand women. They liked to be swept off their feet, but they didn't like you to be too eager.

After a few days in his new role, Mark realised just how much concentration was required to be a programmer, which was just as well, because there was none of the office banter that he had been used to in both of his previous positions. It was going to be a long few days before he could see Melody on Thursday, so he arranged to go out for a mid-week drink with Ray and his girlfriend Val, and they were all able to give each other an update on their lives during the previous three weeks; except that Mark didn't mention Melody. He wanted to be sure things went well on Thursday before he boasted of his new affair. He wasn't superstitious, but he wasn't taking any chances. As Ray himself had once said – 'It's bad luck to be superstitious!'

When Thursday arrived, Mark was just as apprehensive as he had been on his very first date. He still felt the need to make a strong impression on Melody and he determined to let his humour come to the fore, so he lined up a few little quips and stories, but this plan was not aided by the fact that the film they went to see was a real 'weepy' – not really the type of film Mark enjoyed. To make matters worse, Melody seemed visibly upset by the ending. Mark wanted to comfort her, but didn't feel their relationship had developed sufficiently for him to cuddle her as they left the cinema. When Mark suggested a drink, Melody hesitated, but reluctantly agreed.

Mark wondered why and his feelings of anxiety were worsening. He desperately wanted this to succeed, but their relationship was not progressing.

Once they had sat down in the pub, Mark said 'I've got this little joke. There are ten sorts of people in the world; those that understand binary and those that don't.'

Melody just looked at him, expecting a punch-line or something further. 'Is that it?' she asked. This was one of those dreadful moments when one tells a joke and it gets absolutely no reaction.

'Yes, that's the joke,' Mark replied.

'I don't get it. What's binary?'

'That's the point, see. If you understood binary, you would understand the joke.'

'In that case, I don't see the point in telling me a joke that I can't get.'

'No, you're right. It was silly. Binary is a numbering system where ten – that is one zero – equals two in the normal decimal system. But it's not funny unless you know binary. In fact, come to think of it, it's not very funny if you do know binary. I was just trying to lighten the mood after that film.'

'Didn't you enjoy it, then?' Melody asked, looking a little indignant.

'Oh, dear,' thought Mark as he let out a little sigh. Why did he have to say that?

'Well, it wasn't that bad,' he lied. 'It's just not my sort of film. I read a review in the paper that said the critic found it all a bit contrived, so that's probably coloured my view of it. But you enjoyed it, didn't you? That's the main thing. I'm just happy to be with you.'

Melody gave him a little smile. 'I suppose it is more of a girlie type of film. Next time, we'll find something we both like.'

At least she thought there might be a next time, thought Mark.

'Anyway,' she added, 'I must just pay a visit. I'll be back in a minute.'

When she returned, Mark asked 'Could you hear me in there?'

Melody had a very puzzled look on her face. 'What?'

'Because I could hear you.'

Melody didn't look the least bit amused. 'How rude!' she said.

'Sorry,' said Mark and he just went quiet. After a few more seconds, he half mumbled 'Someone used that joke in the office and it got a very good response, but this obviously wasn't the right time to use it again. I am sorry.'

Mark reached for his drink looking a little sulky. After an embarrassing silence that seemed to last forever, Melody said 'Actually, Mark, I can see that it might have been very funny, but do you mind if I say something?'

When someone says that, you're sure that he or she is going to say something unpleasant, but Mark nodded anyway.

'I get the feeling, Mark,' she said slowly, 'that you're trying too hard to make an impression. I think you just need to be yourself. When we first met at South Walton, you swept me off my feet, you know.'

'Really! I've never swept anyone off their feet. Are you getting me mixed up with someone else?'

'No. That's what you did that day. The way you put me at ease and took control of the situation really impressed me. You acted like a real gentleman and made sure I felt comfortable about getting in the car of a total stranger. Then when you disappeared without giving me chance to thank you, I felt very disappointed – not with you, but just the way it turned out.

'You can blame your neighbour for that,' Mark interjected. 'I had every intention of ensuring you could manage before I left, but I felt superfluous after she took control.'

'And that demonstrated something else about you,' Melody continued. 'It showed that you are a very kind-hearted person. So you don't have to keep trying to make a good impression with me. I've already made up my mind about you. So just enjoy yourself and relax. I'm sure you've been out with other girls without feeling you have to keep making a special effort. And just to let you know, I'm not going anywhere.'

Mark reached for her hand. Melody responded with a very firm squeeze and all his concerns seem to evaporate. He looked at her lovely face with her lovely single dimple and that gap-toothed smile and he felt a little aroused. He dearly wanted to explore her lovely body. He knew from her ability to chase a hockey ball that she was reasonably athletic and carried little, if any, excess weight and that suited his tastes.

Mark let go of her hand and sat back feeling more assured of his chances.

'So no more jokes, then,' Mark said.

'Oh, no – I like jokes. Just to prove it, here's one I heard yesterday. Did you hear about the agnostic, dyslexic insomniac? He would lay awake at night and wonder if there was a dog.'

It took Mark a couple of seconds to get the joke, but then he laughed – as much with a feeling of relief as from a sense of humour.

'My turn,' he said and repeated the joke about council workers planting trees – the one which Maggie had told him on their first meeting and Melody laughed as well.

The atmosphere had now changed completely and when they left the pub, Mark reached to hold Melody's hand as they walked across the pub car park. When they reached Mark's car, he put his arm around her back and pulled her closer so that they could kiss. Her lips met his willingly and unlike his kisses with Sandy, their lips felt compatible, which was a great relief to Mark as he had started to wonder if he had forgotten how to kiss properly. He decided his bad experiences with Sandy had been down to her lack of technique – nothing to do with compatibility. After a few seconds, Melody said 'Not out here in the car park. Let's get inside.'

She was right, but Mark had wanted to get his arms around her and hold her close which wouldn't have been so easy in the car. Once in the car, Mark wasn't sure whether she had meant no kissing at all in the car park or just outside of the car. And she had said *'Let's get inside.'* Did she mean get inside her house or just in the car? As things were starting to go so well, he decided not to risk a refusal and started the car to take her home. Surely, this time she would invite him in for coffee?

As they drove back to Melody's cottage, the conversation flowed much freer than the previous date and in much the same way as their first encounter. This was mostly down to Mark's now more relaxed attitude. And sure enough, when they arrived, Melody said 'Are you coming in?' Mark didn't need to be asked twice.

The road was engulfed in darkness and was empty apart from their two vehicles and a light coloured Ford Corsair. Melody stopped as she saw the Ford. 'Oh, not again!' she exclaimed.

'What's the matter?' Mark asked showing genuine concern.

'Let's get inside. I'll tell you about it in there.' She unlocked the door and they went inside. 'That's Trevor. I went out with him a few times and when I could see it wasn't working out, I decided to end it. The trouble is, I was a bit too soft with him and just put him off with excuses. He seems to think we have so much in common that we are destined for each other. At first, it was just a few 'phone calls and then it was letters. Now he turns up in places where he expects to see me and a couple of times, I've seen him outside the cottage – just sitting there in his car.'

'Right,' said Mark. 'I'll go and have a word with him.'

'No, don't do that. He needs careful handling. He might do something really stupid. I wouldn't want that on my conscience.'

'What, you mean he might top himself?'

'I don't know… yes he might. He was always a bit strange.'

'Well, you can't carry on like this. Leave it to me.' Mark was going to be the knight in shining armour again, although he didn't know what he was going to do, except that he knew he had to do something.

'What are you going to do?' She asked.

'I'm just going to deal with it. Will he get violent?'

'I doubt it. He might cry, though. He's done that before now.'

Mark felt relieved that Trevor wasn't going to get violent, but he didn't relish tears either.

As Mark went outside into the dark road, he could just make out Trevor's silhouette sinking down in his seat, but when Mark reached the car, Trevor realised there was no point in hiding. Mark tapped on the side window, Trevor wound it down and let out a feeble 'Hello.'

'What are you doing here?'

'I'm minding my own business,' Trevor replied, trying to sound aggressive but actually coming across as a rather pathetic person.

'No, you're not. You're upsetting my girlfriend and you're going to stop doing it and keep out of her life.' Mark felt very proud of his dynamic stance, emboldened as it was by Trevor's meek demeanour.

'I didn't realise she had a boyfriend. I'm sorry. Can I just have a word with her?'

'Do you really think that will do any good? She's not interested in you and doesn't want you in her life. I'm afraid there has to come a point when you need to just let go and get on with your life. So, no more 'phone calls; no more letters and stay away from Walton.' Mark was speaking from experience because there had been numerous occasions when he had failed to move on when he had been rejected, so he knew it was good advice.

'Yes, you're right. Tell Mel I'm sorry if I've upset her. I won't bother her again.'

Mark stood back so that Trevor could start his engine and drive off, which he did with a squeal of tyres. Mark returned to Melody who had made a point of not showing herself, but had still tried to listen through the open door.

'I heard some of what you told him,' she said, 'but I couldn't hear anything of what he said. How did he take it?'

'I think he realises how silly he has been. I'm sure you won't hear from him again.'

'Thank you, Mark. You've come to my rescue again.'

'Not really – just getting rid of a rival.'

'He was hardly a rival. He was never really in with a chance,' she said as she put her arms around Mark.

'Am I in with a chance?' he asked as his arms went around her waist and down to the small of her lovely strong back.

'Not tonight, I'm afraid. It's the wrong time of the month… but I will make it up to you.'

Mark couldn't believe his ears. A few hours ago, he was worried in case he might blow their relationship and now he was getting a promise of things to come. He thought he might have had to work a lot harder to have his wicked way with her. How refreshing after his struggles with Sandy. However, Melody wasn't on the pill like Maggie, so he would have to start using those horrible condoms again. Mark wondered if the 'wrong time of month' explained some of her tetchy behaviour earlier – or was that just a myth put about by men who knew no better? But he had been thinking that Melody may have been feeling a little upset after that mawkish film. Or had it just been his own behaviour which he realised had been rather poor; or maybe just a combination of everything. The main thing was that everything was now resolved – except that Mark always took things to heart and he would probably agonise over it all instead of sleeping that night.

'So would you like some cocoa?' Melody asked.

'I'd rather have coffee, if I may, please. I need to stay awake for the drive home.'

'I'm afraid I don't have coffee. I don't like it. I never have done. I can make a cup of tea, if you'd rather?'

'No, I'd rather have cocoa, this time of night, thank you.'

'I'll have to get some coffee in, if that's what you prefer.' Again she was sending out signals that she was expecting to see a lot more of Mark and it filled him with wonderful expectations.

'Have you never liked coffee?'

'No, I don't really like the smell.'

'I don't suppose you ever knew Ladyman's in King's Lynn?

'No, what's Ladyman's?'

It was a shop in the High Street. It's closed now, but they sold tea and coffee there. The smell of roasting coffee as you walked past was a real delight, although I don't suppose you would appreciate it. There used to be a big pot hanging outside from the mock Tudor frontage. There were two shops with a mock Tudor frontage – both quite close to each other. The other one was Boots, but they've moved down the road now. I say *mock Tudor*. It may have been real Tudor for all I know.'

'Anyway,' said Melody. 'Take a seat and I'll get us some drinks.'

There was a two-seater settee and two upright chairs, so Mark naturally sat on the settee, assuming Melody would sit next to him when they drank their cocoa.

He looked around the cosy little room. Everything seemed to be on a miniature scale. As well as the small settee, there was a small coffee table, a small bookcase and a small television on top of a small cabinet. But he couldn't see a record player.

He continued talking while Melody occupied herself in the kitchen. 'What did Trevor mean when he said you had a lot in common?'

'Ah, well. I told him I like *'The Sounds of Silence'* by Simon and Garfunkel. It turns out that he's a big fan of theirs.'

'Do you like Bob Dylan, by any chance?' Mark asked.

'No, why do you ask?'

'Oh, it's just that a girl I worked with liked Simon and Garfunkel and she was mad keen on Bob Dylan as well, so I thought you might like both of them. What else did you have in common with loverboy?'

'We met at his judo class. I joined when I first moved here and decided that if I was to live alone, perhaps I ought to be able to look after myself, but I didn't really enjoy it.'

'Did you get any belts?'

'No, I didn't stick at it long enough, but Trev was a brown belt and he ran the class.'

'Now you tell me! After I went out to tackle him in the dark!'

'He wouldn't hurt you. He was a big softie.'

'Yeah, well I'm a big softie, too!'

'In that case, we'll have to see if we can't harden you up a bit,' Melody said as she brought the cocoa in and sat next to him. Mark wasn't sure if he needed her to harden him. He was already part way there.

While they waited for the cocoa to cool down, Melody snuggled up against Mark. He put his arm around her and kissed her fragrant hair. Conversation now seemed irrelevant and Mark no longer felt the pressure to find something to say. But after a few minutes, he did ask 'When am I going to see you again?' He no longer felt the need to ask 'Can I see you again.'

'You were telling me about your horrible time in London and how the one redeeming feature of the trip was the French cuisine in the hotel. I thought I might cook you a nice meal Saturday evening. I'm very proud of my *coq au vin*.'

Mark had never heard of *coq au vin,* but he knew *vin* was French for wine. 'That sounds great,' Mark replied. 'Are you going to be rude when you serve it, like the French waiters at the hotel?'

'I can do if you like that sort of thing.'

'Or you could dress up as a French maid?' Mark asked with a lecherous look on his face.

'Not with my horrible legs,' Melody said.

'Who says you've got horrible legs?'

'I do. They're not very nice.'

'You forget that I've seen your legs in a hockey skirt and I think they're great.' And with that, Mark reached down for a fondle, which he found extremely enjoyable. However, as his hand ventured a little higher, Melody stopped him and said 'No, not tonight Mark.'

He let out a sigh and said 'All right, but I can assure you that you've got great legs and a great figure.'

'No, I haven't. My bum's too big and my breasts are too small. But let's change the subject.'

Mark didn't really want to change the subject, but he said 'All right. Going back to Saturday, do you want me to get some wine?'

'No, it's all right. My parents brought me a nice case when they went to France this year. Are you all right with Saturday night? You can relax after your football and sample my delicious claret.'

'That's sounds great, but I'll be driving, so I can't have too much wine.'

'Well, you don't have to go home... bring your toothbrush.'

Mark was unable to respond. He imagined that his heart had just stopped beating. He couldn't think what to say next. Did this mean what he hoped it meant? Or did she mean he could sleep on the settee – except that he could tell that no one could be expected to sleep on this tiny settee. He wasn't sure if he should demonstrate his excitement or remain cool, but Melody didn't appear to be looking for a response, so he drank his cocoa and when he had finished he leant back and put his arm around her shoulder so they could both snuggle up together again. After a few more minutes of contented silence, he asked 'Haven't you got a record player?'

'No. I keep thinking about buying one, but as I'd have to buy some records as well, it doesn't seem worth the expense.'

'Shall I bring mine on Saturday?'

'Only if you bring some records as well – what have you got? Something like Frank Sinatra or Tony Bennett?'

'The nearest I've got to that is a couple of Dionne Warwick LPs.'

'That will be nice.'

'I'm sure I can dig out a few more ballady things.' Mark didn't want to say *romantic* in case it sounded a little too forward, even though it would have been in keeping with their conversation. And perhaps he could get Melody to appreciate Jerry Butler and Walter Jackson.

Again, there was a period of mutually contented silence and after a few more minutes, Melody asked 'Are you all right, now?'

'Yes, apart from two things.'

'And what are they?'

'Well, first of all, my arm's gone to sleep so I'm afraid I will have to move.'

They both sat up. 'And what's the other thing?'

'I need to use your toilet.'

'Would you mind using the outside loo? The one upstairs is right next to my bedroom and I don't want you to see it in its current state. I left in a bit of a hurry, this evening.'

'Of course I don't mind.' Mark was used to an outside toilet.

'I've got a torch you can use,' she added and got up to open the door to the staircase where she picked up what looked like a bicycle lamp with a twin-cell battery. 'I use this to see my way up the stairs. The bulb on the landing has gone and I can't reach above the stairs to change it.'

'Would you like me to try?' Mark asked.

'Yes, but not tonight. It would be better in daylight.' Again, there were signals that Melody expected to see more of Mark. 'You can wash your hands in the kitchen sink.'

As Mark opened the back door, a furry creature dashed through his legs and he heard Melody say 'Hello Benny. Where have you been?' Mark assumed that Benny was a cat, but all he had seen was a mass of fur. In the toilet, Mark noticed that the seat was up. That bothered him and when he returned, he felt compelled to mention it.

'That was probably my father. He visited about a fortnight ago. I don't use the outside loo. Why, did you think I have loads of male visitors? Are you the jealous sort?'

'No, I'm not the jealous sort. I was just curious.' But Mark did remember Jenny seeing someone behind his back, so he couldn't stop himself asking the question.

'Anyway,' he said. 'I think I ought to be making a move. Can I have a nice cuddle before I go?'

They moved together and it was a very nice warm cuddle, which moved on to a kiss. Mark decided that as it was the 'wrong time of the month' he wouldn't use his tongue, but he still felt the urge to let his hands wander a little and after starting with the small of her back, his hands fell naturally on her delightfully firm buttocks.

'I thought you said your bum was too big. It's absolutely perfect.' And Mark meant it. He could feel himself getting aroused, so he decided to step back, but not before landing another kiss.

'Well, as long as you like it, I suppose that's the main thing,' Melody replied. 'What time can you get here after your football on Saturday?'

'Not before six thirty. It's an away match – probably nearer to seven o'clock, if that's all right?'

'We've got all night, haven't we?'

Mark was reluctant to leave, but eventually he reached the door and after another nice warm embrace and a kiss, he was heading for his car.

There was no risk of the cocoa sending Mark to sleep as he drove home. His mind was racing with all sorts of wonderful thoughts – not least the memory of Melody's wonderful body. He had to admit that he had never noticed her lack of bosom; him being a 'leg and bum' man.

Perhaps he should have mentioned that he had a football match Sunday morning, so he would have to leave soon after breakfast, but he hadn't wanted to mention anything negative that might have spoilt Melody's plans for Saturday evening, and suddenly, Mark was optimistic about his life. He would no longer have to consider his back-up plans of trying again to date Blodwyn or Jane. Although he still felt there was unfinished business with both of them. In Jane's case, he had never got to explore her lovely curves. And as for Blodwyn, he would always have regrets about the one that got away, but Melody was everything he wanted in a girlfriend. Saturday couldn't come soon enough.

Now he faced the old perennial question. Should he save himself for Saturday night, but risk his excitement causing premature conclusion or would an over-indulgence when he got home improve his performance on Saturday. He decided it would depend on how easily he fell asleep.

Meanwhile, Melody was preparing for bed. She opened the door to the stairway and ushered Benny the cat upstairs. Every night she had to weigh up whether to let him sleep upstairs and therefore run the risk of having to get up in the night to let him out; or whether to let him out before she retired and run the risk of having to get up and let him back in. As he had just come in, there was every chance he would stay with her all night – but cats never did what you want them to do. She would leave the door to the stairs open in case Benny wanted to wander around during the night. At that time of the year, she had been told, mice often found a way into a country cottage.

As she turned off all the downstairs lights, the house was enclosed in darkness apart from her cycle lamp which lit the way up the stairs. It would be a great help if Mark could reach to change the bulb on the landing, but she would have to tidy up before Saturday. She looked around the bathroom to ensure there were no signs of her previous boyfriend. She'd nearly been caught out with the toilet seat. She didn't want Mark to discover a discarded men's razor or a half bottle of aftershave. She wouldn't be able to explain those away by blaming her father, since her father could never have stayed in her little one-bedroom abode.

One of the reasons that Melody had moved to Norfolk was to be nearer to Rod, whom she had met during one of her holidays in Norfolk, but at that point she had not known he was married. As soon as she had discovered the unsavoury truth, she ended the relationship without due ceremony. There was no way that she was going to steal another woman's husband, despite Rod's protestations that his wife would understand. Melody was confident that Mark was a person of greater integrity than Rod and hopefully, less clingy than Trevor.

She believed Mark did appreciate her figure, but as she stood in front of her mirror, she couldn't understand why. She looked at her 'fried eggs for breasts' as Rod had described them and sighed. She envied those women who appeared on television in the 'Miss Anglia' competition with their perfect 36-24-36 figures and their slim thighs and small bottoms. Her bottom was twice the size of some of them and her thighs were too fleshy at the top. But Mark liked them. That was important. She was confident that he would be a considerate lover. He had spoken of a previous courtship so she could be sure he was 'off the mark' and they could both look forward to ensuring he became 'further off the mark.' She chuckled to herself at the little pun.